"In this stunning novel . . . the dogged, intuitive Venetian police detective Guido Brunetti, Leon combines an engrossing, complex plot with an indictment of the corruption endemic to Italian society. . . . Many of Leon's favorite characters appear. . . . They balance this dark, cynical tale of widespread secrecy, violence and corruption."
—*Publishers Weekly* (starred review)

"Commissario Guido Brunetti's [latest] case may be his best yet—not that he'd see it that way himself. . . . Leon's most adroit balance of teasing mystery, Brunetti's droll battles with his coworkers and higher-ups, and intimations of something far deeper and darker behind the curtain."
—*Kirkus Reviews* (starred review)

"The appeal of Guido Brunetti, the hero of Donna Leon's long-running Venetian crime series, comes not from his shrewdness, though he is plenty shrewd, nor from his quick wit. It comes, instead, from his role as an everyman. . . . Not so different from our own days at the office or nights around the dinner table. Crime fiction for those willing to grapple with, rather than escape, the uncertainties of daily life."
—Bill Ott, *Booklist* (starred review)

"The evocative Venetian setting and the warmth and humanity of the Brunetti family add considerable pleasure to this nuanced, intelligent mystery; another winner from the Venice-based Leon. Highly recommended."
—Michele Laber, *Library Journal* (starred review)

"Another of her fabulous Italian mysteries . . . She has her finger on the pulse." —*Bookseller*

"Gives the reader a feel for life in Venice. . . . The story is filled with the average citizen's cynicism, knowledge of corruption, and deep distrust and fear of government and police. Characters are brilliantly portrayed. Even bit players become real and individual and Brunetti and his family are multifaceted and layered." —Sally Fellows, *Mystery News*

"The sophisticated but still moral Brunetti, with his love of food and his loving family, proves a worthy custodian of timeless values and verities." —*The Wall Street Journal*

"In her classy, literate, atmospheric Commissario Guido Brunetti series, Donna Leon takes readers . . . to a Venice that tourists rarely see." —*BookPage*

"If you're heading to Venice, take along a few of [Leon's] books to use for both entertainment and travel directions." —*Pittsburgh Post-Gazette*

"A beautifully cadenced mystery . . . no one is more graceful and accomplished than Leon." —*The Washington Post*

"Smuggling, sexual betrayal, high-class fakery and, of course, Mafia money make for a rich brew. . . . Exactly the right cop for the right city. Long may he walk, or wade, through it." —Sarah Dunant, author of *The Birth of Venus*

"Leon's books shimmer in the grace of their setting and are warmed by the charm of their characters." —*The New York Times Book Review*

"Superb. . . . An outstanding book, deserving of the widest audience possible, a chance for American readers to again experience a master practitioner's art." —*Publishers Weekly* (starred review)

"Richly atmospheric, Leon introduces you to the Venice insiders know." —Ellen Hale, *USA Today*

"A new Donna Leon book about . . . Brunetti is ready for our immediate pleasure. She uses the relatively small and crime-free canvas of Venice for riffs about Italian life, sexual styles, and—best of all—the kind of ingrown business and political corruption that seems to lurk just below the surface." —Dick Adler, *Chicago Tribune*

"*Uniform Justice* is a neat balancing act. Its silken prose and considerable charm almost conceal its underlying anger; it is an unlovely story set in the loveliest of cities. . . . Donna Leon is indeed sophisticated."

—Patrick Anderson, *The Washington Post*

"There's atmosphere aplenty in *Uniform Justice*. . . . Brunetti is a compelling character, a good man trying to stay on the honest path in a devious and twisted world."

—*The Baltimore Sun*

"Venice provides a beautifully rendered backdrop for this operatic story of fathers and sons, and Leon's writing trembles with true feeling." —*Star-Tribune* (Minneapolis)

"One of the best international crime writers is Donna Leon, and her Commissario Guido Brunetti tales set in Venice are at the apex of continental thrillers. . . . The author has written a pitch-perfect tale where all the characters are three-dimensional, breathing entities, and the lives they live, while by turns sweet and horrific, are always believable. Let Leon by your travel agent and tour guide to Venice. It's an unforgettable trip." —*Rocky Mountain News*

"Events are powered by Leon's compelling portraits."

—*The Oregonian* (Portland)

"The plot is silky and complex, and the main appeal is the protagonist, Brunetti." —*The Cleveland Plain Dealer*

"Leon, a wonderfully literate writer, sets forth her plot clearly and succinctly. . . . The ending of *Uniform Justice* is not a neat wrap-up of the case with justice prevailing. It is rather the ending that one would expect in real life. Leon says that 'the murder mystery is a craft, not an art,' but I say that murder mystery in her hands is an art." —*The Roanoke Times*

DONNA LEON

QUIETLY IN THEIR SLEEP

A PENGUIN / GROVE PRESS BOOK

For Donald McCall

PENGUIN BOOKS

Published by the Penguin Group

Penguin Group (USA) Inc., 375 Hudson Street, New York, New York 10014, U.S.A.

Penguin Group (Canada), 90 Eglinton Avenue East, Suite 700, Toronto,
Ontario, Canada M4P 2Y3 (a division of Pearson Penguin Canada Inc.)

Penguin Books Ltd, 80 Strand, London WC2R 0RL, England

Penguin Ireland, 25 St Stephen's Green, Dublin 2, Ireland (a division of Penguin Books Ltd)

Penguin Group (Australia), 250 Camberwell Road, Camberwell,
Victoria 3124, Australia (a division of Pearson Australia Group Pty Ltd)

Penguin Books India Pvt Ltd, 11 Community Centre,
Panchsheel Park, New Delhi – 110 017, India

Penguin Group (NZ), 67 Apollo Drive, Rosedale, North Shore 0745,
Auckland, New Zealand (a division of Pearson New Zealand Ltd)

Penguin Books (South Africa) (Pty) Ltd, 24 Sturdee Avenue,
Rosebank, Johannesburg 2196, South Africa

Penguin Books Ltd, Registered Offices: 80 Strand, London WC2R 0RL, England

First published in Great Britain under the title *The Death of Faith*
by Pan Macmillan Ltd 1997
Reprinted by arrangement with Grove/Atlantic, Inc.
Published in Penguin Books 2007

3 5 7 9 10 8 6 4

Copyright © Donna Leon 1997
All rights reserved

PUBLISHER'S NOTE

This is a work of fiction. Names, characters, places, and incidents either are the product
of the author's imagination or are used fictitiously, and any resemblance to actual persons,
living or dead, business establishments, events, or locales is entirely coincidental.

ISBN 978-0-14-311220-4
CIP data available

Printed in the United States of America

È sempre bene
Il sospettare un poco, in questo mondo.

It's always better, in this world,
To be a little suspicious.

                    Così fan tutte, Mozart

Chapter One

Brunetti sat at his desk and stared at his feet. Propped on the bottom drawer of his desk, they each presented him with four horizontal rows of tiny metal-circled round eyes that looked back at him in apparent, multiple reproach. For the last half hour, he'd divided his time and attention between the doors of the wooden *armadio* that stood against the far wall of his office and, when those ceased to hold his attention, his shoes. Occasionally, when the sharp corner of the top of the drawer began to cut into his heel, he crossed his feet the other way, but that merely rearranged the pattern of the eyes and did little to eliminate their reproach or relieve his boredom.

Vice-Questore Giuseppe Patta had been on vacation in Thailand for the last two weeks – gone there on what the staff of the Questura insisted on calling his second honeymoon – and Brunetti had been left in charge of what crime there was in Venice. But crime, it seemed, had boarded the plane with the Vice-Questore, for little of any importance had happened since Patta and his wife (newly restored to his home and – one trembled – his arms) had left, save for the usual break-ins and pick-pocketing. The only interesting crime had taken

1

place at a jewelry store in Campo San Maurizio two days before, when a well-dressed couple pushed in their baby carriage, and, new father blushing with pride, asked to see a diamond ring to give to the even shyer mother. She tried on first one, then another. Finally, selecting a three-carat white diamond, she asked if she could go out and look at it in the light of day. The inevitable followed: she stepped outside the door, flashed her hand in the sunlight, smiled, then waved to the father, who dipped his head into the carriage to rearrange the covers and, with an embarrassed smile to the owner, stepped outside to join his wife. And disappeared, of course, leaving the baby carriage and doll behind, blocking the door.

However ingenious, this certainly did not constitute a crime wave, and Brunetti found himself bored and at a loss, uncertain about whether he preferred the responsibility of command and the mounds of paper it seemed to generate or the freedom of action that his inferior status usually afforded him.

He looked up when someone knocked at his door, then smiled when it opened to present him this morning's first sight of Signorina Elettra, Patta's secretary, who seemed to have taken the Vice-Questore's departure as an invitation to begin her work day at ten, rather than the usual eight-thirty.

'*Buon giorno*, Commissario,' she said as she came in, her smile reminding him, fleetingly, of *gelato all' amarena* – scarlet and white – colours matched by the stripes of her silk blouse. She came into the office and stepped a bit to the side, allowing another woman to come in behind her. Brunetti glanced at the second woman and was briefly conscious of a square-cut suit in cheap grey polyester, its skirt in unfashionable proximity to low-heeled shoes. He noticed the woman's hands clasped awkwardly around a cheap imitation leather handbag, and turned his eyes back to Signorina Elettra.

'Commissario, here's someone who would like to speak to you,' she said.

'Yes?' he asked and looked at the other woman again, not much interested. But then he noticed the curve of her right cheek, and, as she turned her head and glanced around the room, the fine line of her jaw and neck. He repeated, this time with more interest, 'Yes?'

At his tone, the woman turned her head toward him and gave a half-smile and, with it, became strangely familiar to Brunetti, though he was certain he had never seen her before. It occurred to him that she might be the daughter of a friend, come to seek his help, and he thought that what he recognized was not her face but its reflection of her family.

'Yes, Signorina?' he said, rising from his chair and waving a hand toward one that stood on the other side of his desk. When he spoke, the woman gave a quick glance at Signorina Elettra, who responded with the smile she reserved for those nervous of finding themselves in the Questura. She said something about having to get back to work, and let herself out of the office.

The woman moved around to the front of the chair and sat down, pulling her skirt to one side before she did so. Though she was slender, she moved gracelessly, as if unaccustomed to wearing anything other than low-heeled shoes.

Brunetti knew from long experience that it was best to say nothing, that he should wait, face calm and interested, and sooner or later his silence would spur the person in front of him into speech. As he waited, he glanced at her face, away, then back again, trying to remember why it was so familiar to him. He sought some sign of a parent in her face, or perhaps a sales-girl he knew from a shop, unrecognizable now she was not behind the familiar counter that would have identified her. If she did work in a shop, he found himself thinking, it would certainly not be one that had anything to do with clothing or fashion: the suit was a dreadful box-like thing in a style that had disappeared ten years ago; her haircut was simply hair that had been cut very short, and done too carelessly to be either boyish or stylish; her face was absolutely bare of make-up. But, as he took a third glance, he realized that she could be said to be in disguise, and what was hidden was her beauty. Her dark eyes were widely spaced, the lashes so long and thick that they needed no mascara. The lips were pale, but full and smooth. The nose, straight, narrow, and faintly arched, was – he could find no better word for it – noble. And beneath the awkwardly cropped hair, he saw that her brow was wide and unwrinkled. But even his consciousness of her beauty brought memory no closer.

She startled him by asking, 'You don't recognize me, do you, Commissario?' Even the voice was familiar but it, too, was out of place. He cast about in vain to recall it, but he could be certain only that it

4

had nothing to do with the Questura or with his work.

'No, I'm sorry, Signorina. I don't. But I know that I know you and that this isn't where I'd expect to see you.' He smiled a real smile, one that asked her understanding of this common human predicament.

'I wouldn't expect most people you know to have reason to be in the Questura,' she said, but then she smiled to show that she meant it lightly and did understand his confusion.

'No, few of my friends ever come here voluntarily, and, so far, none of them has had to come involuntarily.' This time he smiled to show he could joke about police business, too, and added, 'Fortunately.'

'I've never had anything to do with the police before,' she said, looking around the room again, as if afraid that something bad would happen to her now that she did.

'Most people never do,' Brunetti offered.

'No, I suppose not,' she said, looking down at her hands. With no introduction, she said, 'I used to be immaculate.'

'I beg your pardon.' Brunetti was utterly at a loss, suddenly wondering if something was seriously wrong with this young woman.

'Suor'Immacolata,' she said, glancing up at him and smiling that soft smile which had for so long glowed at him from under the starched white wimple of her habit. The name put her into place and solved the puzzle: the haircut made sense, as did her evident awkwardness with the clothing she wore. Brunetti had been conscious of her beauty since the first time he saw her in that rest home where, for years, his mother had found no rest. But the nature of her religious vows and the long habit that reflected them had hedged her round as if with a taboo, and so Brunetti had registered her beauty as he would that of a flower or a painting, and he had responded to it as a viewer and not as a man. Now, freed of restrictions and disguise, her beauty had slipped into the room, however much her awkwardness and cheap clothing tried to hide it.

Suor'Immacolata had disappeared from his mother's nursing home about a year ago, and Brunetti, upset by his mother's desperation at the loss of the sister who had been most kind to her, could learn only that she had been transferred to another of the order's nursing homes. A long roll of questions ran through his mind, but he discarded them all as inappropriate. She was here: she would tell him why.

'I can't go back to Sicily,' she said abruptly. 'My family wouldn't understand.' Her hands abandoned their hold on her purse and sought comfort from one another. Finding none, they placed themselves on her thighs. Then, as if suddenly conscious of the warmth of the flesh under them, they returned to the hard angles of the bag.

'Have you been . . .' Brunetti began and then, failing to find the correct verb, settled for a pause and the lame finale, ' – long?'

'Three weeks.'

'Are you staying here in Venice?'

'No, not here, out at the Lido. I have a room in a pensione.'

Had she come to him, he wondered, for money.

If so, he would be honoured and glad to give it to her, so vast was the debt incurred by her years of charity to him and to his mother.

As if she'd read his mind, she said, 'I have a job.'

'Yes?'

'In a private clinic on the Lido.'

'A nurse?'

'In the laundry.' She caught his swift glance at her hands and smiled. 'It's all machines now, Commissario. No more taking the sheets down to the river and beating them on the rocks.'

He laughed as much at his own embarrassment as at her answer. That lightened the mood in the room and freed him to say, 'I'm sorry that you had to make this decision.' In the past, he would have added her title, 'Suor'Immacolata', but there was no longer anything he could call her. With her habit had gone her name and he knew not what else.

'My name is Maria,' she said, 'Maria Testa.' Like a singer who paused to follow the lingering sound of a note that marked the change from one key to another, she stopped here and listened to the echo of her name. 'Though I'm not sure it's mine any longer,' she added.

'What?' Brunetti asked.

'There's a process you have to go through when you leave. The order, that is. I suppose it's like deconsecrating a church. It's very complicated, and it can take a long time before they let you go.'

'I suppose they want to be sure that you are. Sure, that is,' Brunetti suggested.

'Yes. It can take months, perhaps years. You've

7

got to give them letters from people who know you and who think you're able to make the decision.'

'Is that what you'd like? Can I help you that way?'

She waved a hand to one side, flicking away his words and, with them, the vow of obedience. 'No, it doesn't matter. It's finished. Over.'

'I see,' Brunetti said, although he didn't.

She looked across at him, her gaze so direct and eyes so startling in their beauty that Brunetti felt a tinge of anticipatory envy for the man who would sweep away her vow of chastity.

'I came because of the *casa di cura*. Because of what I saw there.'

Brunetti's heart surged across the distance to his mother's side, and he was immediately alert for any hint of peril.

But before he could form his terror into a question, she said, 'No, Commissario, it's not your mother. Nothing will happen to her.' She paused then, embarrassed at how that sounded and at the grim truth contained in her words: the only thing that could ever again happen to Brunetti's mother was death. 'I'm sorry,' she added lamely but said nothing more.

Brunetti studied her for a moment, confused by what she had said, but at a loss as to how to ask her what she meant. He remembered the afternoon of his most recent visit to his mother, wishing that he could somehow see the long-absent Suor'Immacolata, knowing that she was the only person who would understand the painful fullness of his soul. But instead of the lovely Sicilian, he had found in

8

the hall only Suor'Eleanora, a woman whom the course of years had turned sour and to whom the vows meant poverty of spirit, chastity of humour, and obedience only to some rigorous concept of duty. The fact that his mother could be, even if for an instant, in the care of this woman enraged him as a man; the fact that the *casa di cura* was considered to be one of the best available shamed him as a citizen.

Her voice pulled him back from his long reverie, but he didn't hear what she said and so had to ask, 'I'm sorry, Suora,' immediately conscious of how long usage had pulled her title from him. 'I wasn't paying attention.'

She began again, ignoring his use of her title. 'I'm talking about the *casa di cura* here in Venice where I was working three weeks ago. But it isn't only that I left, Dottore. I left the order, I left everything. To begin my . . .' Here she paused and glanced out the open window, off to the façade of the church of San Lorenzo, seeking there the name of what she was about to begin. 'My new life.' She looked across at him and gave a small, weak smile. '*La Vita Nuova*,' she repeated but in a tone she struggled to make lighter, as if conscious of the heavy melodrama that had slipped into her voice. 'We had to read *La Vita Nuova* in school, but I don't remember it very well.' She glanced across at him, eyebrows pulled together in interrogation.

Brunetti had no idea where this conversation was going; first there was talk of danger, and now of Dante. 'We read it, too, but I think I was too young.

9

I always preferred *La Divina Commedia*, anyway,' he said. 'Especially *Purgatorio*.'

'How strange,' she said with interest, which might have been real or only an attempt to delay whatever it was she had come to tell him. 'I've never heard anyone prefer that book before. Why?'

Brunetti allowed himself a smile. 'I know, because I'm a policeman, people always assume I'd prefer *Inferno*. The wicked are punished and everyone gets what Dante thought they deserved. But I've never liked it, the absolute certainty of the judgements, all that awful suffering. Forever.' She sat quietly, looking at his face and attending to his words. 'I like *Purgatorio* because there's still the possibility that things will change. For the others, whether they're in Heaven or Hell, it's all finished: that's where they'll be. Forever.'

'Do you believe that?' she asked, and Brunetti knew she wasn't talking about literature.

'No.'

'No part of it?'

'Do you mean if I believe that there's a Heaven or a Hell?'

She nodded, and he wondered if some lingering superstition kept her from uttering the words of doubt.

'No,' he answered.

'Nothing?'

'Nothing.'

After a very long pause, she said, 'How very grim.'

As he had many times since he realized that this was what he believed, Brunetti shrugged.

'I suppose we'll find out,' she said, but her voice was rich with possibility, not sarcasm or dismissal.

Brunetti's impulse was again to shrug, for this was a discussion he had abandoned years ago, while still in university, laying aside the things of a child, out of patience with speculation and eager for life. But a glance at her reminded him that she was, in a sense, just out of the egg, about to begin her own *vita nuova*, and so this sort of question, no doubt unthinkable in the past, must be current and vital to her. 'Perhaps it's true,' he conceded.

Her response was instant and fiery. 'You don't have to condescend to me, Commissario. I left my vocation behind me, not my wits.'

He chose neither to apologize nor to continue this accidental discussion of theology. He shifted a letter from one side of his desk to the other, pushed his chair back, and crossed his legs. 'Shall we talk about that, instead?' he asked.

'About what?'

'About the place where you left your vocation?'

'The nursing home?' she asked unnecessarily.

Brunetti nodded. 'Which one are you talking about?'

'San Leonardo. It's over near the Giustiniani Hospital. The order helps to staff it.'

He noticed that she was sitting with her feet placed one beside the other, both flat on the floor, knees pressed together. She opened the bag with some difficulty and took from it a sheet of paper, unfolded it, and looked down at whatever was written there. 'In the last year,' she began nervously, 'five people have died at San Leonardo.' She turned the paper around and leaned forward to place it in front of him. Brunetti glanced down at the list.

'These people?' he asked.

She nodded. 'I've given their names, their ages, and what they died of.'

He looked down at the list again and saw it gave exactly that information. There were the names of three women and two men. Brunetti recalled reading some sort of statistic that said women were supposed to live longer than men, but these had not. One of the women was in her sixties, the others in their early seventies. Both of the men were older. Two had died of heart attacks, two of strokes, and one of pneumonia.

'Why have you given me this list?' he asked, looking up at her.

Even though she must have been prepared for the question, she took some time to answer it. 'Because you're the only one who might be able to do something about it.'

Brunetti waited a moment for her to explain that remark, and when she didn't, he said, 'I'm not sure what "it" is.'

'Can you find out what they died of?'

He waved the list in the air between them. 'Other than what's written here?' he asked.

She nodded. 'Yes. If what's there isn't true, is there any way that you can find out what they actually died of?'

There was no need for Brunetti to think before he answered: the law about exhumation was clear. 'Not without an order from a judge or a request from the family, no.'

'Oh,' she said. 'I had no idea. I've been – I don't know how to say this – I've been away from the world for so long that I don't know how things work any more, how things are done.' She paused for a moment and added, 'Perhaps I never knew.'

'How long were you in the order?' he asked.

'Twelve years, ever since I was fifteen.' If she saw his surprise, she ignored it. 'That's a long time, I know.'

'But you weren't really away from the world, were you?' Brunetti asked. 'After all, you trained as a nurse.'

'No,' she answered quickly. 'I'm not a nurse. Well, not a trained or professional one, at any rate. The order saw that I had a . . .' she stopped dead, and Brunetti realized she had found herself in the unaccustomed position of acknowledging a talent or giving herself a compliment and had no choice but to stop talking. After a pause that allowed her to remove any praise from her remarks, she continued, 'They decided that it would be good for me to try to help old people, and so I was sent to work in the nursing homes.'

'How long were you there?'

'Seven years. Six out in Dolo, and then one at San Leonardo,' she answered. That would have made Suor'Immacolata, Brunetti realized, twenty when she arrived at the nursing home where his mother was, the age when most women are getting jobs, deciding on professions, meeting lovers, having children. He thought of what those other women would have achieved in those years, and then he thought of what life must have been for Suor'-

Immacolata, surrounded by the howls of the mad and the smells of the incontinent. Had he been a man with a religious sense, a belief in some higher being, perhaps Brunetti could have taken consolation in the ultimate spiritual reward she would receive in return for the years she had given away. He turned from that thought and asked, setting the list down in front of him and smoothing it with the side of his hand, 'What was unusual about the deaths of these people?'

She paused a moment before she answered, and when she did, she confused him utterly. 'Nothing. Usually we have a death every few months, sometimes more than that just after the holidays.'

Decades of experience in questioning the willing and the unwilling underlay the calm with which Brunetti asked, 'Then why have you made out this list?'

'Two of the women were widows, and the other one never married. One of the men never had anyone come to visit.' She looked at him, waiting to be prodded, but still he said nothing.

Her voice grew softer, and Brunetti had a sudden fantasy of Suor'Immacolata, still in her black and white habit, struggling against the admonition never to spread slander, never to speak ill, even of a sinner. 'I heard two of them,' she finally said, 'at one time or another, say that they wanted to remember the *casa di cura* when they died.' She stopped at this and glanced down at her hands, which had abandoned the purse and now held one another in a death grip.

'And did they do that?'

She shook her head from side to side but said nothing.

14

'Maria,' he said, casting his voice intentionally low, 'does that mean they didn't do it or you don't know?'

She didn't look up at him when she answered. 'I don't know. But two of them, Signorina da Prè and Signora Cristanti . . . both of them said that they wanted to.'

'What did they say?'

'Signorina da Prè said, one day after Mass — there's no collection when Padre Pio says the Mass for us, *said* the Mass for us.' Suddenly conscious of the confusion of tenses caused by her having left the order, she stopped. She reached a nervous hand up to her temple, and Brunetti saw her slide her fingers back, seeking the protective comfort of her wimple. But instead, her fingers encountered only her exposed hair, and she pulled them away as though they had been burned.

'After the Mass,' she repeated, 'as I was helping her back to her room, she said that it didn't matter that there was no collection, that they'd find out after she was gone how generous she had been.'

'Did you ask her what she meant?'

'No. I thought it was clear, that she had left them her money, or some of it.'

'And?'

Again, she shook her head. 'I don't know.'

'How long after that did she die?'

'Three months.'

'Did she say this to anyone else, about the money?'

'I don't know. She didn't talk to many people.'

'And the other woman?'

'Signora Cristanti,' Maria clarified. 'She was much more direct. She said that she wanted to leave her money to the people who had been good to her. She said it to everyone, all the time. But she wasn't . . . I don't think she was able to make that decision, not really, not when I knew her.'

'Why do you say that?'

'She wasn't very clear in her mind,' Maria answered. 'At least not all of the time. There were some days when she seemed all right, but most days she wandered; thought she was a girl again, asked to be taken places.' After a moment's pause, in an entirely clinical voice, she added, 'It's very common.'

'Going back into the past?' Brunetti asked.

'Yes. Poor things. I suppose the past is better for them than the present. Any past.'

Brunetti remembered his last visit to his mother but pushed the memory away. Instead, he asked, 'What happened to her?'

'Signora Cristanti?'

'Yes.'

'She died of a heart attack about four months ago.'

'Where did she die?'

'There. At the *casa di cura*.'

'Where did she have the heart attack? In her room or in some place where there were other people?' Brunetti didn't call them 'witnesses', not even in his mind.

'No, she died in her sleep. Quietly.'

'I see,' Brunetti said, not really meaning it. He allowed some time to pass before he asked, 'Does this list mean you think these people died of some-

16

thing else? Other than what's written by their names?'

She looked up at him, and he was puzzled by her surprise. If she had got so far as to come to see him about this, surely she must understand the implications of what she was saying.

In an obvious attempt to stall for time, she repeated, 'Something else?' When Brunetti didn't answer, she said, 'Signora Cristanti never had any trouble with her heart before.'

'And the other people on this list who died of heart attacks or strokes?'

'Signor Lerini had a history of heart trouble,' she said. 'No one else.'

Brunetti looked down at the list again. 'This other woman, Signora Galasso. Did she have trouble with her health before?'

Instead of answering him, she began to run one finger along the top of her bag, back and forth, back and forth.

'Maria,' he said and paused after he said her name, waiting for her to look up at him. When she did, he continued, 'I know it's a serious thing to bear false witness against your neighbour.' That startled her, as if the devil had started to quote the Bible. 'But it is important to protect the weak and those who can't protect themselves.' Brunetti didn't remember that as being in the Bible, though he thought it certainly should be. She said nothing to this, and so he asked, 'Do you understand, Maria?' When she still didn't answer, he changed the question and asked, 'Do you agree?'

'Of course, I agree,' she said, voice edgy. 'But

what if I'm wrong? What if this is all my imagination and nothing happened to those people?'

'If you believed that, I doubt you would be here. And you certainly wouldn't be dressed the way you are.' As soon as he said it, he realized that it sounded like deprecation of the way she was dressed, though his words referred only to her decision to leave the order and remove her habit.

Brunetti pushed the list to the side of his desk and, in a verbal equivalent of that gesture, changed the subject. 'When did you decide to leave?'

If she had been waiting for the question, her answer could have come no more quickly. 'After I spoke to the Mother Superior,' she said, voice rough with some remembered emotion. 'But first I spoke to Padre Pio, my confessor.'

'Can you tell me what you said to them?' Brunetti had been away from the Church and all its works and pomps for so long that he no longer remembered just what could and could not be repeated about a confession or what the penalty for doing so was, but he remembered enough to know that confession was something people were not supposed to talk about.

'Yes, I think so.'

'Is he the same priest who says Mass?'

'Yes. He's a member of our order, but he doesn't live there. He comes twice a week.'

'From where?'

'From our chapter house, here in Venice. He was my confessor in the other nursing home, too.'

Brunetti saw how willing she was to be diverted by details, and so he asked, 'What did you tell him?'

18

She paused a moment, and Brunetti imagined she was remembering her conversation with her confessor. 'I told him about the people who had died,' she said and stopped, looking away from him.

When he saw that she was going to say nothing further, Brunetti asked, 'Did you say anything else, anything about their money or what they had said about it?'

She shook her head. 'I didn't know about it then. That is, I hadn't remembered it then, I was so troubled by their deaths, so that's all I said to him, that they had died.'

'And what did he say?'

She looked at Brunetti again. 'He said that he didn't understand. And so I explained it to him. I told him the names of the people who had died and what I knew of their medical histories, that most of them had been in good health and had died suddenly. He listened to everything I had to say and asked me if I was sure.' In a casual aside, she added, 'Because I'm Sicilian, people up here always assume I'm stupid. Or a liar.'

Brunetti glanced at her to see if there was some reprimand, some comment on his own behaviour hidden in this remark, but there seemed to be none. 'I think he just couldn't believe it, that it was possible. Then, when I insisted that so many deaths were not normal,' she continued, 'he asked me if I was aware of the danger of repeating such things. Of the danger of causing slander? When I told him that I was aware of that, he suggested I pray about it.' She stopped.

'And then?'

'I told him that I had prayed, that I had prayed for days. Then he asked me if I knew what I was suggesting, what a horror it was.' She stopped again and then added as an aside, 'He was shocked. I don't think he could understand the possibility. He's a very good man, Padre Pio, and very unworldly.' Brunetti smothered a smile at hearing this said by someone who had spent the last twelve years in a convent.

'What happened then?'

'I asked to speak to the Mother Superior.'

'And did you?'

'It took two days, but she finally saw me, late one afternoon, after Vespers. I repeated everything to her, about the old people dying. She couldn't hide her surprise. I was glad to see that because it meant Padre Pio hadn't said anything to her. I knew he wouldn't, but what I had said was so terrible, well, I didn't know . . .' Her voice trailed away.

'And?' he asked.

'She refused to listen to me, said she would not listen to lies, that what I was saying would damage the order.'

'And so?'

'She told me, ordered me, under my vow of obedience, to keep full silence for a month.'

'Does that mean what I think it does, that you were not to speak to anyone for a month?'

'Yes.'

'What about your work? Didn't you have to speak to the patients?'

'I wasn't with them.'

'What?'

'The Mother Superior ordered me to spend my time in my room and in the chapel.'

'For a month?'

'Two.'

'What?'

'Two,' she repeated. 'At the end of the first month, she came to see me in my room and asked if my prayers and meditations had shown me the proper path. I told her that I had prayed and meditated – and I had – but that I was still troubled by the deaths. She refused to listen and told me to resume my silence.'

'And did you?'

She nodded.

'And then?'

'I spent the next week in prayer, and that's when I began to try to remember anything those people had told me, and that's when I remembered what Signora da Prè and Signorina Cristanti had said to me, about their money. Before that, I wouldn't let myself think about it, but once I did, I couldn't stop remembering.'

Brunetti considered the wide variety of things she might have 'remembered' after more than a month of solitude and silence. 'What happened at the end of the second month?'

'The Mother Superior came to my room again and asked me if I had come to my senses. I said that I had, which I suppose is true.' She stopped talking and again gave Brunetti that sad, nervous smile.

'And then?'

'And then I left.'

21

'Just like that?' Immediately, Brunetti began to consider the practical details: clothing, money, transportation. Strangely enough, they were the same details that had to be considered by people who were about to be released from prison.

'That same afternoon, I walked out with the people who had been there for visiting hours. No one seemed to think it was strange; no one noticed. I asked one of the women who was leaving if she could tell me where I could buy some clothing. All I had was seventeen thousand lire.'

She stopped speaking and Brunetti asked, 'And did she tell you?'

'Her father was one of my patients, so she knew me. She and her husband invited me to go back to their home with them for supper. I had no place to go, so I went. To the Lido.'

'And?'

'On the boat, I told them what I'd decided to do, but I didn't say anything about the reason. I'm not sure I even knew, or know now. I wasn't slandering the order or the nursing home. I'm not doing that now, am I?' Brunetti, who had no idea, shook his head and she continued. 'All I did was tell the Mother Superior about the deaths, that it seemed strange to me, so many of them.'

In an entirely conversational tone, Brunetti said, 'I've read that old people sometimes die in a series, with no reason.'

'I told you that. It's usually right after the holidays.'

'Could that be the explanation here?' he asked.

Her eyes flashed in what Brunetti believed was anger. 'Of course it could be. But then why did she try to silence me?'

'I think you told me that, Maria.'

'What?'

'Your vow. Obedience. I don't know how important that is to them, but it could be that they were worried about that, more than anything else.' When she didn't answer, he asked, 'Do you think that's possible?' She still refused to answer, so he asked, 'Then what happened? With the people on the Lido?'

'They were very kind to me. After we had dinner, she gave me some of her clothes.' She swept her hands open to show the skirt she was wearing. 'I stayed with them for the first week, and then they helped me get the job at the clinic.'

'Didn't you have to show some sort of identification to get it?'

She shook her head. 'No. They were so glad to find someone willing to do the work that they didn't ask any questions. But I've sent to the city hall in my home town and asked that copies of my birth certificate and *carta d'identità* be sent to me. If I'm going to come back to this life, then I suppose I'll need them.'

'Where did you have them sent, to the clinic?'

'No, to the home of these people.' She had heard the concern in his voice and said, 'Why do you ask?'

He shook her question away with a quick sideways motion of his head. 'Just curiosity. You never know how long that sort of thing can take.' It was a bad lie, but she had been a nun for so long that Brunetti did not believe she would easily recognize one. 'Are you still in contact with anyone from the *casa di cura* or from your order?'

'No. No one.'

'Do they know where you've gone?'

She shook her head. 'I don't think so. There's no way they could know.'

'Would the people on the Lido tell them?'

'No, I asked them not to tell anyone about me, and I think they won't.' Recalling his former uneasiness, she asked, 'Why do you ask about that?'

He saw no reason not to tell her this much, at least. 'If there is any truth in . . .' he began, but then realized that he wasn't at all sure what to call it, for certainly it wasn't an accusation, really no more than a comment on coincidence. He began again. 'Because of what you've told me, it might be wise for you to make no contact with the people at the *casa di cura.*' He realized that he had no idea who these people were. 'When you heard these old women talk, did you have any idea who, and I mean specifically, who they would leave their money to?'

'I've thought about that,' she said in a low voice, 'and I don't like to say.'

'Please, Maria, I don't think you can choose any longer what you do and don't want to say about this.'

She nodded, but very slowly, acknowledging the truth of what he said, though that didn't make it palatable. 'They could have left it to the *casa di cura* itself or to the director. Or to the order.'

'Who's the director?'

'Doctor Messini, Fabio Messini.'

'Is there anyone else?'

She considered this for a moment and then answered, 'Perhaps to Padre Pio. He's so good to the patients that many of them are very fond of him. But I don't think he'd accept anything.'

'The Mother Superior?' Brunetti asked.

'No. The order forbids us to own anything. The women, that is.'

Brunetti pulled a piece of paper toward him. 'Do you know Padre Pio's surname?'

Her alarm was palpable in her eyes. 'But you aren't going to talk to him, are you?'

'No, I don't think so. But I'd like to know it. In case it becomes necessary.'

'Cavaletti,' she said.

'Do you know anything more about him?'

She shook her head. 'No, only that he comes to hear confessions twice a week. If someone is very sick, he comes to give them the Last Rites. I've seldom had time to talk to him. Outside of the confessional, that is.' She stopped for a moment, and then added, 'The last time I saw him was about a month ago, Mother Superior's name day, February twentieth.' Suddenly her mouth drew closed and her eyes tightened, as if she had been struck by a sudden pain. Brunetti leaned forward in his chair, afraid she was going to faint.

She opened her eyes and looked across at him, raising a hand to ward him off. 'Isn't that strange?' she asked. 'That I would remember her feast day.' She looked away and then back at him. 'I can't remember my birthday. Just the feast day of

L'Immacolata, December eighth.' She shook her head, whether in sadness or surprise, he couldn't tell. 'It's as if part of me stopped existing for all those years, got cancelled out. I can't remember any more when it is, my birthday.'

'Maybe you could make it be the date you left the convent,' Brunetti suggested and smiled to show he meant it gently.

She met his glance for a moment and then raised the first two fingers of her right hand to her forehead and rubbed at it, eyes turned down. '*La Vita Nuova*,' she said, more to herself than to him.

With no warning, she got to her feet. 'I think I'd like to leave now, Commissario.' Her eyes were less calm than her voice, so Brunetti made no attempt to stop her.

'Could you tell me the name of the pensione where you're staying?'

'La Pergola.'

'On the Lido?'

'Yes.'

'And the people who helped you?'

'Why do you want their name?' she asked with real alarm.

'Because I like to know things,' he said, an honest answer.

'Sassi, Vittorio Sassi. Via Morosini, number eleven.'

'Thank you,' Brunetti said, not writing these names down. She turned toward the door and for a moment he thought she would ask him what he was going to do about what she had told him, but she said nothing. He got up and came around the desk, hoping at least to open the door for her, but she was too quick for him. She opened it, took one glance back at him, didn't smile, and left the room.

Chapter Two

Brunetti returned to the contemplation of his feet, but they no longer spoke to him of idle things. Like a presiding deity, his mother filled his thoughts, she for years a traveller in the unchartable territory of the mad. Fears for her safety flailed at his mind with their wild wings, though he knew well that only one, final, absolute safety remained for his mother, a safety his heart could not wish for her, no matter how much his mind urged him. He found himself involuntarily pulled toward the memories of the last six years, fingering them like the beads on some horrid rosary.

With a sudden, violent motion, he kicked the drawer shut and got to his feet. Suor'Immacolata – he could not yet call her anything else – had assured him there was no danger to his mother; he had heard no proof that there was danger to anyone at all. Old people died, and it was often a liberation for them and for those around them, as it would be for . . . He went back to his desk and picked up the list she had given him, again ran his eye down the names and ages.

Brunetti began to think of ways to learn more about the people on the list, more about their lives and their deaths. Suor'Immacolata had given the dates of their deaths, which would lead to death certificates at the city hall, the first path in the vast bureaucratic labyrinth that would lead him eventually to copies of their wills. Gossamer, his curiosity would have to be as light and airy as gossamer, his questions as delicate as the touch of a cat's whiskers. He tried to remember ever having told Suor'-Immacolata that he was a *commissario* of police. Perhaps he had mentioned it during one of those long afternoons when his mother allowed him to take her hand, but only if the young woman who was her favourite remained in the room with them. They, the two of them, had to talk about something, since Brunetti's mother often remained silent for hours, crooning a tuneless melody to herself. As if the habit she wore had amputated her personality, Suor'Immacolata had never said anything about herself, at least nothing that Brunetti remembered, so it must have been then that he had told her what he did, as he cast about for topics to fill those endless, ragged hours. And she had heard and remembered and so had come to him, a year later, with her story and her fear.

Years before, there had been certain things that Brunetti had found it difficult, sometimes impossible, to believe people capable of doing. He had once believed, or perhaps had forced himself to believe, that there were limits to human vice. Gradually, as he was exposed to ever more horrible examples of crime, as he saw the lengths to which people would go to feed their various lusts – greed, though the most common, was hardly the most compelling – he had seen this illusion eaten away by the mounting tide until he sometimes felt himself in the position of that daft Irish king, the one whose name he could never pronounce correctly, who stood at the edge of the sea, beating at the encroaching tide with his sword, maddened by the defiance of the mounting waters.

It no longer surprised him, therefore, that old people might be killed for their wealth; what surprised him was the technique, for at least at first glance it was replete with possibility for error or discovery.

He had also learned, during the years he had practised this profession of his, that the important trail to follow was the one left by money. The place where it began was usually a given: the person from whom the money was taken, either by force or by craft. The other end, where the trail finished, was the difficult one to find, just as it was the more vital one, for it was there that would also be found the person who had practised the craft or the force. *Cui bono?*

If Suor'Immacolata was right – he forced himself into the conditional mode – then the first thing he had to find was the end of the trail, and that search could begin only with their wills.

He found Signorina Elettra at her desk, and the sight of her busy at her computer surprised him, almost as if he had expected her to be reading the newspaper or working on a crossword puzzle as a way to celebrate Patta's continuing absence. 'Signorina, what do you know about wills?' he asked as he came in.

'That I don't have one,' she said lightly and

smiled, tossing her answer over her shoulder and treating the question lightly, as would anyone still in their early thirties.

And may you never need one, Brunetti found himself wishing. He returned her smile and then allowed his own to fade away. 'Well, about other people's wills, then?'

Seeing his seriousness, she swivelled around in her chair and faced him, waiting for an explanation.

'I'd like to find out the contents of the wills of five people who died here this year, in the San Leonardo nursing home.'

'Were they residents of Venice?' she asked.

'I don't know. Why? Does it make a difference?'

'Wills are made public by the notory who drew them up, regardless of where the person dies. If they made their wills here in Venice, then all I need is the name of the notory.'

'And if I don't have that?' he asked.

'Then that will make it harder.'

'Harder?'

Her smile was open, her voice level. 'The fact that you didn't simply contact the heirs and ask for copies, Commissario, makes me think that you don't want anyone to know you're asking questions.' She smiled again. 'There's a central office where copies are recorded. Their files were computerized two years ago, so there's no problem there, but if the notaries work out in some little *paese* out on the mainland that hasn't been computerized yet, then it might be more difficult.'

'If they were recorded here, can you get the information?'

'Of course.'

'How?'

She looked down at her skirt and brushed away an invisible speck. 'I'm afraid it's illegal.'

'What's illegal?'

'The way I get the information.'

'Which is . . .?'

'I'm not sure you can understand, Commissario, or that I could explain it to you adequately, but there are ways of discovering the codes which give access to almost all information. The more public the information is — a city hall, public records — the easier it is to discover the code. And once a person has that, it's as if . . . well, it's as if they'd gone home and left the door to the office open and the lights on.'

'Is this true of all government agencies?' he asked uneasily.

'I think you'd prefer not to know the answer,' she said, her smile gone.

'How easy is it to get this information?' he asked.

'I'd say it's in direct proportion to the skill of the person looking for it.'

'And how skilled are you, Signorina?'

The question summoned back a smile, a very small one. 'I think that's a question I'd prefer not to answer, Commissario.'

He studied the soft contours of her face, noticed for the first time two faint lines that extended down from the outside corners of her eyes, no doubt the result of frequent smiles, and found it difficult to believe that this was a person possessed of criminal craft and, in all likelihood, of criminal intent.

Not for a moment reflecting upon his oath of

office, Brunetti asked, 'But if they lived here, then you can get the information?'

He noticed the way she struggled to keep all evidence of pride out of her voice, struggled and failed. 'The records in the registry office, Commissario?'

Amused at the tone of condescension which a former employee of the Banca D'Italia used when speaking the name of a mere government office, he nodded.

'I can get you the names of the principal heirs after lunch. Copies of the wills might take a day or two.'

Only the young and attractive can risk showing off, he realized. 'After lunch will do nicely, Signorina.' He left the list with the names and dates of death on her desk and went back up to his office.

When he sat at his desk, he looked at the names of the two men he'd written down: Dr Fabio Messini, and Father Pio Cavaletti. Neither of them was familiar to him, but in a city as socially incestuous as Venice, that was meaningless to a person in pursuit of information.

He called down to the office where the uniformed police had their desks. 'Vianello, could you come up here for a moment? And bring Miotti along with you, would you?' While he waited for the two policemen to arrive, Brunetti drew a row of checks under the names, and it was not until Vianello and Miotti appeared at his door that he realized they were crosses. He set his pen down and motioned the two policemen to the chairs in front of his desk.

As Vianello sat, his unbuttoned uniform jacket swung open, and Brunetti noticed that he looked thinner than he had during the winter.

'You on a diet, Vianello?' he asked.

'No, sir,' the Sergeant replied, surprised that Brunetti had noticed. 'Exercise.'

'What?' Brunetti, to whom the idea of exercise bordered on the obscene, made no attempt to disguise his shock.

'Exercise,' Vianello repeated. 'I go over to the *palestra* after work and spend a half hour or so.'

'Doing what?' Brunetti asked.

'Exercising, sir.'

'How often?'

'As often as I can,' Vianello answered, sounding suddenly evasive.

'How often is that?'

'Oh, three or four times a week.'

Miotti sat silent, his head turning back and forth as he followed this strange conversation. Is this how crime was fought?

'And what do you do when you're there?'

'I exercise, sir,' coming down on the verb with impressive force.

Interested now, however perversely so, Brunetti leaned forward, elbows on his desk, chin cupped in one hand. 'But how? Running in place? Swinging from ropes?'

'No, sir,' Vianello answered, not smiling. 'With machines.'

'What kind of machines?'

'Exercise machines.'

Brunetti turned his eyes to Miotti who, because

he was young, might understand some of this. But Miotti, whose youth took care of his body for him, looked away from Brunetti and back to Vianello.

'Well,' Brunetti concluded, when it was evident that Vianello was going to be no more forthcoming, 'you look very good.'

'Thank you, sir. You might want to think about giving it a try yourself.'

Tucking in his stomach and sitting up straighter in his chair, Brunetti turned his attention back to business. 'Miotti,' he began, 'your brother is a priest, isn't he?'

'Yes, sir,' he answered, evidently surprised that his superior would know.

'What kind?'

'A Dominican, sir.'

'Is he here in Venice?'

'No, sir. He was here for four years, but then they sent him to Novara, three years ago, to teach in a boys' school.'

'Are you in touch with him?'

'Yes, sir. I speak to him every week, and I see him three or four times a year.'

'Good. The next time you talk to him, I'd like you to ask him something.'

'What about, sir?' Miotti asked, taking a notebook and a pen from his jacket pocket and pleasing Brunetti by not asking why.

'I'd like you to ask him if he knows anything about Padre Pio Cavaletti. He's a member of the Order of the Sacred Cross here in the city.' Brunetti saw Vianello's raised eyebrows, but the Sergeant remained silent, listening.

'Is there anything specific you'd like me to ask him, sir?'

'No, anything at all that he can think of or remember.'

Miotti started to speak, hesitated, then asked, 'Can you tell me anything more about him, sir? That I can tell my brother?'

'He's the chaplain for the *casa di cura* over near the Ospedale Giustiniani, but that's all I know about him.' Miotti kept his head down, writing, so Brunetti asked, 'Do you have any idea about who he could be, Miotti?'

The young officer looked up. 'No, sir. I never had much to do with my brother's clerical friends.'

Brunetti, responding more to his tone than to the words, asked, 'Is there any reason for that?'

Instead of answering, Miotti shook his head quickly and then looked down at the pages of his notebook, adding a few words to what he had written.

Brunetti glanced at Vianello over the lowered head of the younger man, but the Sergeant gave a barely perceptible shrug. Brunetti opened his eyes and nodded briefly toward Miotti. Vianello, interpreting this as a signal that he discover the reasons for the young man's reticence when they went back downstairs, nodded in return.

'Anything else, sir?' Vianello asked.

'This afternoon,' Brunetti said, answering his question but thinking of the copies of the wills Signorina Elettra had promised him, 'I should have the names of some people I'd like to go and talk to.'

'Would you like me to come with you, sir?' Vianello asked.

Brunetti nodded. 'Four o'clock,' he decided, thinking that would give him plenty of time to get back from lunch. 'Good. I think that's all for now. Thank you both.'

'I'll come up and get you,' Vianello said. As the younger man moved toward the door, Vianello turned, gestured toward the disappearing Miotti with his chin, and nodded to Brunetti. If there was anything to be discovered about Miotti's reluctance to spend time with his brother's clerical friends, Vianello would find it out that afternoon.

When they were gone, Brunetti opened a drawer and pulled out the Yellow Pages. He looked under doctors but found no listing in Venice for Messini. He checked the white pages and found three of them, one a Doctor Fabio, with an address in Dorsoduro. He made a note of Messini's phone number and address, then picked up the phone and dialled a different number from memory.

The phone was picked up on the third ring, and a man's voice said, '*Allò?*'

'*Ciao*, Lele,' Brunetti said, recognizing the painter's gruff voice. 'I'm calling about one of your neighbours, Dottor Fabio Messini?' If someone lived in Dorsoduro, Lele Bortoluzzi, whose family had been in Venice since the Crusades, would know who they were.

'Is he the one with the Afghan?'

'Dog or wife?' Brunetti asked with a laugh.

'If it's the one I'm thinking of, the wife's a Roman, but the dog's an Afghan. Beautiful, graceful thing. Just like the wife, if you think about it. She walks it past the gallery at least once a day.'

'The Messini I'm looking for has a nursing home over near the Giustiniani.'

Lele, who knew everything, said, 'He's the same one who runs the place Regina's in, isn't he?'

'Yes.'

'How is she, Guido?' Lele, only a few years younger than Brunetti's mother, had known her all his life and had been one of her husband's best friends.

'She's the same, Lele.'

'God save her, Guido. I'm sorry.'

'Thank you,' Brunetti said. There was nothing else to be said. 'What about Messini?'

'As far as I can remember, he started with an *ambulatorio* over here, about twenty years ago. But then after he married the Roman, Claudia, he used her family's money to start the *casa di cura*. After that, he gave up private practice. Well, I think he did. And now I believe he's the director of four or five of them.'

'Do you know him?'

'No. I see him every once in a while. Not often. Certainly not as often as I see the wife.'

'How do you know who she is?' Brunetti asked.

'She's bought a few paintings from me over the course of the years. I like her. Intelligent woman.'

'With good taste in paintings?' Brunetti asked.

Lele's laugh came down the phone. 'Modesty prevents my answering that question.'

'Is there any talk about him? Or about them?'

There was a long pause, at the end of which Lele

said, 'I've never heard anything. But I can ask around if you'd like me to.'

'Not so that anyone knows you're asking,' Brunetti said, even though he knew it was unnecessary.

'My tongue shall be as gossamer,' Lele said.

'I'd appreciate it, Lele.'

'It doesn't have anything to do with Regina, does it?'

'No, nothing.'

'Good. She was a wonderful woman, Guido.' Then, as if suddenly realizing he'd used the past tense, Lele quickly added, 'I'll call you if I learn anything.'

'Thanks, Lele.' Brunetti came close to reminding him about being delicate, but he reflected that anyone who had thrived as Lele had in the world of Venetian art and antiquities had to have as much gossamer as steel in his nature, and so all he said was a quick goodbye.

It was still well before twelve, but Brunetti felt himself lured from his office by the scent of spring that had been laying siege to the city for the last week. Besides, he was the boss, so why couldn't he just up and leave if he chose to? Nor did he feel himself obliged to stop and tell Signorina Elettra where he was going; she was probably elbow-deep in computer crime, and he didn't want to be either an accessory or, truth be told, an impediment, so he left her to it and headed toward the Rialto and home.

It had been cold and damp when he left the apartment that morning, and now, in the growing warmth of the day, he felt himself burdened by his jacket and his overcoat. He loosened both, removed his scarf and stuffed it in his pocket, but still it was so warm that he sensed the year's first perspiration break out across his back. He felt trapped in his woollen suit, and then the traitorous thought came to him that both slacks and jacket were tighter than they had been in early winter when he had first worn the suit. When he got to the Rialto Bridge, he pushed ahead in a sudden surge of buoyant energy and started to trot up the steps. After a dozen steps, he found himself winded and had to slow down to a walk. At the top, he paused and gazed off to the left and up toward the curve that took the Grand Canal off toward San Marco and the Doge's Palace. The sun glared up from the surface of the water on which bobbed the first black-headed gulls of the season.

His breath caught, he started down the other side, so pleased with the softness of the day that he felt none of his usual irritation with the crowded streets and milling tourists. Walking between the double bank of fruit and vegetable stalls, he saw that the first asparagus had arrived and wondered if he could persuade Paola to get some. A glance at the price made him realize he had no hope of that, at least for another week, when it would flood into the market and the price be cut in half. Ambling along, he studied the vegetables and their prices, occasionally nodding or exchanging a greeting with people he knew. In the last stall on the right, he saw a familiar leaf and went over to have a closer look.

'Is that *puntarelle*?' he asked, surprised to find it in the market this early.

'Yes, and the best in Rialto,' the vendor assured him, his face flushed with years of wine drinking. 'Six thousand a kilo and cheap at the price.'

Brunetti refused to respond to this absurdity. When he was a boy, *puntarelle* cost a few hundred lire a kilo, and few people ate it; those who bought it generally took it home to give to the rabbits kept illegally in courtyards or back gardens.

'I'll take half a kilo,' Brunetti said, pulling some bills from his pocket.

The vendor leaned forward over the piles of vegetables displayed in front of him and grabbed up an abundant handful of the pungent green leaf. Magician-like, he pulled a sheet of brown paper from nowhere and plunked it onto the scale, dropped the leaves into it, then quickly wrapped it together into a neat package. He laid it on top of a box of neatly ordered rows of baby courgettes and extended his palm. Brunetti gave him three thousand-lire notes, didn't ask for a plastic bag, and set off toward home.

At the clock high on the wall, he turned left and headed up toward San Aponal and home. Without thinking, he took the first right and went into Do Mori, where he had a piece of prosciutto wrapped around a thin breadstick and a glass of Chardonnay to wash away the salty taste of the meat.

A few minutes later and newly winded by the more than ninety stairs that led to it, he opened the door to his apartment and was greeted by the mingled smells that warmed his soul and sang to him of home, hearth, family, and joy.

Though the delirious odour of garlic and onions told him that she was in, Brunetti still called out, 'Paola, are you here?'

A shouted '*Sì*' from the kitchen answered him and drew him down the corridor toward her. He set the paper-wrapped package on the kitchen table, went across the room to kiss her and have a look at what was frying in the pan in front of her.

Yellow and red strips of pepper simmered in a rich tomato sauce, and from it rose the aroma of sausage. 'Tagliatelle?' he asked, naming his favourite fresh pasta.

She smiled and bent to stir the sauce. 'Of course.' Then, turning to the table, she saw the package. 'What's that?'

'Puntarelle. I thought we could have that salad with the anchovy sauce.'

'Good idea,' she said, voice filled with delight. 'Where'd you find them?'

'That guy who beats his wife.'

'I beg your pardon,' came her confused response.

'The last one on the right as you're heading toward the fish market, the one with the veins in his nose.'

'Beats his wife?'

'Well, we've had him down at the Questura three times. But she always drops the charges after she sobers up.'

Brunetti watched as she ran through a mental file of the different vendors on the right side of the market. 'The woman with the mink jacket?' she finally asked.

'Yes.'

'I had no idea.'

Brunetti shrugged.

'Can't you do anything about it?' she asked.

Because he was hungry and because discussion would delay his meal, he was curt. 'No. Not our business.'

He tossed his overcoat, and then his jacket, across the back of a kitchen chair and went to the refrigerator to get himself some wine. Moving around her to get a glass, he murmured, 'Smells good.'

'It's really none of your business?' she asked, and he knew, both from her tone and from long experience, that she had found A Cause.

'No, it's not, not unless she makes a formal *denuncia*, which she has never been willing to do.'

'Perhaps she's afraid of him.'

'Paola,' he answered, having hoped to avoid this, 'she's two of him, must weigh a hundred kilos. I'm sure she could toss him out a window if she wanted to.'

'But?' she asked, hearing the unspoken words in his voice.

'But she doesn't want to, I'd say. They fight, it gets out of control, and she calls us.' He filled a glass and took a swallow, hoping it was over.

'And then?' Paola asked.

'And then we come and pick him up and take him down to the Questura and hold him until she comes to get him in the morning. It happens every six months or so, but there are never any serious signs of violence on her, and she's glad enough to have him go back home with her.'

Paola thought about this for a while but finally shrugged the subject away. 'Strange, isn't it?'

'Very,' Brunetti agreed, knowing from long experience that Paola had decided not to pursue the subject.

Bending down to pick up his coat and jacket and take them back into the hall, he saw a brown manila envelope on the table.

'Is that Chiara's report card?' he asked as he reached toward it.

'Um huh,' Paola said, adding salt to the pot of water that boiled on a back burner.

'How is it?' he asked. 'Good?'

'Excellent in everything except one subject.'

'Physical Education?' he guessed, at a loss, for Chiara had catapulted to the head of her first class in grammar school and had remained there for the last six years. Like him, his daughter preferred lolling about to exercise, and so that was the only subject he could imagine her not doing well in.

He opened the envelope, pulled out the page, and cast his eye across it.

'Religious instruction?' he asked. 'Religious instruction?'

Paola said nothing and so he continued and read the notes added by the teacher in explanation of her grade of 'unsatisfactory'.

' "Asks too many questions?"' he read. And then, ' "Disruptive behaviour." What's this all about?' Brunetti demanded, holding the page out toward Paola.

'You'll have to ask her when she gets home.'

'She isn't back yet?' Brunetti asked, and the wild thought came to him that Chiara knew of the bad report and was hiding out somewhere, refusing to come home. He glanced at his watch and saw that it was still early; she wouldn't be back for another fifteen minutes.

Paola, who was setting four plates onto the table, nudged him gently aside with her hip.

'Has she said anything about this to you?' he asked, moving out of her way.

'Nothing special. She said that she didn't like the priest, but she never said why. Or I didn't ask her why.'

'What kind of priest is he?' Brunetti asked, pulling out a chair and sitting at his place.

'What do you mean, "what kind"?'

'Is he, what do you call it, regular clergy, or a member of an order?'

'I think he's just a regular parish priest, from the church by the school.'

'San Polo?'

'Yes.'

As they spoke, Brunetti read through the comments of the other teachers, all forthright in their praise of Chiara's intelligence and industry. Her mathematics teacher, in fact, referred to her as 'an extraordinarily talented pupil, with a gift for mathematics,' and her Italian teacher went so far as to use the word 'elegance' when speaking of Chiara's written expression. In none of the comments was there a word of qualification, no evidence of that natural inclination of teachers to deliver a stern warning to offset the danger of vanity that was sure to result from each word of praise.

'I don't understand it,' Brunetti said, slipping the

pagella back in its envelope and tossing it gently back down onto the table. He thought for a moment, considering how to phrase his question, and asked Paola, 'You haven't said anything to her, have you?'

Paola was known to her wide circle of friends as many things, and those things varied, but everyone who knew Paola considered her '*una mangia-preti*', an eater of priests. The anti-clerical rage that sometimes flashed out from her still managed to surprise Brunetti, even though it was not often that he could any longer be surprised by anything Paola said or did. But this was the red flag subject which, more than any other, could launch her – with no warning and almost without fail – into fulminant rage.

'You know I agreed,' she said, turning away from the stove and facing him. It had always surprised Brunetti that Paola had so readily acquiesced to their families' suggestion that the children be baptized and sent to religious instruction classes at their schools. 'It's part of Western Culture,' Paola often said with chilling blandness. No fools, the children had quickly learned that Paola was not the person to ask about matters of religious faith, though they had just as quickly realized that her knowledge of ecclesiastical history and theological disputation was virtually encyclopaedic. Her clarification of the theological foundations of the Arian heresy was a study in level-headed objectivity and scholarly attention to detail; her denunciation of the centuries of slaughter that had resulted from that the Church's different opinion was, to use a temperate word, intemperate.

All of these years, she had kept her word and never spoken openly, at least in the presence of the children, against Christianity or, in fact, against any religion. And so whatever antipathy toward religion or any ideas that might have led Chiara toward 'disruptive behaviour' had not come from anything Paola had ever said, at least not openly.

Both turned toward the sound of the opening door, but it was Raffi, not Chiara, who let himself into the apartment. '*Ciao, Mamma!*' he called, heading back toward his own room to put down his books. '*Ciao, Papà.*' A short time later, he came down the hall and into the kitchen. He bent down and kissed Paola on the cheek, and Brunetti, still seated, saw his son from a different perspective and saw him taller.

Raffi lifted the top on the frying pan and, seeing what was inside, kissed his mother again. 'I'm dying, *Mamma*. When are we going to eat?'

'As soon as your sister gets here,' Paola said, turning back to lower the flame under the now-boiling water.

Raffi pushed back his sleeve and checked the time. 'You know she's always on time. She'll walk through the door in seven minutes, so why don't you put the pasta in now?' He reached down onto the table and ripped open a cellophane package of bread sticks and pulled out three of the thin *grissini*. He put the ends between his teeth and, like a rabbit chewing at three longs stalks of grass, nibbled at them until they were gone. He grabbed three more and repeated the process. 'Come on, *Mamma*, I'm starved, and I've got to go over to Massimo's this afternoon to work on physics.'

Paola placed a platter of fried aubergine on the

table, nodded in sudden agreement, and began to drop the newly made strips of pasta into the boiling water.

Brunetti pulled the *pagella* from the envelope and handed it to Raffaele. 'You know anything about this?' he asked.

It was only in recent years and with the abandonment of what his parents referred to as his 'Karl Marx Period' that Raffi's own report cards had come to take on the repetitive perfection his sister's had had from her first days in school, but even in the worst academic disasters of that period, Raffi had never felt anything but pride in his sister's achievements.

He looked up and down the page and handed it back to his father, saying nothing.

'Well?' Brunetti asked.

'Disruptive, huh?' was his only response.

Paola, stirring the pasta, managed to give the side of the pot a few heavy clangs.

'You know anything about it?' Brunetti repeated.

'No, not really,' Raffi said, obviously reluctant to explain whatever it was he knew. When neither of his parents said anything, Raffi said, voice aggrieved, '*Mamma* will just get mad.'

'At what?' Paola asked with false lightness.

'At . . .' Raffi was cut off by the sound of Chiara's key in the door.

'Ah, the guilty one arrives,' Raffi said and poured himself a glass of mineral water.

All three of them watched Chiara hang her jacket on a hook in the hall, drop her books, then pick them up and set them on a chair. She came down the corridor toward them and stopped at the door. 'Somebody die?' she asked with no hint of irony in her voice.

Paola reached down and pulled a colander from a cabinet. She set it in the sink and poured the pasta and boiling water through it. Chiara remained at the door. 'What's wrong?' she asked.

As Paola busied herself pouring the pasta and then the sauce into a large bowl, Brunetti explained. 'Your report card came.'

Chiara's face fell. 'Oh,' was the best she could say. She slid past Brunetti and took her place at the table.

Starting with Raffi's plate, Paola served up four heaping dishes of pasta and then offered them grated parmegiano, which she sprinkled liberally over their pasta. She began to eat. They all began to eat.

When her plate was empty and she was holding it out to her mother for more, Chiara asked, 'Religion, huh?'

'Yes. You got a very low grade,' Paola answered.

'How low?'

'Three.'

Chiara stopped herself from wincing, but just barely.

'Do you know why the grade is so low?' Brunetti asked, placing his hands over his empty plate to tell Paola he wanted no more.

Chiara started on her second helping while Paola spooned the rest into Raffi's dish. 'No, I guess I don't have a reason.'

'Don't you study?' Paola asked.

'There's nothing to study,' Chaira said, 'just that

dumb catechism. You can memorize that in an afternoon.'

'Then?' Brunetti asked.

Raffi took a roll from the basket at the centre of the table, broke it in half, and began to wipe the pasta sauce from his plate. 'Is it Padre Luciano?' he asked.

Chiara nodded and set her fork down. She looked over toward the stove to see what else was for lunch.

'Do you know this Padre Luciano?' Brunetti asked Raffi.

The boy rolled his eyes in his head. 'Oh, God, who doesn't know him?' Then, turning to his sister, he asked, 'You ever go to confession to him, Chiara?'

She shook her head quickly from side to side but said nothing.

Paola got up from the table and took their pasta dishes from the plates on which they rested. She went to the oven, opened it, and brought out a platter of *cotoletta milanese*, placed some sliced lemon wedges around the edge of the platter, and set it on the table. While Brunetti took two cutlets, Paola helped herself to some aubergine, saying nothing.

Seeing that Paola was keeping out of this, Brunetti asked Raffi, 'What's it like, to go to confession to him?'

'Oh, he's famous with the kids,' Raffi said, spooning two cutlets onto his plate.

'Famous for what?' Brunetti asked.

Instead of answering, Raffi shot a glance toward Chiara. Both of her parents saw her give a barely

50

perceptible shake of her head and then bend down and devote her attention to her lunch.

Brunetti set his fork down. Chiara didn't look up, and Raffi glanced over to Paola, who still said nothing. 'All right,' Brunetti said, voice heavier than he would have liked to hear it. 'What's going on here, and what aren't we supposed to know about this Padre Luciano?'

He looked from Raffi, who refused to meet his eyes, to Chiara and was surprised to see that her face was suffused with a dark blush.

Softening his voice, he asked, 'Chiara, can Raffi tell us what he knows?'

She nodded but didn't look up.

Raffi imitated his father and set his fork down, too. But then he smiled. 'It's not like it's any big thing, *Papà*.'

Brunetti said nothing. Paola might as well have been mute.

'It's what he says to the kids. When they confess sex things.' He stopped.

'Sex things?' Brunetti repeated.

'You know, *Papà*. Things they do.'

Brunetti knew. 'What does he do – Padre Luciano?' Brunetti asked.

'He makes them describe them. You know, talk about them.' Raffi made a noise, something between a snicker and a groan, and stopped talking.

Brunetti glanced at Chiara and saw that the blush had grown even deeper.

'I see,' Brunetti said.

'It's really sort of sad,' Raffi said.

'Has he ever done this to you?' Brunetti asked.

'Oh, no, I stopped going to confession years ago. But he does it to the young boys.'

'And the girls,' Chiara added in a very soft voice, so soft that Brunetti asked her nothing.

'Is that all he does?' Brunetti asked Raffi.

'That's all I know, *Papà*. I had him for religious instruction about four years ago, and the only thing he made us do then was memorize the book and recite it back to him. But he used to say nasty things to the girls.' Turning to his sister, he asked, 'He still do that?'

She nodded.

'Would anyone like another cutlet?' Paola asked in an entirely normal voice. She got two shaken heads and a grunt and took that as sufficient response to remove the platter. There was no salad that day, and she had planned to serve only fruit for dessert. Instead, she opened a paper package on the counter and pulled out a heavy cake, laden with fresh fruit and filled with whipped cream, which she had intended to take back to the university that afternoon to offer to her colleagues after the monthly faculty meeting.

'Chiara, dear, would you get plates?' she asked while taking a broad silver knife from a drawer.

The pieces she cut them, Brunetti noticed, were large enough to catapult the entire lot of them into insulin shock, but the sweetness of the cake, and then the coffee, and then the talk of the equal sweetness of the first real day of springtime were enough to restore some sort of tranquillity to the family. After it, Paola said she would do the dishes, and Brunetti decided to read the paper. Chiara disappeared into her room, and Raffi went off to study physics with his friend. Neither Brunetti nor Paola said anything further about the subject, but they both knew that they had not heard the last of Padre Luciano.

Chapter Three

Brunetti took his overcoat with him after lunch and walked back to the Questura with it draped over his shoulders, revelling in the softness of the day, comfortable and warm after the large meal. He forced himself to ignore the tightness of his suit, insisting to himself that it was no more than the unaccustomed warmth of the day that made him so sensitive to the weight of the heavy wool. Besides, everyone gained a kilo or two during the winter; probably did a person good: built up resistance to disease and things like that.

As he started the descent from the Rialto Bridge, he saw a number eighty-two pulling up to the *embarcadero* on his right and, without thinking, ran to get it, which he managed to do just as it was starting to pull away from the dock and out into the centre of the Grand Canal. He moved to the right side of the boat but stayed outside on the deck, glad of the breeze and the light that danced up from the water. He watched Calle Tiepolo approaching on the right side and peered up the narrow *calle*, searching for the railing of his terrace, but they were past it too quickly for him to see it, and so he turned his attention back to the canal.

Brunetti often wondered what it must have been

like to live in the days of the Most Serene Republic, to have made this grand passage by means of the power of oars alone, to move in silence without motors or horns, a silence broken by nothing more than the shouted '*Ouie*' of boatmen and the slip of oars. So much had changed: today's merchants kept in touch with one another with the odious '*telefonini*', not by means of slant-rigged galleons. The very air stank of the miasma of exhaust and pollution that drifted over from the mainland; no sea breeze seemed any longer able to sweep the city entirely clean. The one thing that the ages had left unchanged was the city's thousand-year-old heritage of venality, and Brunetti always felt uncomfortable at his inability to decide whether he thought this good or bad.

It had been his original intention to get off at San Samuele and take the long walk up toward San Marco, but the thought of the crowds that would have been induced out onto the streets by the mellow weather kept him on the boat, and he didn't get off until San Zaccaria. He cut back toward the Questura, arriving there a little after three and apparently in advance of most of the uniformed staff.

In his office, he found that the papers on his desk had proliferated – perhaps they actually bred? – while he was at lunch. As promised, Signorina Elettra had given him a neatly typed list, providing the names of the principal heirs of the people Suor'Immacolata – he corrected himself: Maria Testa – had given him. She had also supplied addresses and phone numbers. Casting his eye down the list, Brunetti saw that three of them lived in Venice. The fourth lived in Torino, and the last will listed the names of six people, none of them resident in Venice. Underneath, a typed note from Signorina Elettra told him that she would have copies of the wills by the following afternoon.

For a moment, he thought of calling ahead, but then he reflected that a certain advantage was always to be gained by arriving, at least for the first interview, unannounced and, if possible, unexpected, and so he did no more than arrange the addresses in the most convenient geographic order on his mental map of the city and then slip the list into his jacket pocket. The advantage given by surprise was in no way related to the guilt or innocence of the people he spoke to, but long experience had taught him that surprise often spurred people toward the truth.

He bent his head over the remaining official papers and began to read. After the second, he sat back in his seat, pulled the stack toward him, and continued to read. It was after only a few minutes that the tedium of their contents, the warmth of the office, and the aftermath of his lunch lured Brunetti's hands down onto his lap and his chin onto his chest. Some time later, he was shocked awake by the sound of a door slamming out in the corridor. He shook his head, ran his hands across his face a few times, and wished he had a coffee. Instead, he looked up to see Vianello standing at the door, the door Brunetti realized had stood open during his entire nap.

'Good afternoon, Sergeant,' he said, giving Vianello the smile of a man who felt fully in control of everyone at the Questura. 'What is it?'

'I said I'd come and get you, sir. It's quarter to four.'

'That late?' Brunetti said, glancing down at his watch.

'Yes, sir,' Vianello said. 'I came up before, but you were busy.' Vianello waited a minute for that to sink in and then added, 'I've got the boat outside, sir.'

As they walked down the steps of the Questura, Brunetti asked, 'Did you speak to Miotti?'

'Yes, sir. It's what I expected.'

'His brother's gay?' Brunetti asked, not even bothering to look at Vianello.

Vianello stopped in the middle of the staircase. When Brunetti turned to him, the sergeant asked, 'How did you know that, sir?'

'He seemed nervous about his brother and his clerical friends, and I couldn't think of anything else about a priest that would make Miotti nervous. It's not as if he's the most open-minded man we have.' After a moment's reflection, Brunetti added, 'And it's not as if it's a surprise when a priest is gay.'

'It's the opposite that's a surprise, I'd say,' Vianello remarked and started back down the steps. He turned his attention back to Miotti, not needing to explain the leap to Brunetti. 'But you've always said he's a good policeman, sir.'

'He doesn't have to be open-minded to be a good policeman, Vianello.'

'No, I suppose not,' Vianello agreed.

They emerged from the Questura a few minutes later and found Bonsuan, the pilot, waiting for them aboard a police launch. Everything glistened: the brass fittings on the boat, one of the metal tags on Bonsuan's collar, the new green leaves on the vine coming back to life on the wall across the canal, a wine bottle drifting by on the surface of the water, itself a gleaming field. For no reason other than the light, Vianello spread his arms wide and smiled.

Bonsuan's attention was drawn by the movement, and he stared. Caught between embarrassment and joy, Vianello began to turn his motion into the tired stretch of a deskbound man, but then a pair of amorous swifts flashed by, low to the water, and Vianello dropped all pretence. 'It's springtime,' he called happily to the pilot and leaped onto the deck beside him. He clapped Bonsuan on the shoulder, his own joy suddenly overflowing.

'Do we owe all of this to your exercise class?' Brunetti asked as he came aboard.

Bonsuan, who apparently knew nothing about Vianello's latest enthusiasm, gave the sergeant a disgusted look, turned, hit the motor into life, and pulled the launch out into the narrow canal.

Spirits undampened, Vianello remained on deck while Brunetti went down into the cabin. He pulled down a city guide that rested on a shelf running along one side of the cabin and checked the locations of the three addresses on the list. From inside, he watched the interaction between the two men: his sergeant, as unashamedly filled with high spirits as an adolescent; the dour pilot, staring ahead as they pulled out into the *bacino* of San Marco. As he watched, Vianello placed a hand on Bonsuan's shoulder and pointed off to the east, calling his attention to a thick-masted sailboat that came toward them, its sails fat-cheeked with the fresh spring breeze. Bonsuan nodded once but turned his attention back to their course. Vianello tossed his head back and laughed, sending the deep sound spilling down into the cabin.

Brunetti resisted until they were in the middle of the *bacino*, but then he gave in to the magnet of Vianello's happiness and came up on deck. Just as he stepped outside, the wake of a passing Lido ferry caught them broadside, knocking Brunetti off balance and toward the boat's low railing. Vianello's hand shot out; he grabbed Brunetti by the sleeve and pulled him back. He held his superior's arm until the boat steadied, then let him go, saying, 'Not in that water.'

'Afraid I'd drown?' Brunetti asked.

Bonsuan broke in. 'More likely the cholera would get you.'

'Cholera?' Brunetti asked, laughing at his exaggeration, the first joke he'd ever heard Bonsuan attempt.

Bonsuan swung his head around and gave Brunetti a level glance. 'Cholera,' he repeated.

When Bonsuan turned back to the wheel, Vianello and Brunetti stared at one another like guilty schoolboys, and Brunetti had the impression that it was with difficulty that Vianello stopped himself from laughing.

'When I was a boy,' Bonsuan said with no introduction, 'I used to swim in front of my house. Just dive into the water from the side of the Canale di Cannaregio. You could see to the bottom. You could see fish, crabs. Now all you see is mud and shit.'

Vianello and Brunetti exchanged another glance.

'Anyone who eats a fish from out of that water is crazy,' Bonsuan said.

Late last year, there had been numerous cases of cholera reported, but in the south, where that sort of thing happened. Brunetti remembered that the health authorities had closed the fish market in Bari and warned the local people to avoid eating fish, which had seemed to him like telling cows to avoid eating grass. The autumn rains and floods had driven the story from the pages of the national newspapers, but not before Brunetti had begun to wonder whether the same thing was possible, here in the north, and how wise it was to eat anything that came from the increasingly putrid waters of the Adriatic.

When the boat pulled up at the gondola stop to the left of Palazzo Dario, Vianello grabbed the end of a coiled rope and leaped onto the dock. Leaning back, he held the rope taut and the boat close to the dock as Brunetti stepped ashore.

'You want me to wait for you, sir?' Bonsuan asked.

'No, don't bother. I don't know how long we'll be,' Brunetti told him. 'You can go back.'

Bonsuan raised a hand languidly toward the peak of his uniform cap, a gesture that served as both salute and farewell. He slipped the motor into reverse and arched the boat out into the canal, not bothering to look back at the two men who stood on the landing.

'Where first?' Vianello asked.

'Dorsoduro 723. It's up near the Guggenheim, on the left.'

The men walked up the narrow *calle* and turned

right at the first intersection. Brunetti found himself still wanting a coffee, then surprised that there were no bars to be seen on either side of the street.

An old man walking his dog came toward them, and Vianello moved behind Brunetti to give them room to pass, though they continued to talk about what Bonsuan had said. 'You really think the water is that bad, sir?' Vianello asked.

'Yes.'

'But some people still swim in the Canale della Giudecca,' Vianello insisted.

'When?'

'Redentore.'

'They're drunk, then,' Brunetti said dismissively.

Vianello shrugged and then stopped when Brunetti did.

'I think this is it,' Brunetti said, pulling the paper from his pocket. 'Da Prè,' he said aloud, looking at the names engraved on the two neat rows of brass plates that stood to the left of the door.

'Who is it?' Vianello asked.

'Ludovico, heir to Signorina da Prè. Could be anyone. Cousin. Brother. Nephew.'

'How old was she?'

'Seventy-two,' Brunetti answered, remembering the neat columns on Maria Testa's list.

'What did she die of?'

'Heart attack.'

'Any suspicion that this person,' Vianello began, nodding with his chin toward the brass plate beside the door, 'had anything to do with it?'

'She left him this apartment and more than five hundred million lire.'

'Does that mean that it's possible?' Vianello asked.

Brunetti, who had recently learned that the building in which they lived needed a new roof and that their share of it would be nine million lire, said, 'If the apartment's nice enough, I might kill someone to get it.'

Vianello, who knew nothing about the roof, gave his commissario a strange look.

Brunetti pressed the bell. Nothing happened for a long time, so Brunetti pressed it again, this time holding it for much longer. The two men exchanged a glance, and Brunetti pulled out the list, looking for the next address. Just as he turned away to the left and up toward the Accademia, a disembodied, high-pitched voice called out from the speaker above the name plates.

'Who is it?'

The voice was imbued with the asexual plaint of age, providing Brunetti with no idea of how to address the speaker, whether Signora or Signore. 'Is that the da Prè family?' he asked.

'Yes. What do you want?'

'There are some questions about the estate of Signorina da Prè, and we need to talk to you.'

Without further question, the door clicked open, letting them into a broad courtyard with a vine-covered well in the centre. The only staircase was through a door on the left. On the landing at the second floor, a door stood open, and in it stood one of the smallest men Brunetti had ever seen.

Though neither Vianello nor Brunetti was particularly tall, they both towered over this man, who seemed to grow even smaller as they drew near him.

'Signor da Prè?' Brunetti asked.

'Yes,' he said, coming a step forward from the door and extending a hand no larger than a child's. Because the man raised his hand almost to the height of his own shoulder, Brunetti did not have to lean down to take it; otherwise, he would certainly have had to do so. Da Prè's handshake was firm, and the glance he shot up toward Brunetti's eyes was clear and direct. His face was narrow, almost blade-like in its thinness. Either age or prolonged pain had cut deep grooves on either side of his mouth and scooped out dark circles under his eyes. His size made his age impossible to determine: he could have been anywhere from fifty to seventy.

Taking in Vianello's uniform, Signor da Prè did not extend his hand and did no more than nod in his direction. He stepped back through the door, opening it wider and inviting the two men into the apartment.

Muttering '*Permesso,*' the two policemen followed him into the hall and waited while he closed the door.

'This way, please,' the man said, heading back down the corridor.

From behind him, Brunetti saw the sharp hump that stuck up through the cloth of the left side of his jacket like the breastbone of a chicken. Though da Prè did not actually limp, his whole body canted to the left when he walked, as though the wall were a magnet and he a sack of metal filings pulled toward it. He led them into a living room that had windows on two sides. Rooftops were visible from those on the left, while the others looked across to the shuttered windows of a building on the other side of the narrow *calle*.

All of the furniture in the room was on the same scale as two monumental cupboards that filled the back wall: a high-backed sofa that seated six; four carved chairs which, from the ornamental work on their armrests, must have been Spanish; and an immense Florentine sideboard, its top littered with countless small objects at which Brunetti barely glanced. Da Prè climbed up into one of the chairs and waved Brunetti and Vianello into two of the others.

Brunetti's feet, when he sat down, just barely reached the floor, and he noticed that da Prè's hung midway between the seat and the floor. Somehow, the intense sobriety of the man's face kept the wild disparity in scale from being in any way ridiculous.

'You said there is something wrong with my sister's will?' da Prè began, voice cool.

'No, Signor da Prè,' Brunetti returned, 'I don't want to confuse the issue or mislead you. Our curiosity has nothing to do with your sister's will or with any stipulations that might be made in it. We're interested, instead, in her death, or with the cause of her death.'

'Then why didn't you say that at the beginning?' the little man asked, voice warmer now, but not in a way that Brunetti liked.

'Are those snuff boxes, Signor da Prè?' Vianello interrupted, getting down from his chair and going over to the sideboard.

'What?' the little man said sharply.

'Are these snuff boxes?' Vianello asked, bending

down over the surface, bringing his face closer to the small objects that covered it.

'Why do you ask?' da Prè said, voice no warmer but certainly curious.

'My uncle Luigi, in Trieste, collected them. I always loved going to visit him when I was a boy because he'd show them to me and let me touch them.' As if to eliminate that fearful possibility from taking root in Signor da Prè's mind, Vianello grasped his hands behind his back and did no more than lean closer to the boxes. He pulled his hands apart and pointed to one, careful to keep his finger at least a handsbreadth away from the box. 'Is this one Dutch?'

'Which one?' da Prè asked, getting down from his chair and going over to stand beside the sergeant.

Da Prè's head came barely to the top of the sideboard, so he had to stand on tiptoe to see to the back of the surface, to the box that Vianello was pointing at. 'Yes, it's Delft. Eighteenth-century.'

'And this one?' Vianello asked, pointing still and not presuming to touch. 'Bavarian?'

'Very good,' da Prè said, picking up the tiny box and handing it to the sergeant, who was careful to take it in both cupped hands.

Vianello turned it over and looked at the bottom. 'Yes, there's the mark,' he said, tilting it toward da Prè. 'It's a real beauty, isn't it?' he said in a voice rich with enthusiasm. 'My uncle would have loved this one, especially the way it's divided into two chambers.'

As the two men, heads close together, continued to examine the small boxes, Brunetti looked around the room. Three of the paintings were seventeenth-century, very bad paintings and very bad seventeenth-century: the death of stags, boars, and then more stags. There was too much blood in them and far too much artistically posed death to interest Brunetti. The others appeared to be biblical scenes, but they too all had to do with the shedding of great quantities of blood, this time human. Brunetti turned his attention to the ceiling, which had an elaborately stuccoed centre medallion, from the middle of which hung a Murano glass chandelier made of hundreds of small-petalled pastel flowers.

He glanced again at the two men, now crouched down in front of an open door on the right side of the cupboard. The shelves inside held what seemed to Brunetti to be hundreds more of the tiny boxes. For a moment, Brunetti felt himself suffocated with the strangeness of this giant's living room in which a tiny doll of a man had trapped himself, with only these bright enamelled momentos of a forgotten age to remind himself of what must be, for him, the true scale of things.

The two men got to their feet as Brunetti watched. Da Prè closed the door of the cabinet and came back to his chair and with a little, practised hop resumed his place in it. Vianello lingered a moment, giving a last admiring glance at the boxes arrayed across the top, but then returned to his own chair.

Brunetti dared a smile for the first time, and da Prè, returning it and glancing toward Vianello, said, 'I didn't know such people worked for the police.'

Neither did Brunetti, but that didn't for a moment stop him from saying, 'Yes, the sergeant is quite well known at the Questura for his interest in snuff boxes.'

Hearing in Brunetti's tone the irony with which the unenlightened perpetually regard the true enthusiast, da Prè said, 'They're an important part of European culture, snuff boxes. Some of the finest craftsmen on the continent devoted years of their lives – decades – to making them. There was no better way for a person to show appreciation than by giving a snuff box. Mozart, Haydn . . .' Da Prè's enthusiasm overcame his words, and he finished with a wild flourish of one of his little arms toward the laden sideboard.

Vianello, who had nodded in silent assent through all of this speech, said to Brunetti, 'I'm afraid you don't understand, Commissario.'

Brunetti, who had no idea how he had deserved to be sent this clever man who could so easily disarm even the most antagonistic witness, nodded in humble agreement.

'Did your sister share your enthusiasm?' Vianello's question was seamless.

The little man kicked one tiny foot at the rung of his chair. 'No, my sister had no enthusiasm for them.' Vianello shook his head at such an error, and da Prè, encouraged by that, added, 'And no enthusiasm for anything else.'

'None at all?' Vianello asked, with what sounded like real concern.

'No,' da Prè repeated. 'Not unless you count her enthusiasm for priests.' The manner in which he pronounced the last word suggested that the only enthusiasm he was likely to have for priests would arise from signing the orders for their execution.

Vianello shook his head, as if he could think of no greater peril, especially for a woman, than to fall into the hands of priests.

Voice filled with horror, Vianello asked, 'She didn't leave them anything, did she?' Then, just as quickly, he added, 'I'm sorry. It's not my place to ask.'

'No, that's quite all right, Sergeant,' da Prè said. 'They tried, but they didn't get a lira.' A smirk filled his face, and he added, 'No one who tried to get anything from her estate succeeded.'

Vianello smiled broadly to show his joy at this narrow avoidance of disaster. Propping his elbow on the arm of his chair and his chin on his palm, he settled in to hear the tale of Signor da Prè's triumph.

The little man pushed himself back in his own chair until his legs were almost completely parallel with the seat. 'She always had a weakness for religion,' he began. 'Our parents sent her to convent schools. I think that's why she never married.' Brunetti glanced at da Prè's hands, gripped atop the arms of his chair, but there was no sign of a wedding ring.

'We never got along,' he said simply. 'She had her interest in religion. And I had mine in art.' By which, Brunetti assumed, he meant enamelled snuff boxes.

'When our parents died, they left this apartment to us jointly. But we couldn't live together.' Vianello nodded here, suggesting how difficult it was to live with a woman. 'So I sold her my share. Twenty-three years ago. And I bought a smaller apartment. I needed the money to add to my collection.' Again, Vianello nodded, this time in understanding of the many demands of art.

'Then, three years ago, she fell and broke her hip, and it wouldn't heal right, so there was no choice but to put her in the *casa di cura*.' He stopped speaking here, an old man thinking about the things that made the nursing home inescapable. 'She asked me to move in here to keep an eye on her things,' he continued, 'but I refused. I didn't know if she'd come back, and then I'd have to move out again. And I didn't want to have to move the collection in here – I wouldn't live anywhere without it – and then move it again, should she recover. Too risky, too much chance of breaking something.' Da Prè's hands gripped tighter in unconscious terror at this possibility.

Brunetti found that, as the story progressed, he too began to nod in agreement with Signor da Prè, drawn into the lunatic world where a broken lid was a greater tragedy than a broken hip.

'Then, when she died, she named me her heir, but she tried to give them a hundred million. She'd added that to her will while she was there.'

'What did you do?' Vianello asked.

'I took it to my lawyer,' da Prè answered instantly. 'He had me declare that her mind was unsound during the last months of her life – that's when she signed that thing.'

'And?' Vianello prompted.

'It was thrown out, of course,' the little man said with great pride. 'The judges listened to me. It

69

was lunacy on Augusta's part. So they denied the bequest.'

'And you inherited everything?' Brunetti asked.

'Of course,' da Prè answered shortly. 'There's no one else in the immediate family.'

'Was her mind unsound?' Vianello asked.

Da Prè glanced over at the sergeant and answered immediately. 'Of course not. She was as lucid as she ever was, right up to the last time I saw her, the day before she died. But the bequest was insane.'

Brunetti wasn't sure he understood the distinction, but instead of seeking clarification, he asked, 'Did the people at the nursing home appear to know about the bequest?'

'What do you mean?' da Prè asked suspiciously.

'Did anyone from there ask you about the will, or did they oppose your decision to have the bequest denied?'

'One of them called me before the funeral and asked to give a sermon during the mass. I told him there wasn't going to be any sermon. Augusta had left instructions in the will about the funeral, wanted a requiem mass, so there was no way I could get around that. But she didn't say anything specific about a sermon, so at least I stopped them from standing up there and prattling on about another world where all the happy souls will meet again.' Da Prè smiled here; it was not a pretty smile.

'One of them came to her funeral,' he went on. 'Big man, fat. He came up to me after it and said how great a loss Augusta had been to the "community of Christians".' The sarcasm with which da Prè pronounced the words scalded the air around him.

'Then he said something about how generous she had always been, what a good friend she had been to the order.' Da Prè stopped talking here and his mind seemed to wander away in pleased recollection of the scene.

'What did you say?' Vianello finally asked.

'I told him the generosity was going into the grave with her,' da Prè said with another bleak smile.

Neither Vianello nor Brunetti said anything for a moment, and then Brunetti asked, 'Did they take any legal action?'

'Against me, do you mean?' da Prè asked.

Brunetti nodded.

'No. Nothing.' Da Prè was silent for a moment and then added, 'Just because they got their hands on her, that doesn't mean they could get their hands on her money.'

'Did she ever talk about this what you call "getting their hands on her"?' Brunetti asked.

'What do you mean?'

'Did she tell you that they were after her to give them her money?'

'Tell me?'

'Yes, did she ever say anything, while she was at the *casa di cura*, about their trying to get her to leave her money to them.'

'I don't know,' da Prè answered.

Brunetti didn't know how to ask. He left it for da Prè to explain, which he did. 'It was my duty to go and see her every month, which was all the time I could afford, but we had nothing to say to one another. I'd bring her any post that had accumulated, but it was always just religious things: magazines, requests for money. I'd ask her how she was. But there was nothing we could talk about, so I'd leave.'

'I see.' Brunetti saw, getting to his feet; she had been there three years and had left everything to this brother who had been too busy to visit her more than once a month, no doubt occupied with his little boxes.

'What's this all about?' da Prè asked before Brunetti could move away from him. 'Are they going to try to contest the will?' Da Prè started to say something else but stopped himself, and Brunetti thought he saw him begin to smile, but then the little man covered his mouth with his hand, and the moment was gone.

'Nothing, really, Signore. Actually, we're interested in someone who worked there.'

'I can't help you there. I didn't know any of the staff.'

Vianello got to his feet and came to stand by Brunetti, the warmth of his previous conversation with da Prè serving to mitigate the badly disguised indignation which emanated from his superior.

Da Prè asked no more questions. He got to his feet and led the two men out of the room and then down the corridor to the door of the apartment. There, Vianello took his upraised hand and shook it, thanking him for having shown him the lovely snuff boxes. Brunetti, too, shook the upraised hand, but he gave no thanks and was the first one through the door.

Chapter Four

'Horrible little man, horrible little man,' Brunetti heard Vianello muttering as they walked down the steps.

Outside, it was cooler, as though da Prè had stolen the warmth from the day. 'Disgusting little man,' Vianello continued. 'He thinks he owns those boxes. The fool.'

'What, Sergeant?' Brunetti asked, not having followed Vianello's leap of thought.

'He thinks he owns those things, those stupid little boxes.'

'I thought you liked them.'

'God, no; I think they're disgusting. My uncle had scores of them, and every time we went there, he insisted on making me look at them. He was just the same, acquiring things, and things, and things, and believing he owned them.'

'Didn't he?' Brunetti asked, pausing at a corner the better to hear what Vianello was saying.

'Of course he owned them,' Vianello said, stopping in front of Brunetti. 'That is, he paid for them, had the receipts, could do with them whatever he wanted. But we never really own anything, do we?' he asked, looking directly at Brunetti.

'I'm not sure what you mean, Vianello.'

'Think about it, sir. We buy things. We wear them or put them on our walls, or sit on them, but anyone who wants to can take them away from us. Or break them.' Vianello shook his head, frustrated by the difficulty he had in explaining what he thought was a relatively simple idea. 'Just think of da Prè. Long after he's dead, someone else will own those stupid little boxes, and then someone after him, just as someone owned them before he did. But no one ever thinks of that: objects survive us and go on living. It's stupid to believe we own them. And it's sinful for them to be so important.'

Brunetti knew the sergeant to be as godless and irreverent as he was himself, knew that the only religion he had was family and the sanctity of the ties of blood, and so it was strange to hear him speak of sin or define things in terms of it.

'And how could he leave his own sister in a place like that for three years and visit her once a month?' Vianello asked, as if he actually believed the question could admit an answer.

Brunetti's voice was non-committal when he said, 'I imagine it's not such a bad place,' in a tone so cool it reminded the sergeant that Brunetti's mother was in a similar place.

'I didn't mean that, sir,' Vianello hastened to explain. 'I meant any place like that.' Hearing how little better that was, he continued, 'I mean, and not go and visit her more than that, just leave her there by herself.'

'There's usually a large staff,' was Brunetti's reply as he started off again and turned left at Campo San Vio.

'But they're not family,' Vianello insisted in the full belief that familial affection had a far greater therapeutic value than did any amount of service to be bought from the 'caring' professions. For all Brunetti knew, the sergeant could be right, but it was not a subject he wanted to pursue, not now, and not in the immediate future.

'Who's next?' Vianello asked, agreeing by that question to change the subject and get them both away, at least temporarily, from subjects that led, if anywhere, to pain.

'It's up here, I think,' Brunetti said, turning into a narrow *calle* that cut back from the canal they were walking along.

Had the heir of Conte Egidio Crivoni been standing at the door waiting for them, the voice that responded to their ring could have come no more swiftly. Just as quickly the massive door snapped open when Brunetti explained that he had come seeking information about the estate of Conte Crivoni. Up two flights of stairs and then two more they went; Brunetti was struck by the fact that there was only one door on each landing, this a suggestion that each apartment comprised an entire floor, and that in its turn a suggestion of the wealth of the tenants.

Just as Brunetti set his foot on the top landing, a black-suited major domo opened the single door in front of them. That is, from his sombre nod and the distant solemnity of his bearing, Brunetti assumed him to be a servant, a belief that was confirmed when he offered to take Brunetti's overcoat and said that 'La Contessa' would see them in her study. The man disappeared behind a door for a moment but immediately reappeared, this time without Brunetti's coat.

Brunetti had time to take in no more than soft brown eyes and a small gold cross on the left lapel of his jacket before the man turned and led them down the hall. Paintings, all portraits from different centuries and in different styles, lined the walls of both sides of the corridor. Though he knew it was the way of portraits, Brunetti was struck by how unhappy most of these people looked, unhappy and something more; restless, perhaps, as though they believed their time would be better spent conquering the savage or converting the heathen, not posing for some vain, earthly memorial. The women seemed convinced they could do it by the mere example of blameless lives; the men appeared to place greater faith in the power of the sword.

The man stopped in front of a door, knocked once, then opened it without waiting for a reply. He held it open and waited for Brunetti and Vianello to enter, then pulled the door silently closed behind them.

A verse from Dante leaped to Brunetti's mind:

> Oscura e profonda era e nebulosa
> Tanto che, per ficcar lo viso a fondo
> Io non vi discernea alcuna cosa.

So too was this room dark, as though by entering this place they, like Dante, had left behind the light of the world, the sun, and joy. Tall windows lined one wall of the room, all hidden behind velvet drapes of a particularly sober brown, something between sepia and dried blood. What light filtered in illuminated the leather backs of hundreds of very serious-looking volumes that lined the remaining walls from floor to ceiling. The floor was parquet, not thin strips of laminated wood laid down in sheets but the real thing, each cube carefully cut and positioned into place.

In one corner of the room, sitting behind a massive desk covered with books and papers, Brunetti saw the top half of a large woman dressed in black. The severity of her dress and expression rendered the rest of the room suddenly cheerful.

'What do you want?' she asked, Vianello's uniform, apparently, enough to obviate the need to ask who they were.

From where he stood, Brunetti could get no clear idea of the woman's age, though her voice – deep, resonant, and imperious – suggested maturity, if not advanced age itself. He took a few steps across the room until he was only a few metres from her desk. 'Contessa?' he began.

'I asked you what you wanted,' was her only response.

Brunetti smiled. 'I'll try to take as little of your time as possible, Contessa. I know how very busy you are. My mother-in-law often speaks of your dedication to good works and of the stamina with which you so generously aid Holy Mother Church.' He tried to make his pronunciation of that last sound reverent, no easy feat.

'Who is your mother-in-law?' she demanded, speaking as if she expected it to be her seamstress.

Brunetti took careful aim and hit her right between her close-set eyes: 'Contessa Falier.'

'Donatella Falier?' she asked, making a bad business of her attempt to hide her astonishment.

Brunetti pretended not to have noticed it. 'Yes. It was just last week, I think, that she was talking about your latest project.'

'You mean the campaign to ban the sale of contraceptives in pharmacies?' she asked, supplying Brunetti with the information he needed.

'Yes,' he said, nodded as if in full approval, and smiled.

She rose from her chair and walked around the desk, her hand extended to him now that his humanity had been proven by his being related, if only by marriage, to one of the best-born women in the city. Standing, she revealed the full extent of the body that had been hidden by the desk. Taller than Brunetti, she outweighed him by twenty kilos. Her bulk, however, was not the heavy, compact flesh of the healthy fat person but the loose, jiggling suet of the perpetually immobile. Her chins rode one another down the front of her dress, itself little more than an immense tube of black wool that hung suspended from the immense buttress of her bosom. Brunetti did not sense that there had been much joy, nor even much pleasure, in the creation of all that flesh.

'You're Paola's husband, then?' she asked as she came up to him. As she drew closer, she pushed ahead of her the acrid scent of unwashed flesh.

'Yes, Contessa. Guido Brunetti,' he said, taking her offered hand. Holding it as he would a piece of the True Cross, he bowed over her hand and raised it to within a centimetre of his lips. Straightening himself, he said, 'It's an honour to meet you,' managing to sound as though he meant it.

He turned to Vianello. 'And this is Sergeant Vianello, my assistant.' Vianello gave a smart bow, face as solemn as Brunetti's, managing to look as though he had been struck to silence by the honour of the presentation, and he but a lowly policeman. The Contessa barely glanced at him.

'Please sit down, Dottor Brunetti,' she said, waving one fat hand toward a straight-backed chair that stood in front of her desk. Brunetti moved toward the chair then turned and waved Vianello to another one that stood nearer the door, where he would probably be safer from the refulgent glow of her nobility.

The Countess returned to her seat behind the desk and lowered herself slowly into her chair. She shifted some papers to her right and looked at Brunetti. 'Did you tell Stefano there was some problem with my husband's estate?'

'No, Contessa, nothing as serious as that,' Brunetti said with what he hoped was an easy smile. She nodded, waiting for his explanation.

Brunetti smiled again and began to explain, inventing as he went. 'As you know, Contessa, there is an increasing tendency toward criminality in this country.' She nodded. 'It seems that nothing is any longer sacred, no one safe from those who will go to any lengths to extort and trick money from those who rightfully possess it.' The Contessa nodded in sad agreement.

'The latest form this sort of chicanery has taken is seen in those who prey upon the trust of older people, who try, and too often succeed, in deceiving them and swindling them.'

The Countess held up a thick-fingered hand. 'Are you warning me that this is going to happen to me?'

'No, Countess. You can rest assured of that. But what we want to be sure about is that your late husband' – and here Brunetti permitted himself two slow shakes of his head, lamenting the fact that the virtuous are too soon taken from us – 'that your late husband was not a victim of this sort of heartless duplicity.'

'Are you telling me that you think Egidio was robbed? Deceived? I don't understand what you're talking about.' She leaned forward and her bosom came to rest on the top of the desk.

'Then let me speak plainly, Contessa. We want to be sure that no one managed to persuade the Count, before his death, to make a bequest to them, that no one exerted undue influence on him in order to obtain part of his estate and to prevent its going to his rightful heirs.'

The Contessa considered this but said nothing.

'Is it possible that something like this could have happened, Contessa?'

'What has caused you to have these suspicions?' she asked.

'Your husband's name came up almost accidentally, Contessa, as we were pursuing another investigation.'

'About people who are cheated out of their estates?' she asked.

'No, Contessa, of something else. But before acting officially, I wanted to come to you personally – because of the high regard in which you are held – and, if I could, assure myself that there was nothing to investigate.'

'And what do you need from me?'

'Your assurances that there was nothing untoward about your late husband's will.'

'Untoward?' she repeated.

'A bequest to someone not a part of the family?' Brunetti suggested.

She shook her head.

'Someone who was not a close friend?'

Again, a shake so definite as to set her jowls swinging.

'An institution to which he extended charity?' Brunetti saw her eyes light up here.

'What do you mean by an institution?'

'Some of these swindlers deceive people into making contributions to what they present as worthy charities. We've had cases of people being persuaded to give money to children's hospitals in Rumania or to what they were told was one of Mother Teresa's hospices.' Brunetti pumped his voice full of indignation as he added, 'Terrible. Shocking.'

The Countess met his eye and expressed the same judgement with a nod. 'There was nothing like that. My husband left his estate to his family, as a man should. There were no strange bequests. No one got anything who shouldn't have.'

Because he was in the Countess's line of vision,

Vianello took the liberty of nodding in strong affirmation of the propriety of this.

Brunetti got to his feet. 'You've relieved me greatly, Contessa. I was afraid that a man as generous as the Count was known to be might have become a victim of these people. But after speaking to you, I'm glad to learn that we can cancel his name from our investigation.' He injected greater warmth into his voice and continued, 'Speaking as a public official, I'm always glad when that happens, but I speak as a private citizen when I say that I am personally very pleased with this.' He turned back toward Vianello and waved him to his feet.

When he turned around, the Contessa had come around her desk again and was heaving her mountainous girth toward him.

'Can you tell me any more about this, Dottore?'

'No, Contessa, so long as I know your husband had nothing to do with these people, I can tell my colleague—'

'Your colleague?' she interrupted.

'Yes, one of the other *commissari* is handling the investigation into this ring of swindlers. I'll send him a memo that your husband had nothing to do with them, thank God, and then I'll get back to my own cases.'

'If this isn't your case, why did you come here?' she asked bluntly.

Brunetti smiled before he answered. 'I hoped that it would be less troubling for you if the questions were put to you by a person who, that is to say, by a person who is sensitive to your position in the community. I didn't want you to be burdened with worry, however momentary I knew it would be.'

Rather than thanking Brunetti for this courtesy, the Contessa nodded in acceptance of what was no more than her due.

Brunetti extended his hand and, when she put hers out to meet his, he bent over it again, resisting the impulse to click his heels.

He backed toward the door, where Vianello awaited him. There, both men gave small bows and let themselves back into the hall. Stefano, if that was the name of the man with the cross on his lapel, was waiting for them there, not leaning against the wall but standing in the middle of the corridor, Brunetti's overcoat in his arms. When he saw them emerge, he opened Brunetti's coat and held it while he put it on. Without speaking, he led them to the end of the corridor and held the door for them while they left the apartment.

Chapter Five

Neither spoke as they went down the steps and out into the street, where the sudden spring night had fallen upon the city.

'Well?' Brunetti asked as he took the list from his pocket again. He checked the next address and set off toward it; Vianello fell into step beside him.

'Is that what's known as an important personage in the city?' was Vianello's attempt at an answer.

'I think so.'

'Poor Venice, then.' So much for the magic effect of the patent of nobility upon Vianello. 'She the one who paid Lucia's ransom?' the sergeant asked, referring to the famous case of kidnapping, more than a decade ago, when the bones of Santa Lucia were taken from her church and held for ransom. A never-disclosed sum was paid to the thieves, and the police were directed to some bones, presumably those of the blessed Lucia, lying in a field on the mainland. These bones were restored to the church with great solemnity and the case closed.

Brunetti nodded. 'I heard a rumour that she did, but you never know, do you?'

'Probably pig bones, anyway,' Vianello offered, his tone suggesting that he hoped this had been the case.

Since Vianello seemed unwilling to answer an indirect question, Brunetti made it a direct one. 'What'd you think of the Countess?'

'She became interested when you suggested that something might have been given to an institution. Didn't seem worried about people or relatives.'

'Yes,' Brunetti agreed, 'those hospitals in Rumania.'

Vianello turned to Brunetti and gave him a long look. 'Where'd all these people who are tricked into giving money to Mother Teresa come from?'

Brunetti smiled and shrugged away the question. 'I had to tell her something. That sounded as good as anything.'

'Doesn't much matter, does it?' Vianello asked.

'What doesn't much matter?'

'Whether Mother Teresa gets the money or it goes to crooks.'

Surprised, Brunetti asked, 'What do you mean?'

'No one ever finds out where that money goes, do they? She's won all those prizes, and someone's always collecting money for her, but there never seems to be anything to show for it, does there?'

This was a depth of cynicism even Brunetti had never managed to reach, and so he said, 'Well, at least they have a decent death, those people she takes in.'

Vianello's answer was immediate. 'They'd probably rather have a decent meal, if you ask me.' Then, looking pointedly down at his watch and making no attempt to disguise his mounting scepticism at how Brunetti was using their time, he added, 'Or a drink.'

Brunetti took the hint. Neither of the two people

they'd spoken to, however unpleasant they'd been, had the look or feel of guilt about them. 'One more,' he said, glad it came out sounding like a suggestion and not a request.

Vianello's nod was tired, his shrug a comment on how boring and repetitive was much of the work they did. 'And then *un' ombra*,' he said, neither suggestion nor request.

Brunetti nodded, glanced down again at the address, and turned into the *calle* on their right. They found themselves in a courtyard and paused, searching for some indication of a house number on the first door they came to.

'What number are we looking for, sir?'

'Three hundred and twelve,' Brunetti answered, reading from the sheet of paper.

'Must be that one over there,' Vianello said, placing his hand on Brunetti's arm and pointing across the courtyard.

As they crossed it, they noticed that narcissi and daffodils were popping up from the dark earth in the centre, the smaller flowers now closed against the approaching chill of the night.

On the other side, they found the number they sought, and Brunetti rang the bell.

After a moment, a voice came through the speakerphone, asking who it was.

'I've come about Signor Lerini,' Brunetti answered.

'Signor Lerini is no longer of this world,' the voice answered.

'I know that, Signora. I've come to ask questions about his estate.'

'His estate is in heaven,' the voice answered. Brunetti and Vianello exchanged a glance.

'I've come to discuss the one he left behind him here,' Brunetti said, making no attempt to disguise his impatience.

'Who are you?' the voice demanded.

'Police,' he answered just as quickly.

The speakerphone clicked as the woman put it down sharply. Nothing happened for what seemed a long time, and then the door snapped open.

Again, they climbed stairs. Like the corridor in Contessa Crivoni's home, these stairs too were lined with portraits, but they were all of the same person: Jesus, as he made his way through the increasingly bloody Stations of the Cross to his death on Calvary and the third-floor landing. Brunetti paused long enough to examine one of them, and saw that, instead of the cheap reproductions from a religious magazine that he had expected to find, these were carefully detailed drawings in coloured pencil, pencils which, though lingering lovingly upon the wounds, thorns, and nails, still managed to convey a saccharine sweetness to the face of the suffering Christ.

When Brunetti turned his attention from the crucified Christ, he saw that a woman stood at an open door, and for an instant he thought that he had somehow managed to stumble upon Suor'-Immacolata again, and she had returned to her order and her habit. But a closer look showed him that it was an entirely different woman and the only resemblance came from her clothing: a long white skirt that fell to the floor and a shapeless black sweater buttoned over a high-necked white blouse. All the woman needed was a wimple and a long rosary hanging from her waist, and the habit would have been complete. The skin of her face was papery and too white, as though it seldom, if ever, saw the light of day. Her nose was long and pink at the tip, her chin too small for the rest of her face. The curious untouched quality of her face made it difficult for Brunetti to tell her age, but he guessed she was somewhere between fifty and sixty.

'Signora Lerini?' Brunetti asked, not bothering to waste a smile on her.

'Signorina,' she corrected him with an immediacy that suggested she had often made this same correction and perhaps looked forward to making it as well.

'I've come to ask you some questions about your father's estate,' Brunetti said.

'And may I ask who you are?' she enquired in a tone that managed to mix meekness and aggression.

'Commissario Brunetti,' he answered and then turned to Vianello. 'And this is my sergeant, Vianello.'

'I suppose you have to come in,' she said.

When Brunetti nodded, she stepped back and held the door for them. Muttering '*Permesso,*' they went into the apartment. Brunetti was immediately struck by an odour which, for all its being familiar, he could not immediately recognize. A mahogany sideboard stood in the hallway, its surface covered with photographs in elaborate silver frames. Brunetti cast his eyes over them for a second, looked away, but then turned back to study them more closely.

All of the subjects seemed to be in clerical garb: bishops, cardinals, four nuns standing in a stiff line, even the Pope. The woman turned to lead them to another room, and Brunetti bent down to take a closer look at the photos. All of them were auto-graphed, and many of them bore dedications to 'Signorina Lerini', one Cardinal going so far as to address her as 'Benedetta, beloved sister in Christ'. Brunetti had the odd sensation of being in a teenager's room, its walls filled with giant posters of rock stars, they too dressed in the wild costumes of their profession.

Quickly, he caught up with Signorina Lerini and Vianello and followed them into a room that at first appeared to be a chapel but, upon closer examin-ation, revealed itself to be a sitting room. In one corner stood a wooden Madonna, beside whom burned six tall candles, the source of the scent Bru-netti had been unable to identify. In front of the statue stood a prie-dieu, no soft cushion upon the wooden kneeler.

Against another wall stood a different sort of shrine, this one apparently to her late father; at any rate, to the photo of a bull-necked man in a business suit posed heavily at his desk, hands clasped tightly together in front of him. Instead of candles, two soft spotlights were directed at it from some place high up in the ceiling beams; Brunetti had the distinct impression that they were left burning day and night.

Signorina Lerini lowered herself into a chair but sat at the front of it, her back upright and straight as a sword.

'I'd like to begin,' Brunetti said when they were

all seated, 'by extending my condolences on your loss. Your father was a well-known man, certainly an asset to the city, and I'm sure his absence must be very hard to bear.'

She brought her lips together and bowed her head at this. 'The Lord's will must be welcomed,' she said.

From beside him, Brunetti heard Vianello whisper, just at the level of audibility, 'Amen,' but he resisted the impulse to glance at his sergeant. Signorina Lerini, however, did turn to Vianello and saw a face that matched her own for solemnity and piety. Her face relaxed visibly at this, and some of the rigidity went out of her spine.

'Signorina, I do not wish to intrude upon your grief, for I know it must be very great, but there are some questions I would like to ask about your father's estate.'

'As I told you,' she said, 'his estate is now with the Lord.'

This time, Brunetti heard a breathed '*Sì, sì,*' from beside him and wondered if Vianello was perhaps overplaying his part. Apparently not, for this time Signorina Lerini looked at the sergeant and nodded in his direction, no doubt acknowledging the presence of the other Christian in the room.

'Unfortunately, Signorina, those of us who remain behind must still concern ourselves with earthly things,' Brunetti said.

Hearing this, Signorina Lerini glanced at her father's photo, but he seemed unable to give her any help. 'What is it you are concerned about?' she asked.

'Through information gained during another investigation,' Brunetti began, repeating his lie, 'we have learned that some people in the city have fallen victim to swindlers who approach them under the false guise of charity. That is, they present themselves as the representatives of various charities and in this way succeed in obtaining sums of money, often very large sums of money, from their victims.' He waited for Signorina Lerini to display some sign of curiosity at what he was saying, but he waited in vain and so continued. 'We have reason to believe that one of these persons managed to gain the confidence of some of the patients at the *casa di cura* where your father was a patient.'

At this, Signorina Lerini looked up at him, eyes wide with curiosity.

'Signorina, could you tell me if these people ever approached your father?'

'How would I know something like that?'

'I thought perhaps your father might have discussed making changes in his will, perhaps some sort of bequest to a charity you had never heard him speak of before.' She said nothing here. 'Were there any charitable bequests in your father's will, Signorina?'

'What do you mean by charitable bequests?' she asked.

Brunetti thought it a relatively simple question, but he still explained. 'To a hospital, perhaps, or an orphanage?'

She shook her head.

'I'm sure he must have left money to some worthy religious organization,' Brunetti suggested.

She shook her head again but offered no explanation.

Suddenly Vianello broke in. 'If I might be allowed to interrupt you, sir, I'd like to suggest that a man like Signor Lerini would certainly not wait until his death to begin to share the profits of his labours with Holy Mother Church.' Having said that, Vianello bowed the top half of his seated body toward Signor Lerini's daughter, who smiled graciously in response to this tribute to her father's generosity.

'It seems to me,' continued Vianello, encouraged by her smile, 'that our duty to the Church is one we carry with us all through our lives, not only at the hour of our death.' Having said this, Vianello returned to his respectful silence, the Church defended and he content with having been the one to do it.

'My father's life,' Signorina Lerini began, 'was a shining example of Christian virtue. Not only was his entire life an exemplary model of industry, but his loving concern for the spiritual welfare of everyone he came in touch with, either personally or professionally, set a standard which will be hard to exceed.' She went on in this vein for another few minutes, but Brunetti tuned out, letting his attention wander around the room.

The heavy furniture, relics from a previous era, was familiar to him, all of it built to endure through the ages and devil take the ideas of comfort or beauty. After a quick survey of the room, which showed him a number of paintings more concerned with piety than beauty, Brunetti confined his attention to a study of the bulbous, four-clawed feet that reached out from the legs of tables and chairs.

He turned his attention back just as Signorina Lerini was coming to the peroration of this speech she must have delivered countless times before. So pat was her delivery that Brunetti wondered if she was any longer conscious of what she was saying and tended to suspect that she might not be.

'I hope that satisfies your curiosity,' she said, finally coming to an end.

'It certainly is a very impressive catalogue of virtues, Signorina,' Brunetti said. Signorina Lerini contented herself with the words and smiled in response, her father having received his due.

Since he hadn't heard her mention it, Brunetti asked, 'Could you tell me if the *casa di cura* was a recipient of your father's generosity?'

Her smile disappeared. 'What do you mean?'

'Did he remember it in his will?'

'No.'

'Could he perhaps have given them something while he was still there?'

'I don't know,' she said, speaking in a soft voice and, by that, meaning to suggest lack of interest in such worldly things but, by the sharp look she gave him at the mention of such a possibility, succeeding only in looking wary and displeased.

'How much control did your father have over his finances while he was there?' Brunetti asked.

'I'm not sure I understand your question,' she said.

'Was he in contact with his bank, could he write cheques? If he was no longer capable of doing those things, did he ask you, or whoever was handling his affairs, to pay bills or make gifts?' He doubted that he could make the question any clearer to her.

That she didn't like this was evident, but Brunetti was out of patience with her protestations and her virtue.

'I thought you said this was an investigation of swindlers, Commissario,' she said in a voice so sharp that Brunetti immediately regretted his own tone.

'It is, Signorina, it certainly is. And I wanted to know if they could possibly have taken advantage of your father and of his generosity while he was in the *casa di cura*.'

'How could that happen?' Brunetti noticed that her right hand held the fingers of the left in a vice-like grip, bunching the skin together like the wattle of a chicken.

'If these people had come to visit other patients, or found themselves there for any reason, they could have had contact with your father.' When she said nothing, Brunetti asked, 'Isn't that possible?'

'And he could have given them money?' she asked.

'It's possible, but only theoretically. If there were no strange bequests in his will, and if he gave no unusual instructions about his finances, I don't think there's anything to worry about.'

'You can rest assured, then, Commissario. I was in charge of my father's finances during his last illness, and he never spoke of anything like that.'

'And his will? Did he make any changes to it during the time he was there?'

'None.'

'And you were his heir?'

'Yes. I am his only child.'

Brunetti had come to the end of both his patience and his questions. 'Thank you for your time and for your cooperation, Signorina. What you've told us puts an end to any suspicions we might have had.' After he said this, Brunetti got to his feet, followed instantly by Vianello. 'I feel very much better, Signorina,' Brunetti continued, smiling with every appearance of sincerity. 'What you've told me reassures me because it means that your father was not taken advantage of by these despicable people.' He smiled again and turned toward the door. He sensed Vianello's presence close behind him.

Signorina Lerini got up from her chair and came with them to the door. 'It's not that any of this matters,' she said, waving a hand to encompass the room and everything in it, perhaps hoping to dismiss it all with that gesture.

'Not when our eternal salvation is at stake, Signorina,' Vianello said. Brunetti was glad his back was to both of them because he was not sure he had been fast enough to hide both his shock and disgust at Vianello's remark.

Chapter Six

When they were outside, Brunetti turned to Vianello and asked, 'And might I be so bold as to ask where that sudden burst of piety came from, Sergeant?' He shot an impatient glance at Vianello, but the sergeant answered him with a grin. Brunetti insisted, 'Well?'

'I don't have the patience I used to have, sir. And she's so far gone I figured she wouldn't realize what I was doing.'

'I suspect you succeeded in that,' Brunetti said. 'It was a wonderful performance. "Our eternal salvation is at stake,"' Brunetti repeated, making no attempt to hide his disgust. 'I hope she believed you, because you sounded as false as a snake to me.'

'Oh, she believed me, sir,' Vianello said, heading out of the courtyard and back toward the Accademia Bridge.

'Why are you so sure?' Brunetti asked.

'Hypocrites never think that other people can be just as false as they are.'

'Are you sure that's what she is?'

'Did you see her face when you suggested that her father, her sainted father, might have given some of the loot away?'

Brunetti nodded.

'Well?' Vianello asked.

'Well what?'

'I think it's enough to show what all that crap about religion is really all about.'

'And what do you think that is, Sergeant?'

'That it makes her special, makes her stand out from the crowd. She's not beautiful, not even pretty, and there's no indication that she's smart. So the only thing that can make her stand out from other people, the way we all want to do, I suppose, is to be religious. That way everyone who meets her says, "Oh, what an interesting, intense person." And she doesn't have to do anything or learn anything or even work at anything. Or even be interesting. All she does is say things, pious things, and everyone jumps up and down saying how good she is.'

Brunetti wasn't persuaded, but he kept his opinion to himself. There had certainly been something excessive and out of tune about Signorina Lerini's piety, but Brunetti didn't think it was hypocrisy. To Brunetti, who had seen his fair share of it in his work, her talk of religion and God's will had the ring of simple fanaticism. He had found her lacking the intelligence and self-involvement that were usually present in the real hypocrite.

'It sounds like you're pretty familiar with that sort of religion, Vianello,' Brunetti said, turning into a bar. After their prolonged exposure to sanctity, he needed a drink. So, apparently, did Vianello, who ordered them two glasses of white wine.

'My sister,' Vianello said in explanation. 'Except that she grew out of it.'

'What happened?'

'It started about two years before she got married.' Vianello sipped at the wine, set his glass down on the bar, and nibbled at a cracker he picked up from a bowl. 'Luckily, it ended when she got married.' Another sip. A smile. 'No room for Jesus in bed, I guess.' A larger sip. 'It was awful. We had to listen to her for months, going on and on about prayer and good works and how much she loved the Madonna. It got to a point that even my mother – who really is a saint – couldn't stand to listen to her.'

'What happened?'

'As I said, she got married, and then the children started coming, and then there was no time to be holy or pious. Then I guess she forgot about it.'

'You think that could happen with Signorina Lerini?' Brunetti asked, sipping at his wine.

Vianello shrugged. 'At her age – what is she, fifty?' he asked and then continued after Brunetti nodded, 'The only reason I could see anyone marrying her would be for the money. And there's not much chance of her giving any of that up, is there?'

'You really didn't like her, did you, Vianello?'

'I don't like hypocrites. And I don't like religious people. So you can imagine what I think about the combination.'

'But your mother is a saint, you said. Isn't she religious?'

Vianello nodded and pushed his glass across the bar. The bartender filled it, glanced at Brunetti, who held his own out to be refilled.

'Yes. But hers is real faith, belief in human kindness.'

'Isn't that what Christianity is supposed to be all about?'

The only answer Vianello gave to this was an angry snort. 'You know, Commissario, I meant that when I said my mother is a saint. She raised two kids along with the three of us. Their father worked with mine, and when his wife died, he started to drink and didn't take care of the kids. So my mother just took them home and raised them along with us. No big fuss, no speeches about generosity. And one day she caught my brother making fun of one of them, saying his father drank. At first, I thought she was going to kill Luca, but all she did was call him into the kitchen and tell him she was ashamed of him. That's all, just that she was ashamed of him. And Luca cried for a week. She was pleasant to him, but she made it clear how she felt.' Vianello sipped at his drink again, his memory back in their youth.

'What happened?' Brunetti asked.

'Hum?'

'What happened? To your brother?'

'Oh, about two weeks later, we were all walking home from school together, and some of the bigger boys in the neighbourhood started saying things to the boy, the same one Luca had been teasing.'

'And?'

'And Luca went crazy, I guess. He beat two of them bloody, chased one of them halfway to Castello. And all the time, he was yelling at them that they couldn't say those things about his brother.' Vianello's eyes brightened with the story. 'Well, when he got home, he was awfully bloody. I think he broke one of his fingers in the fight; anyway, my father had to take him to the hospital.'

'And?'

'Well, while they were there, at the hospital, Luca told my father what had happened, and when they came home, my father told my mother.' Vianello finished his wine and pulled some bills from his pocket.

'What did your mother do?'

'Oh, nothing special, really. Except that night she made *risotto di pesce*, Luca's favourite. We hadn't had it for two weeks, like she was on strike or something. Or putting us all on a hunger strike because of what Luca said,' he added with a loud laugh. 'But after that, Luca started smiling again. My mother never said anything about it. Luca was the baby, and I've always thought he was her favourite.' He picked up the change and slipped it into his pocket. 'She's like that. No big sermons. But good, good to her soul.'

He walked to the door and held it open for Brunetti. 'Are there any more names on the list, Commissario? Because you're not going to get me to believe that one of those people is capable of anything worse than false piety.' Vianello turned to look at the clock on the wall above the bar.

Just as tired of piety as his sergeant was, Brunetti said, 'No, I don't think so. The fourth will divided everything equally among six children.'

'And the fifth?'

'The heir lives in Torino.'

'That doesn't leave many suspects, does it, sir?'

'No, I'm afraid not. And I'm beginning to think there's not much to be suspicious of.'

'Should we bother going back to the Questura?' Vianello asked, this time pushing back his sleeve to look at his watch.

It was quarter after six. 'No, no sense in bothering to do that,' Brunetti answered. 'You might as well get home at a decent hour, Sergeant.'

Vianello smiled in answer, started to say something, stopped himself, but then gave in to the impulse and said, 'Give me more time at the gym.'

'Don't even say such things to me,' Brunetti insisted, pulling his face together in an expression of exaggerated horror.

Vianello laughed aloud as he started up the first steps of the Accademia Bridge, leaving Brunetti to make his way home by way of Campo San Barnaba.

It was in this *campo*, standing in front of the newly restored church and seeing its freshly scrubbed façade for the first time, that the idea came to Brunetti. He cut into the *calle* beside the church and stopped at the last door before the Grand Canal.

The door clicked open on his second ring, and he entered the immense courtyard of his parents-in-law's *palazzo*. Luciana, the maid who had been with the family since before Brunetti met Paola, opened the door at the top of the stairs that led up to the *palazzo* and smiled a friendly greeting. '*Buona sera*, Dottore,' she said, stepping back to allow him into the hall.

'*Buona sera*, Luciana. It's good to see you again,' Brunetti said, giving her his coat, conscious of how many times he'd handed it back and forth that afternoon. 'I'd like to speak to my mother-in-law. If she's home, that is.'

If Luciana was surprised by this request, she gave no sign of it at all. 'The Contessa is reading. But I'm sure she'd be glad to see you, Dottore.' As she led Brunetti back into the living portion of the *palazzo*, Luciana asked, voice warm with real affection, 'How are the children?'

'Raffi's in love,' Brunetti said, warmed by Luciana's answering smile. 'And so is Chiara,' he added, this time amused to see her shock. 'But luckily, Raffi's in love with a girl, and Chiara's in love with the new polar bear in the Berlin Zoo.'

Luciana stopped and placed one hand on his sleeve. 'Oh, Dottore, you shouldn't play tricks like that on an old woman,' she said, taking her other hand, the one for melodrama, from her heart.

'Who's the girl?' she asked. 'Is she a good girl?'

'Sara Paganuzzi. She lives on the floor under us. Raffi's known her since they were kids. Her father has a glass factory out on Murano.'

'That Paganuzzi?' Luciana asked with real curiosity.

'Yes. Do you know them?'

'No, not personally, but I know his work. Beautiful, beautiful. My nephew works out on Murano, and he's always saying that Paganuzzi is the best of the glass-makers.' Luciana stopped in front of the Contessa's study and knocked on the door.

'*Avanti*,' the Contessa's voice called from inside. Luciana opened the door and allowed Brunetti to go in unannounced. After all, there was very little danger that he would find the Contessa doing something she shouldn't be doing or secretly reading a body-building magazine.

Donatella Falier looked across the top of her reading glasses, set her book face down beside her on the sofa, the glasses on top of it, and got immediately to her feet. She came quickly toward Brunetti and lifted up her face to receive his two light kisses. Though he knew she was in her mid-sixties, the Contessa looked at least a decade younger; there was not a white hair to be seen, wrinkles were reduced to insignificance by carefully applied make-up, and her small body was trim and straight.

'Guido, is anything wrong?' she asked with real concern, and Brunetti felt a moment's regret that he was such a stranger to this woman's life that his very presence would speak only of danger or loss.

'No, nothing at all. Everyone's fine.'

He saw her relax visibly as he answered. 'Good, good. Would you like something to drink, Guido?' She looked toward the window as if to tell the time by the quantity of light that remained and thus know what sort of drink to offer, and he saw that she was surprised to find the windows of the room dark. 'What time is it?' she asked.

'Six-thirty.'

'Is it really?' she asked rhetorically, going back toward the sofa where she had been sitting. 'Come and sit here and tell me how the children are,' she said. She resumed her place, closed the book, and set it on the table beside her. She folded the glasses and set them beside the book. 'No, sit here, Guido,' she insisted when she saw him move toward a chair on the opposite side of the low table in front of the sofa.

He did as she told him and sat beside her on the

sofa. In his many years of marriage to Paola, Brunetti had spent very little time alone with her mother, and so the impression he had of her was confused. At times, she seemed the most empty-headed of social butterflies, unable to do something so simple as get herself a drink, yet at other times she had amazed Brunetti with summations of people's motivations or characters that stunned him with their icy penetration and accuracy. He was kept off balance because he could never tell if her remarks were intentional or accidental. It was this woman who had, a year ago, referred to Fini, the Neo-fascist parliamentarian, as 'Mussofini', giving no indication of whether the mistaken name was the result of confusion or contempt.

He told her how the children were, assuring the Contessa that both of them were doing well in school, were sleeping with their windows closed against the night air, and eating two vegetables with every meal. That, apparently, was enough to assure the Contessa that all was well with her grandchildren, and so she turned her attention to their parents. 'And you and Paola? You certainly are looking robust, Guido,' she said, and Brunetti found himself sitting up a bit straighter.

'Now tell me, what would you like to drink?' she asked.

'Nothing, really. I've come to ask you about some people you might know.'

'Really?' she said, turning her jade-green eyes toward him and opening them wide. 'Whatever for?'

'Well, the name of one of them has come up in

104

another investigation we're conducting . . .' he began and let the sentence trail out.

'And you've come to see if I know anything about them?'

'Well, yes.'

'What could I possibly know that could be of help to the police?'

'Well, personal things,' Brunetti said.

'You mean gossip?' she asked.

'Um, yes.'

She looked aside for a moment and straightened a minuscule wrinkle in the fabric on the arm of the sofa. 'I didn't know the police interested themselves with gossip.'

'It's probably our richest source of information.'

'Really?' she asked, and when he nodded, added, 'How very interesting.'

Brunetti said nothing, and to avoid meeting the Contessa's glance, he looked across her to the spine of the book on the table, expecting to find a romance or a mystery. '*The Voyage of the Beagle*,' he asked aloud, unable to contain his astonishment and pronouncing the title in English.

The Contessa glanced at the book and then back to Brunetti. 'Why, yes, Guido. Have you read it?'

'When I was in university, years ago, but in translation,' he managed to say, voice under control and all astonishment removed from it.

'Yes, I've always enjoyed reading Darwin,' the Contessa explained. 'Did you like the book?' she continued, all discussion of gossip and police business suspended.

'Yes, I did, at the time. I'm not sure my memory of it is all that clear, though.'

'You should read it again, then. It's an important book, probably one of the most important books of the modern world. That and the *Origin of Species*, I'd say.' Brunetti nodded in agreement. 'Would you like to borrow it when I'm finished with it?' she asked. 'You wouldn't have any trouble with the English, would you?'

'No, I don't think so, but I've got quite a lot to read at the moment. Perhaps later in the year.'

'Yes, it would be a lovely book to read on vacation, I think. All those beaches. All those lovely animals.'

'Yes, yes,' Brunetti agreed, utterly at a loss as to what to say.

The Contessa saved him. 'Who is it you wanted me to gossip about, Guido?'

'Well, not exactly gossip, just tell me if you've heard anything about them that might be interesting to the police.'

'And what sort of thing is interesting to the police?'

He hesitated a moment but then had to confess, 'Everything, I suppose.'

'Yes, I thought that might be the case,' she answered. 'Well?'

'Signorina Benedetta Lerini,' he said.

'The one who lives over in Dorsoduro?' the Contessa asked.

'Yes.'

The Contessa thought for a moment and then said, 'All I know about her is that she is very gen-

106

erous to the Church, or is said to be. Much of the money she inherited from her father – dreadful, vicious man – has been given to the Church.'

'Which one?'

The Contessa paused for a moment. 'Isn't that strange?' she asked with mingled surprise and curiosity, 'I don't have any idea. All I've heard is that she's very religious and gives a lot of money to the Church. But for all I know, it could be the Waldensians or the Anglicans or even those dreadful Americans who stop you on the street, you know, the ones who have lots of wives but don't let them drink Coca Cola.'

Brunetti wasn't sure how much this advanced his understanding of Signorina Lerini, and so he tried the other name. 'And Contessa Crivoni?'

'Claudia?' the Contessa asked, making no attempt to disguise her first reaction, which was surprise, nor her second, which was delight.

'If that's her name. She's the widow of Conte Egidio.'

'Oh, this is too, too delicious,' the Contessa said with a fluty laugh. 'How I wish I could tell the girls at bridge.' Seeing Brunetti's look of sheer panic, she instantly added, 'No, don't worry, Guido. I won't say a thing about this. Not even to Orazio. Paola has told me how she can never tell me anything you tell her.'

'She has?'

'Yes.'

'But does she ever tell you anything?' Brunetti asked before he could stop himself.

The Contessa smiled in response and placed her

ring-covered hand on his sleeve. 'Now, Guido, you're loyal to your oath to the police, aren't you?'

He nodded.

'Well, then, I'm loyal to my daughter.' She smiled again. 'Now tell me what you'd like to know about Claudia.'

'I'd like to know about her husband, how she got on with him.'

'No one got on with Egidio, I'm afraid,' the Contessa said without hesitation, then added with reflective slowness, 'But I suppose the same thing could probably be said of Claudia.' She considered this, as though she hadn't realized it until she'd said it. 'What do you know about them, Guido?'

'Nothing more than the usual gossip in the city.'

'Which is?'

'That he made his money in the sixties by putting up illegal buildings in Mestre.'

'And what about Claudia?'

'That she is interested in public morality,' Brunetti said blandly.

The Contessa smiled at this, 'Oh, yes, she certainly is.'

When she added nothing to this, Brunetti asked, 'What do you know about her, or how do you know her?'

'Because of the church, San Simone Piccolo. She's on the committee that's trying to raise enough money for the restoration.'

'Are you a member, as well?'

'Good heavens, no. She asked me to join, but I know the talk about restoration is just a ruse.'

'To cover up what?'

'It's the only church in the city where they say the mass in Latin. Did you know that?'

'No.'

'I think they had something to do with that cardinal in France – Lefevre – the one who wanted to go back to Latin and incense. So I assume that any money they raised would be sent to France or used for incense, not to restore the church.' She considered this for a moment and then added, 'The church is so ugly, it ought not to be restored anyway. Just a bad imitation of the Pantheon.'

However interesting he might have found this architectural digression, Brunetti pulled the Contessa away from it. 'But what do you know about her?'

The Contessa looked away from him, toward the row of quatrefoil windows that gave an unimpeded view to the *palazzi* on the other side of the Grand Canal. 'What use is going to be made of this, Guido? Can you tell me that?'

'Can you tell me why you want to know?' he asked by way of answer.

'Because, unpleasant a creature as Claudia is, I don't want her to suffer unjustly as a result of some gossip that proves to be false.' Before Brunetti could say anything, she raised a hand and said, voice a bit louder. 'No, I think it's closer to the truth to say that I don't want to be responsible for that suffering.'

'I can assure you that she will suffer nothing unmerited.'

'I find that a very ambiguous remark.'

'Yes, I suppose it is. The truth is that I don't have any idea if she could have done anything or, in fact, any idea of *what* sort of thing she might have

109

done. I don't even know if anything wrong *has* been done.'

'But you're coming to ask questions about her?'

'Yes.'

'Then you must have reason to be curious about her.'

'Yes, I am. But I promise you that it is no more than that. And if what you tell me removes my curiosity, whatever it is, it will not go any further than me. I promise you that.'

'And if it doesn't?'

Brunetti pulled his lips together while he thought this through. 'Then I'll look into whatever you tell me and see what truth lies under the gossip.'

'Very often there is none,' she said.

He smiled to hear her say that. Certainly the Contessa needed no one to tell her that, just as often, truth provided a rock-like foundation to gossip.

After a long pause, she said, 'There's talk about a priest,' but said nothing more.

'What kind of talk?'

She waved a hand in the air by way of answer.

'Which priest?'

'I don't know.'

'What do you know?' he asked softly.

'There have been a few remarks dropped. Nothing overt, you understand, nothing that could be interpreted as anything other than the deepest and most sincere concern for her welfare.' Brunetti was familiar with remarks like this: crucifixion was kinder. 'You know how these things get said, Guido. If she fails to come to a meeting, someone will ask if anything is wrong, or someone else will say that

110

they hope it's not a sickness of some sort, then add, in that voice women have, that they know it would have to be illness, her spiritual health being so well looked after.'

'Is that all?' Brunetti asked.

She nodded. 'It's enough.'

'Why do you think it's a priest?'

Again, the Contessa waved her hand. 'It's the tone. The words don't really mean anything; it's all done with the tone, the inflection, the hint that lies lurking under the surface of the most innocent remark.'

'How long has this been going on?'

'Guido,' she said, sitting up straighter, 'I don't know that anything at all is going on.'

'Then how long have these remarks been going on?'

'I don't know. More than a year, I think. I was very slow to notice them. Or perhaps people were careful about making them in front of me. They know I don't like that sort of thing.'

'Has anything else been said?'

'What do you mean?'

'At the time of her husband's death?'

'No, nothing that I can remember.'

'Nothing?'

'Guido,' she said, leaning toward him and putting her bejewelled hand on his sleeve, 'please try to remember that I am not a suspect and do try not to talk to me like one.'

He felt his face grow red and he said immediately, 'I'm sorry. I'm sorry. I forget.'

'Yes, Paola's told me.'

'Told you what?' Brunetti asked.

'How important it is to you.'

'How important what is?'

'What you see as justice.'

'What I see?'

'Ah, I'm sorry, Guido. I'm afraid I've offended you now.'

He shook this away with a quick motion of his head, but before he could ask her what she meant by 'his' idea of justice, she got to her feet and said, 'How dark it's getting.'

She seemed to forget about him and went over to stand in front of one of the windows, her back to Brunetti, her hands clasped behind her. Brunetti studied her, the raw silk suit, high heels, and the back of her perfect chignon. The Contessa could have been a young woman standing there, so slender and straight was her outline.

After a long time, she turned, glancing down at her watch. 'Orazio and I have a dinner invitation, Guido, so if you have no other questions, I'm afraid I have to change.'

Brunetti got to his feet and walked across the room. Behind the Contessa, boats moved up and down the canal, and light spilled from the windows of the buildings on the other side. He wanted to say something to her, but before he could speak, she said, 'Please give Paola and the children our love.' She patted his arm and moved past him. Before he could say anything, she was gone, leaving him to study the view from the *palazzo* which would someday be his.

Chapter Seven

Brunetti let himself into the apartment a little before eight, hung up his coat, and went immediately down the hall to Paola's study. He found her, as he knew he would, sprawled in her tattered armchair, one leg curled under her, a pen in one hand, book open on her lap. She glanced up when he came in, made an exaggerated kissing motion in his direction, but looked down at her book again. Brunetti sat on the sofa opposite her, then turned and stretched himself out across its surface. He grabbed up two velvet pillows and pounded them into shape under his head. First he looked at the ceiling, and then he closed his eyes, knowing that she would finish whatever passage she was interested in and then devote herself to him.

A page turned. Minutes passed. He heard the book drop to the floor and said, 'I never knew your mother read.'

'Well, she asks Luciana to help her with the big words.'

'No, I mean read books.'

'As opposed to what? Palms?'

'No, really, Paola, I never knew she read serious books.'

'She still reading Saint Augustine?'

Brunetti had no idea if this was meant to be a joke or not and so he answered, 'No. Darwin. *The Voyage of the Beagle.*'

'Oh, really?' Paola said with what seemed little interest.

'Did you know she read things like that?'

'You make it sound like she's reading kiddie-porn, Guido.'

'No, I just wondered if you knew she read books like that, that she was a serious reader?'

'She is my mother, after all. Of course I knew it.'

'But you never told me.'

'Would that make you like her any more than you do?'

'I like your mother, Paola,' he said, voice perhaps a bit too insistent. 'What I'm talking about is that I never knew who she was. Or,' he corrected himself, 'what she was.'

'And will knowing what she reads make you know who she is?'

'Can you think of a better way to tell?'

Paola considered this for a long time and then gave him the answer he expected. 'No, I suppose I can't.' He heard her move around on her chair, but Brunetti kept his eyes closed. 'What were you doing, talking to my mother? And how did you find out about the book? Surely you didn't call her up to ask her for some reading suggestions.'

'No, I went to see her.'

'My mother? You went to see my mother?'

Brunetti grunted.

'Whatever for?'

'To ask her about some people she knows.'

'Who?'

'Benedetta Lerini.'

'Ou la la,' Paola sang out. 'What's she done, finally confessed she beat that old bastard's head in with a hammer?'

'I believe her father died of a heart attack.'

'To universal rejoicing, I'm sure.'

'Why universal?' When Paola didn't answer him for a long time, Brunetti opened his eyes and glanced across toward her. She sat with the other leg under her now, chin propped on one hand. 'Well?' he asked.

'It's funny, Guido. Now that you ask, I don't know why it should be. I guess it's just because I've always heard that he was a terrible man.'

'Terrible in what way?'

Again, her answer was long delayed. 'I don't know. I can't remember anything, not a single specific thing I might have heard about him, just this general impression that he was bad. That's strange, isn't it?'

Brunetti closed his eyes again. 'I'd say so, especially in this city.'

'You mean everybody knows everybody?'

'Pretty much. Yes.'

'I suppose so.' Both stopped talking, and Brunetti knew she was running her mind back down the long passages of her memory, trying to hunt out the comment, the remark, some trace of the opinion of the late Signor Lerini which she seemed to have taken on, unexamined, as her own.

115

Paola's voice called Brunetti back from near sleep. 'It was Patrizia.'

'Patrizia Belloti?'

'Yes.'

'What did she say?'

'She worked for him, for about five years before he died. That's how I know about him and his daughter. Patrizia said she'd never known a person so awful and that everyone in his office hated him.'

'He was in real estate, wasn't he?'

'Yes, among other things.'

'Did she say why?'

'Why what?'

'People hated him?'

'Let me think for a minute,' Paola said. Then, after a pause, she added, 'I think it had to do with religion.'

Brunetti had been half expecting this. If the daughter was any indication, he would have been one of those sanctimonious bigots who forbade swearing in the office and gave rosaries as Christmas presents. 'What did she say?'

'Well, you know Patrizia, don't you?' A childhood friend of Paola's, she had never seemed very interesting to Brunetti, though he had to confess he had seen her no more than a dozen times in all these years.

'Um hum.'

'She's very religious.'

Brunetti remembered: it was one of the reasons he didn't like her.

'I think she said that he made a scene one day because someone, a new secretary or something, put

116

some sort of religious picture on the wall in her office. Or a cross. I really don't remember now what she told me. It was years ago. But he made a scene, made her take it down. And he swore terribly, too, I think I remember her telling me. Really a foul mouth – "the Madonna this, the Madonna that". Things that Patrizia wouldn't even repeat. Things that would offend even you, Guido.'

Brunetti ignored this casual revelation that Paola appeared to consider him some sort of arbiter of scurrility and directed his thoughts, instead, to this revelation about Signor Lerini. From this drifty world Brunetti was called back by the soft press of Paola's body as she sat down on the sofa near his hip. He pulled himself closer to the back of the sofa to allow her more room without bothering to open his eyes, then felt her elbow, arm, breast lean across his chest.

'Why did you go to see my mother?' her voice asked from just below his chin.

'I thought she might know the Lerini woman, and the other one.'

'Who?'

'Claudia Crivoni.'

'And did she know Claudia?'

'Uh hum.'

'What did she say?'

'Something about a priest.'

'A priest?' Paola said, exactly as had Brunetti when he heard the same thing.

'Yes. But only rumour.'

'That means it's probably true.'

'What's true?'

'Oh, don't be a goose, Guido. What do you think is true?'

'With a priest?'

'Why not?'

'Aren't they supposed to take a vow?'

She pushed herself away. 'I don't believe you. Do you actually believe that makes any difference?'

'It's supposed to.'

'Yes, and children are supposed to be obedient and dutiful.'

'Not ours,' he said and smiled.

He felt Paola's body shake in a quick laugh. 'That's true enough. But really, Guido, you really don't mean that about priests, do you?'

'I don't think she's involved with anyone.'

'Why are you so sure?'

'I've had a look at her,' he said and made a sudden grab at Paola, catching her around the waist and pulling her on top of him.

Paola squealed aloud in surprise, but the noise had much the same delighted horror as did the shrieks Chiara made whenever Raffi or Brunetti tickled her. She squirmed, but Brunetti tightened his arms around her and forced her to lie still.

After a while, he said, 'I never knew your mother.'

'You've known her for twenty years.'

'No, I mean I never knew her as a person. All these years and I had no idea of who she was.'

'You sound sad,' Paola said, pushing herself up on his chest, the better to see his face.

He released his hold on her. 'It is sad, to know

a person for twenty years and never have any idea of what they're like. All that time wasted.'

She lay back down and moved around until her curves fitted more easily into his body. At one point, he let out a sudden, 'Ouf,' as her elbow dug into his stomach, but then she lay still and he wrapped his arms around her again.

Chiara, who came in a half hour later, hungry and looking for dinner, found them asleep like that.

Chapter Eight

The next day, Brunetti woke with a strange, clear-headed sensation, as if a sudden fever had passed in the night and he'd been returned to his senses. He lay in bed for a long time, running through all of the information he had accumulated during the last two days. Rather than come to the conclusion that he had spent his time well, that the Questura and its doings were in safe hands and he in pursuit of crime, he felt himself suddenly embarrassed by his having run off in pursuit of what he now admitted gave every indication of being a wild-goose chase. Not content with believing Maria Testa's story, he had commandeered Vianello and gone off to question people who obviously had no idea what he was talking about nor any idea of why a *commissario* of police would come unannounced to their door.

Patta was due back in ten days, and Brunetti had no doubt what his response would be when he learned how police time had been spent. Even in the warmth and safety of his bed, Brunetti could feel the icy chill of Patta's remarks: 'You mean you believed this story told by a *nun*, by a woman who's been hiding in a convent all her life? And you went and hounded those people, made them think their relatives had been murdered? Are you out of your mind, Brunetti? Do you know who these people *are*?'

He decided that, before abandoning everything, he would speak to one last person, someone who might be able to corroborate, if not Maria's story, then at least her reliability as a witness. And who would know her better than the man to whom she had confessed her sins for the last six years?

The address Brunetti sought was toward the end of the *sestiere* of Castello, near the church of San Francesco della Vigna. The first two people he asked had no idea where the number was, but when he asked where he could find the Fathers of the Sacred Cross, he was immediately told they were at the foot of the next bridge, the second door on the left. So it proved, announced by a small brass plate that bore the name of the order beside a small Maltese cross.

The door was answered after his first ring by a white-haired man who could well have been that figure so common in medieval literature – the good monk. His eyes radiated kindness as the sun radiates warmth, and the rest of his face glowed in a broad smile, as if truly made glad by the arrival of this stranger at his door.

'May I help you?' he asked as if nothing could give him more joy than to be able to do just that.

'I'd like to speak to Padre Pio Cavaletti, Brother.'

'Yes, yes. Come in, my son,' the monk said, opening the door even wider and holding it open for Brunetti. 'Careful there,' he said, pointing down and reaching out instinctively to put a steadying hand on Brunetti's arm as he stepped over the wooden cross bar which formed the bottom of the frame of the heavy wooden door. He wore the long white skirt of Suor'Immacolata's order, but his was covered by a tan apron stained by years of work in grass and dirt.

Brunetti stepped into sweetness and stopped, looking around, trying to identify the odour.

'Lilac,' the monk explained, taking joy in the pleasure he read on Brunetti's face. 'Padre Pio is mad for them, has them sent to him from all over the world.' And so, as Brunetti looked around, it proved to be. Shrubs, bushes, even tall trees filled the entire courtyard in front of them, and the scent swirled around him in waves. As he looked, he saw that only a few of the bushes were bent under the magenta clusters; most of them were not yet in flower.

'But there are so few of them to give such a strong smell,' Brunetti said, unable to disguise his astonishment at the strength of their perfume.

'I know,' the monk said with a proud smile. 'They're the first bloomers, the dark ones: Dilatata and Claude Bernard and Ruhm von Horstenstein.' Brunetti assumed that the monk's linguistic flight had to do with the names of the lilacs he was smelling. 'Those white ones, over there against the far wall,' he began, taking Brunetti's elbow and pointing off to their left, to a dozen green-leafed shrubs that huddled up against the high brick wall, 'White Summers, and Marie Finon, and Ivory Silk – they won't bloom until June, and we'll probably have some still in flower until July, so long as it doesn't get too hot too soon.' Looking around with pleasure that filled both his voice and his face, he said, 'There are twenty-seven different varieties in this courtyard. And in our chapter house up by Trento, we've got another thirty-four.' Before Brunetti could say anything, he went on, 'They come from as far away as Minnesota,' which he pronounced with an entirely Italian crispness of consonant, 'and Wisconsin,' which he could barely get his tongue around.

'And you're the gardener?' Brunetti asked, though it was hardly necessary.

'By the goodness of God, I am that. I've worked in this garden,' he began, giving Brunetti a closer look, 'since the time you were a boy.'

'It's beautiful, Brother. You should be proud of it.'

The old man gave Brunetti a sudden look from under his thick eyebrows. Pride was, after all, one of the seven deadly sins. 'Proud that beauty like this gives glory to God, that is,' Brunetti amended, and the monk's smile was restored.

'The Lord never makes anything that isn't beautiful,' the old man said as he started across the brick path that led across the garden. 'If you have any doubt of that, all you've got to do is look at His flowers.' He nodded in affirmation of this simple truth and asked, 'Do you have a garden?'

'No, I'm afraid I don't,' Brunetti answered.

'Ah, that's a shame. It's good to see things grow. Gives a sense of life.' He came to a door and opened it, standing aside to allow Brunetti to pass into the long corridor of the monastery.

'Do children count?' Brunetti asked with a smile. 'I've got two of those.'

'Oh, they count more than anything in the world,' the monk said, smiling at Brunetti. 'Nothing is more beautiful, and nothing gives greater glory to God.'

Brunetti smiled at the monk and nodded in full agreement with at least the first proposition.

The monk stopped in front of a door and knocked. 'Go right in,' he said without bothering to wait for an answer. 'Padre Pio tells us never to stop anyone who wants to see him.' With a smile and a pat on Brunetti's arm, the monk was gone, back toward the garden and his lilacs – what Brunetti had always believed was the scent of paradise.

A tall man sat at a desk, writing. He looked up when Brunetti came in, set his pen down, and stood. He came out from behind the desk and walked toward his unknown visitor, hand extended, a smile beginning in his eyes, then moving to his mouth.

The priest's lips were so red and full that anyone seeing him for the first time would immediately centre their attention on them, but it was his eyes that revealed his spirit. Somewhere between grey and green, his eyes were alive with a curiosity and interest in the world around him that Brunetti suspected would characterize everything he did. He was tall and very thin, this last emphasized by the long folds of the habit of the Order of the Sacred Cross. Though the priest must have been in his forties, his hair was still black, the only sign of age a thinning natural tonsure at the crown.

'*Buon giorno*,' the priest said in a warm voice. 'How may I help you?' His voice, though it moved in the undulant Veneto cadence, did not have the accent of the city. Perhaps from Padova, Brunetti thought, but before he could begin to answer, the priest continued. 'But excuse me. Let me offer you a seat. Here.' Saying this, he pulled out one of two small cushioned chairs that stood to the left of the desk and waited until Brunetti was seated before he lowered himself into the one opposite.

Suddenly Brunetti was filled with the desire to do this quickly and have done with it, finish with Maria Testa and her story. 'I'd like to speak to you about a member of your order, Father.' A puff of wind blew into the room, rustling the papers on the desk and reminding Brunetti of the rich promise of the season. He felt how warm it was and, looking around him, saw that the windows were open to the courtyard to allow the scent of the lilacs to flood in.

The priest noticed his glance. 'I seem to spend my entire day holding papers down with one hand,' he said with an embarrassed smile. 'But the season for the lilacs is so short, I like to appreciate them as much as I can.' He looked down for a moment, then up at Brunetti. 'I suppose it's a form of gluttony.'

'I don't think it's a serious vice, Father,' Brunetti said with an easy smile.

The priest nodded his thanks for Brunetti's remark. 'I hope this doesn't sound rude, Signore, but I think I have to ask who you are before I can discuss a member of our order with you.' His smile was an embarrassed one, and he extended a hand half-way across the distance that separated them, palm open in a request for Brunetti's understanding.

'I'm Commissario Brunetti,' he said by way of explanation.

'Of the police?' the priest asked, making no attempt to hide his surprise.

'Yes.'

'Good heavens. No one's been hurt, have they?'

'No, not at all. I've come to ask you about a young woman who was a member of your order.'

'Was, Commissario?' he asked. 'A woman?'

'Yes.'

'Then I'm afraid I can't be much help to you. The Mother Superior could give you more information than I can. She is the spiritual mother of the sisters.'

'I believe you know this woman, Father.'

'Yes, who is it?'

'Maria Testa.'

The priest's smile was a completely disarming attempt to apologize for his own ignorance. 'I'm afraid the name doesn't mean anything to me, Commissario. Could you give me her name when she was still a member of our order?'

'Suor'Immacolata.'

The priest's face lit up with recognition. 'Ah yes, she worked at the San Leonardo nursing home. She was a great help to the patients. Many of them loved her deeply, a feeling I think she returned. I was saddened to learn of her decision to leave the order. I've prayed for her.' Brunetti nodded, and the priest went on, voice suddenly alarmed, 'But what do the police want with her?'

This time it was Brunetti who extended a hand across the distance between them. 'We're merely asking some questions about her, Father. She hasn't done anything, believe me.' The priest's relief was visible. Brunetti continued. 'How well did you know her, Father?'

Padre Pio considered the question for several moments. 'That's difficult to answer, Commissario.'

'I thought you were her confessor.'

The priest's eyes opened wide at this, but he quickly glanced down to disguise his surprise. He folded his hands, considering what to say, and then looked back up at Brunetti. 'I'm afraid this might seem needlessly complicated to you, Commissario, but it is important that I distinguish here between my knowledge of her as a superior in the order and my knowledge of her as her confessor.'

'Why is that?' Brunetti asked, though he knew.

'Because I cannot, under pain of serious sin, reveal to you anything she has told me under the seal of confession.'

'But those things you know as her religious superior, can you tell me those?'

'Yes, certainly, especially if they will be of any help to her.' He unfolded his hands, and Brunetti noticed one of them reach for the beads of the rosary that hung from his belt. 'What is it you'd like to know?' the priest asked.

'Is she an honest woman?'

This time the priest made no attempt to hide his surprise. 'Honest? Do you mean if she'd steal?'

'Or lie.'

'No, she'd never do either of those things.' The priest's answer was immediate and unqualified.

'What about her vision of the world?'

'I'm afraid I don't understand the question,' he said with a small shake of his head.

'Is she, do you think, an accurate judge of human nature? Would she be a reliable witness?'

After a long moment's thought, the priest said, 'I think that would depend on what she was judging. Or whom.'

'Meaning?'

'I think she is, well, I suppose "excitable" is as good a word as any. Or "emotional". Suor'Immacolata is very quick to see the good in people, a quality beyond price. But,' and here his face clouded, 'she is often just as ready to suspect the bad.' He stopped, measuring out the next words. 'I'm afraid this next is going to sound terrible, like the worst sort of prejudice.' The priest paused, evidently uncomfortable about what he was going to say. 'Suor'Immacolata is from the South, and I think, because of that, she has a certain vision of mankind or of human nature.' Padre Pio looked away and Brunetti saw the way his teeth caught at his bottom lip, as if he wanted to bite the offending part and thus punish himself for having said what he just had.

'Wouldn't the convent be a strange place to take that vision?'

'You see?' the priest said, obviously embarrassed. 'I don't know how to say what I want to say. If I could speak in theological terms, I'd say she suffers from lack of hope. If she had more hope, then I think she would have more faith in the goodness of people.' He stopped talking and fingered his beads. 'But I'm afraid I cannot say any more than that, Commissario.'

'Because of the danger of revealing something to me that I shouldn't know?'

'That you can't know,' the priest said, voice filled with the ring of absolute certainty. When he saw the look Brunetti gave him, he added, 'I know this seems strange to many people, especially in today's world. But it is a tradition as old as the Church, and I think it is one of the traditions we strive most strongly to maintain. And must maintain.' His smile was sad. 'I'm afraid I can't say more than that.'

'But she wouldn't lie?'

'No. You can be sure of that. Never. She might misinterpret or exaggerate, but Suor'Immacolata would never knowingly lie.'

Brunetti got to his feet. 'Thank you for your time, Father,' he said, extending his hand.

The priest took it; his grasp was firm and dry. He accompanied Brunetti across the room and, at the door, said only 'Go with God,' in response to Brunetti's renewed thanks.

As he emerged into the courtyard, Brunetti saw the gardener kneeling in the dirt beside the back wall of the monastery, hands digging at the roots of a rose bush. The old man saw Brunetti and pushed one hand flat on the ground in an attempt to push himself to his feet, but Brunetti called across to him, 'No, Brother, I'll let myself out.' When he did that, the scent of the lilacs trailed him down the *calle* until he turned the first corner, following him like a benediction.

The next day, the current Minister of Finance visited the city, and even though it was an entirely personal visit, the police were still responsible for his safety while he was there. Because of this and because of a late winter outbreak of flu that had five policemen in bed and one in the hospital, the copies of the wills of the five people who had died at the San Leonardo Casa di Cura lay unnoticed on Brunetti's desk until early the next week. He did manage to think about them, even asked Signorina Elettra about them once, only to receive the brisk reply that they had been placed on his desk two days before.

It was not until the Minister had returned to Rome and the Augean Stables of the Ministry of Finance that Brunetti thought again about the copies of the five wills, and he did that only because his hand fell upon them when he was searching his desk for some missing personnel files. He decided to take a look at them before giving them to Signorina Elettra and asking her to find some place to file them.

His university degree was in law, and so he was familiar with the language, the clauses which provided, bestowed, granted possession of bits and tatters of the world to people not yet dead. Reading through the cautious phrases, he could not help thinking of what Vianello had said about the impossibility of ever really owning anything, for here was proof of that impossibility. They had passed on the fiction of ownership to their heirs and had thus perpetuated that illusion, until more time passed, when the heirs too would have ownership stolen from them by death.

Maybe those Celtic chieftains had it right, Brunetti speculated, when they had all their treasure piled on a barge with their bodies and the whole thing set ablaze to drift to sea. It occurred to him that this sudden turning against material possessions was perhaps no more than a response to having spent time in the company of the Minister of Finance, a man so crass, vulgar, and stupid as surely to turn anyone against wealth. Brunetti laughed aloud at this and returned his attention to the wills.

Aside from that of Signorina da Prè, two of the wills mentioned the *casa di cura*. Signora Cristanti had left five million lire, certainly not an enormous sum, and Signora Galasso, who had given the bulk of her estate to a nephew in Torino, had left it two million lire.

Brunetti had worked for the police for too long not to know that people would kill for sums this small, and many quite casually, but he had also learned that few careful killers would risk detection for such trifles. It seemed unlikely, therefore, that these sums could have served as sufficient motive for anyone involved with the *casa di cura* to be moved to take the risk of killing these old people.

Signorina da Prè sounded, from her brother's description, like an abandoned old woman who had been moved, toward the end of her life, to act charitably toward the institution where she had spent her last lonely years. Da Prè had said no one had opposed his having contested his sister's will. Brunetti could not imagine that anyone who would kill in order to inherit would allow their bequest so easily to be taken from them.

He checked the dates and saw that both the Lerini and Galasso wills that contained the bequests to the *casa di cura* had preceded their deaths by considerably more than a year. Of the remaining wills, two had been signed more than five years before death, and in the last case, twelve. It would take greater imagination and cynicism than Brunetti's to invent a sinister scenario here.

The fact that nothing criminal had taken place made sense, though rather perverse sense, to Brunetti, for by imagining secret, malign events at the *casa di cura*, events which she alone could see, Suor'-Immacolata could thus justify her decision to leave the order that had been her spiritual and physical home from the time she was an adolescent. Brunetti had seen guilt present itself in stranger forms, surely, but he had seldom seen so little real reason for guilt. He realized that he did not believe her, and it filled him with heavy sadness that she would have so soured the beginning of her *vita nuova*. She deserved better of life, and of herself, than this dangerous invention.

The papers, copies of the five wills and the few notes he had sketched after his visits to the people he and Vianello had visited, found their way, not into the hands of Signorina Elettra, but into his bottom drawer, where they rested for another three days.

Patta returned from vacation, less interested in police work than when he left. Brunetti profited from this by making no mention of Maria Testa or her story. Spring advanced, and Brunetti went to visit his mother in the nursing home, a visit made more painful by his renewed awareness of the absence of the instinctive charity of Suor'Immacolata.

The young woman made no further attempt to contact him, and so Brunetti allowed himself to indulge in the virtue of hope, hope that she had abandoned her story, forgotten her fears, and begun her new life. Brunetti even went so far one day as to decide to go out to the Lido to visit her, but when he looked for the file, he couldn't find it or the piece of paper with her address on it, nor could he remember the name of the people who had helped her find a job. Rossi, Bassi, Guzzi, a name that sounded something like that, Brunetti recalled, but then the irritation of Vice-Questore Patta's return to the Questura caught up with him, and he forgot all about her until, two days later, he answered his phone and found himself speaking to a man who identified himself as Vittorio Sassi.

'Are you the man that Maria talked to?' Sassi asked.

'Maria Testa?' Brunetti asked in return, though he knew which Maria the man meant.

'Suor'Immacolata.'

'Yes, she came to see me a few weeks ago. Why are you calling me, Signor Sassi? What's wrong?'

'She's been hit by a car.'

'Where?'

'Out here on the Lido.'

'Where is she?'

'They took her to the emergency ward. That's where I am now, but I can't get any information about her.'

'When did this happen?'

'Yesterday afternoon.'

'Then why have you waited so long to call me?' Brunetti demanded.

There was a long silence.

'Signor Sassi?' Brunetti said, and when he had no answer, he asked in a softer voice, 'How is she?'

'Bad.'

'Who hit her?'

'No one knows.'

'What?'

'She was going home from work late yesterday afternoon, on her bicycle. It looks like a car hit her from behind. It was going very fast. Whoever was driving didn't stop.'

'Who found her?'

'A man in a truck. He saw her lying in a ditch at the side of the road. He brought her to the hospital.'

'How bad is she?'

'I don't know, not really. When they called me this morning, they told me that one of her legs was broken. But they think there might be brain damage.'

'Who thinks that?'

'I don't know. What I'm telling you is what the person I talked to on the phone told me.'

'But you're at the hospital?'

'Yes.'

'How did they know to get in touch with you?' Brunetti asked.

'The police went to her pensione yesterday – her address was in her bag, I think – and the owner gave them my wife's name. He remembered that we'd taken her there. But they didn't bother to call me until this morning, and I came right over here.'

'Why did you call me?'

'When she went into Venice last month, we asked her where she was going, and she said she was going to talk to a policeman named Brunetti. She didn't say what it was about, and we didn't ask, but we thought, well, we thought that if you're a policeman you'd want to know about what happened to her.'

'Thank you, Signor Sassi. I'm very glad you called me,' Brunetti said, then asked, 'How has she been acting since she saw me?'

If Sassi thought this a peculiar question, his voice gave no hint of it. 'Just the same as always. Why?'

Brunetti chose not to answer this and, instead, asked, 'How long are you going to be there?'

'Not much longer. I've got to get back to work, and my wife has the grandchildren.'

'What's the name of her doctor?'

'I don't know that, Commissario. It's chaos out here. The nurses are on strike today, so it's hard to find someone who will tell me anything. And no one seems to know anything about Maria. Can you come out here? Maybe they'd pay some attention to you.'

'I'll be there in half an hour.'

'She's a very good woman,' Sassi said.

Brunetti, who had known her for six years, understood fully how true those words were.

When Sassi hung up, Brunetti called down to Vianello and told him to get a pilot and a boat and be ready to leave for the Lido in five minutes. He had the operator connect him with the hospital at the Lido and asked to speak to the person in charge of the emergency ward. His call was transferred to gynaecology, surgery, and the kitchen before he hung up in disgust and ran down the steps to Vianello, Bonsuan, and the waiting launch.

As they surged across the *laguna*, Brunetti told Vianello about Sassi's call.

'Bastards,' Vianello said when he heard about the hit-and-run driver. 'Why didn't they stop? Just leave her for dead at the side of the road.'

'Maybe that's what they wanted to do,' Brunetti said and watched as the sergeant suddenly understood.

'Of course,' he said, eyes closing at the simplicity of it. 'But we didn't even go to the *casa di cura* to ask any questions. How would they know she'd talked to us?' Vianello asked.

'We don't have any idea of what she's done since she came to see me, do we?'

'No, I suppose we don't. But she couldn't have been foolish enough to just go and accuse someone, could she?'

'She's been in a convent most of her life, Sergeant.'

'What does that mean?'

'It means that she probably thinks it's enough to tell someone that they've done wrong, and they'll march down to the police, say they're sorry, and hand themselves over.' When he heard how flippant he sounded, Brunetti immediately regretted having spoken so lightly. 'I mean she's probably not a very good judge of character, and most motives wouldn't make much sense to her.'

'I suppose you're right, sir. A convent probably

isn't the best preparation for this filthy world we've made.'

Brunetti could think of no response to make to this, so he said nothing until the boat pulled into one of the landings restricted for ambulances at the back of the Ospedale al Mare. They jumped from the boat, telling Bonsuan to wait until they had some idea of what was going on. A gaping door led to a white, cement-floored corridor.

A white-coated attendant came hurrying down it toward them. 'Who are you? What are you doing down here? No one's allowed to come into the hospital this way.'

Ignoring what he said, Brunetti pulled out his warrant card and flashed it at the man. 'Where's the emergency ward?'

He watched as the man thought about resisting or opposing them, but then he saw the usual Italian refusal to resist authority, especially uniformed authority, assert itself, and the man gave them directions. Within minutes, they were standing at a nurses' desk, behind which double doors opened onto a long, brightly lit corridor. No one was at the desk, and no one answered Brunetti's repeated calls for attention.

After a few minutes, a man in a rumpled white coat pushed his way out through the doors. 'Excuse me,' Brunetti said, holding up a hand to stop the man.

'Yes?' he asked.

'How do I find out who's in charge of the emergency room?'

'Why do you want to know?' the man asked in a harried voice.

Again, Brunetti pulled out his warrant card and showed it. The man peered at it and then back to Brunetti. 'What is it you want to know, Commissario? I'm the person doomed to be in charge of this ward.'

'Doomed?' Brunetti asked.

'Sorry. That's an exaggeration. I've been here for the last thirty-six hours because the nurses have decided to go on strike. I'm trying to take care of nine patients with the help of one orderly and one intern. But I don't think telling you all this is going to help me much.'

'Sorry, doctor. I can't arrest your nurses.'

'Pity. How can I help you?'

'I've come to see a woman who was brought in here yesterday. Hit by a car. I was told she has a broken leg and some damage to the brain.'

The doctor recognized the description immediately. 'No, her leg's not broken. It was her shoulder, and it's only dislocated. And there are a few ribs that might be broken. But the head injury's the thing I was worried about.'

'Was, doctor?'

'Yes. We sent her over to the Ospedale Civile less than an hour after she was brought in here. Even if I had the staff to work on her, we don't have the equipment to treat a cranial injury like that.'

Not without difficulty, Brunetti bridled his anger at having come out here on a fool's errand and asked, 'How bad is it?'

'She was unconscious when they brought her in.

I put her shoulder back in place and bandaged her ribs, but I don't know enough about head injuries. I did some tests. I wanted to see what was going on inside her head, to see why she wouldn't come out of it. But she was in and out of here so quickly I had no time to be sure.'

'A man came here a few hours ago to look for her.' Brunetti said. 'No one told him that she'd been sent to Venice.'

The doctor shrugged away all responsibility. 'I told you, there's only the three of us. Someone should have told him.'

'Yes,' Brunetti agreed, 'someone should have told him.' Then he asked, 'Is there anything else you can tell me about her condition?'

'No, you'll have to ask the people over at Civile.'

'Where is she?'

'If they've found a neurologist, she'll be in the intensive care ward. Or she should be.' The doctor shook his head, whether from tiredness or the memory of Maria's injuries, Brunetti wasn't sure. Suddenly one of the doors was pushed open from the inside, and a young woman in an equally rumpled coat appeared. 'Dottore,' she said in an urgent, high voice, 'we need you. Quickly.'

He turned and followed the woman back through the door, not bothering to say anything further to Brunetti. Brunetti turned and went back the way they had come, back out to the launch. He stepped on board and, giving no explanation at all to the pilot of what had happened, said, 'Back to the Ospedale Civile, Bonsuan.' As they cut their way through the freshening waves, Brunetti remained below, but he watched through the glass windows of the doors of the cabin as Vianello told Bonsuan what had just happened. By the end of the tale, both men were shaking their heads disgustedly, no doubt the only possible response to any protracted contact with the public health system.

A quarter of an hour later, the boat pulled up alongside the Civil Hospital, and Brunetti again told Bonsuan to wait for them. Both he and Vianello knew from long experience where the intensive care ward was, and they quickly made their way through the labyrinthine corridors.

A doctor Brunetti knew stood in the corridor outside the ward, and Brunetti went quickly up to him.

'*Buon giorno*, Giovanni,' he said when the doctor recognized him and smiled. 'I'm looking for a woman who was sent over from the Lido yesterday.'

'The one with the head injury?' the young man asked.

'Yes. How is she?'

'It looks like she hit her head against her bicycle and then again when she hit the ground. There's a gash above her ear. But we can't get her out of it, can't get her to wake up.'

'Does anyone know . . .?' Brunetti began but stopped because he didn't know what to ask.

'We don't know anything, Guido. She could come out of it today. Or she could stay in it. Or she could die.' He stuffed his hands into the pockets of his jacket.

'What do you do in a case like this?' Brunetti asked.

'Doctors?'

Brunetti nodded.

'We do tests and more tests. And then we pray.'

'Can I see her?'

'There's not much to see except bandages,' the doctor said.

'I'd still like to see her.'

'All right. But only you,' he said, looking in Vianello's direction.

Vianello nodded and went over to sit in a chair against the wall. He picked up the second section of a two-day-old newspaper and began to read.

The doctor led Brunetti down the corridor and stopped in front of the third door on the right. 'We're crowded, so we've got her in here.' Saying that, he pushed open the door and went in before Brunetti.

Everything was familiar: the smell of flowers and urine, the plastic bottles of mineral water lined up against the windows to keep cool, the sense of expectant misery. There were four beds in the room, one empty. Brunetti saw her instantly, lying in the bed against the far wall. He didn't notice when the doctor left and closed the door but walked over and stood first at the foot of her bed, then moved up beside her head.

Her thick lashes were almost invisible against the dark shadows under both eyes; one short tuft of dark hair sneaked out from under the bandage that covered her hair. The side of her nose was discoloured by the Mercurochrome painted across a scrape that began there and ran down to her chin.

The black threads of stitches began just above her left cheekbone and disappeared under the bandage.

Under the light blue blanket, her body seemed no larger than a child's, weirdly distorted by the thick bandage that bound one shoulder. Brunetti stared first at her mouth and then, when he could detect no motion there, at her chest. He wasn't sure at first, but then he saw the blanket rise as she breathed silently in and then out. When he saw that, he relaxed.

Behind him, one of the other women moaned, and another, perhaps disturbed by the sound, called out for 'Roberto'.

After a time, Brunetti went back into the hall, where Vianello was still reading the paper. Brunetti nodded to him, and together they went out to the waiting boat and back to the Questura.

Chapter Nine

Brunetti and Vianello's agreement not to bother with lunch was as mutual as it was unspoken. As soon as they got back to the Questura, Brunetti sent Vianello to adjust the duty roster and see that a guard be put in front of Maria Testa's room immediately and kept there day and night.

Brunetti called the police on the Lido, gave his name and the reason for his call, and asked if they had learned anything about the hit-and-run accident the day before. They had nothing: no witnesses, no one calling to report a suspicious dent in a neighbour's car, nothing, even though there had been a story in that morning's paper listing a number to call if anyone had information about the accident. Brunetti left his number and, more importantly, his rank, and told them he was to be informed as soon as anything was learned about the driver or the car.

Brunetti opened his drawer and pushed things around until he found the abandoned file. He turned to the copy of the first will, that of Fausta Galasso, the woman who had left everything to her nephew in Torino, and read carefully through the items named: three apartments in Venice, two farms up near Pordenone, and the savings in three bank accounts in the city. He studied the addresses of the apartments, but they told him nothing.

He picked up the phone and dialled a number from memory.

'Bucintoro Real Estate,' a woman's voice answered on the second ring.

'*Ciao*, Stefania,' he said. 'It's Guido.'

'I knew from your voice,' she said. 'How are you and before you tell me, do you want to buy a lovely apartment in Canaregio, one hundred-fifty metres, two bathrooms, three bedrooms, kitchen, dining room, and living room with a view of the *laguna*?'

'What's wrong with it?' Brunetti asked.

'Guido?' she asked in shocked amazement, drawing out the first syllable to three times its normal length.

'Occupied and no way to get the tenant out? Needs a new roof? Dry rot in the walls?' he asked.

There was a short silence and then a short, shocked laugh. '*Acqua alta*,' Stefania said. 'If the water goes above one metre fifty, you'll have fish in your bed.'

'There are no more fish in the *laguna*, Stefania. They've all been poisoned.'

'Seaweed, then. But it's really a beautiful apartment, believe me. An American couple bought it three years ago, spent a fortune restoring it, hundreds of millions, but no one told them about the water. Then, last winter, when we had *acqua alta*, they lost their parquet, their new paint job, and about fifty million in furniture and carpets. Finally they called in an architect, and the first thing he told them was

144

that there was nothing they could do about it. So they want to sell it.'

'How much?'

'Three hundred million.'

'A hundred and fifty metres?' Brunetti asked.

'Yes.'

'That's nothing.'

'I know. You know anyone who might be interested?'

'Stefania, it's cheap for a hundred-fifty square metres. But it's also worthless.' She didn't deny this, didn't say anything. 'You got anyone interested?' he finally asked.

'Yes.'

'Who?'

'Some Germans.'

'Good. I hope you sell it to them.' Stefania's father had been a prisoner of war in Germany for three years. Brunetti's remark needed no clarification.

'If you don't want an apartment, what do you want? Information?'

'Stefania,' he sang back, doing the same to the second syllable of her name as she had done to the first of his. 'Do you think I'd call you for any reason other than hearing your sweet voice?'

'You do feed a girl's dreams, Guido. Hurry up, what do you want to know?'

'I've got three addresses and the name of the last owner. I'd like to know if they're on the market and, if so, what they're worth. Or if they've been sold in the last year, what they sold for.'

'It'll take me a day or two,' she said.

'A day?' he asked.

'All right. A day. What are the addresses?'

Brunetti gave her the three addresses and explained that they had all been left to the nephew by a woman named Galasso. Before she hung up, Stefania told Brunetti that, if the deal with the Germans fell through, she'd expect him to find someone to take the apartment off her hands. He agreed to consider it but stopped short of saying he'd suggest it to his vice-questore.

The next will was that of Signora Renata Cristanti, widow of Marcello. Whatever Signor Cristanti had done while still alive to work, he must have done very well at it, for Signora Cristanti's estate included a long list of apartments, four stores, and investments and savings totalling more than half a billion lire, all left in equal shares to her six children, the same ones who had never troubled to visit her. Reading this, the first thing that occurred to Brunetti was to wonder why a person this wealthy and with six children could come to finish her days in a nursing home run by an order of nuns vowed to poverty, rather than in some ultra modern clinic possessed of every treatment and convenience known to geriatric medicine.

Conte Crivoni had left his widow the apartment in which she lived, as well as two other apartments and various investments the value of which it was impossible to determine merely from reading the will. No other beneficiaries were named.

As Signor da Prè had said, his sister had left everything – aside from the contested bequest to the nursing home – to him. Naming him as sole heir, the will did not list any specific property or holdings, and so it was impossible to know how large the estate had been.

Signor Lerini had left everything to his daughter Benedetta, and again, the fact that the contents were not listed separately made it impossible to know its total value.

The buzzer on his intercom rang. 'Yes, Vice-Questore?' he said as he picked it up.

'I'd like to speak to you for a moment, Brunetti.'

'Yes, sir. I'll be right down.'

Patta had been back in control of the Questura for more than a week, but Brunetti had so far managed to avoid any personal dealings with him. He had prepared, for Patta's arrival, a long report of what the various *commissari* had done during Patta's absence, making no mention of Maria Testa, her visit, or of the interviews it had led him to make.

Signorina Elettra was at her desk in the small office outside Patta's door. Today she was wearing the most feminine of dark-grey business suits, almost a parody of the double-breasted pinstripes Patta affected. Like him, she had a white handkerchief folded in her breast pocket and, like him again, she had a small jewelled stickpin in the centre of her silk tie.

'All right, sell the Fiat,' he heard her saying as he came in. Surprised, he almost interrupted to say he didn't know she had a car, when she added, 'But turn it around immediately and buy a thousand shares of that German biotech stock I told you about last week.' She raised a hand and signalled Brunetti that she had something to tell him before he went into Patta's office. 'And get me out of Dutch guilders before the end of the day. A friend called me and told me what their Finance Minister is going to announce at the cabinet meeting tomorrow.' The person she was speaking to said something, and she answered angrily, 'I don't care if there's a loss. Dump them.'

Saying nothing else, she put the phone down and turned her attention to Brunetti.

'Dutch guilders?' he asked politely.

'If you've got any, get rid of them,' she said.

Brunetti had none but he nodded his thanks for the suggestion anyway. 'You dressing for success?' he asked.

'How kind of you to notice, Commissario. Do you like it?' She stood and took a few steps away from her desk. Complete to Cinderella-sized wingtips.

'It's very nice,' he said. 'Perfect for talking to your broker.'

'Yes, it is, isn't it? Pity he's such a fool. I have to tell him everything.'

'What was it you wanted to tell me?' Brunetti asked.

'Before you speak to the Vice-Questore, I thought I'd tell you that we're about to have a visit from the Swiss police.'

Before she could say anything further, Brunetti smiled and quipped, 'Found out about your numbered accounts, has he?' casting an artificially furtive glance toward Patta's office.

Signorina Elettra's eyes flew open in shock and then as quickly veiled themselves in displeasure. 'No,

Commissario,' she said in an entirely business-like voice, 'it has something to do with the European Commission, but perhaps Vice-Questore Patta can tell you more about it.' She sat back down at her desk, turned her attention to the computer, her back to Brunetti.

Brunetti knocked and, when told to, went into Patta's office. The Vice-Questore, it appeared, had been much restored by his recent vacation. His classic nose and imperious chin glowed with a tan made all the more impressive by its having been acquired in March. It appeared, as well, that the Vice-Questore had shed a few kilos, or else the tailors of Bangkok could better disguise his embonpoint than could those of London.

'Good morning, Brunetti,' Patta said in an entirely pleasant voice.

Taking warning from this, Brunetti did no more than mumble something inaudible and take a seat without bothering to be asked to do so. The fact that Patta didn't bother to show his disapproval for this put Brunetti even more on his guard.

'I'd like to compliment you for the help you gave while I was away,' Patta began, and the alarm bells in Brunetti's mind raised themselves to such a pitch that it was almost impossible to pay attention to what Patta said. Brunetti nodded.

Patta took a few steps away from his desk and then turned back toward it. He took his seat behind the desk, but suddenly disliking the artificial advantage of height it gave him over the person sitting in front of him, he got up again and came to sit in the chair beside Brunetti.

'As you know, Commissario, this is the year of international police cooperation.'

As a matter of fact, Brunetti didn't know this. What is more, he didn't much care, for he knew that, whatever year it was, it was going to end up costing him something, probably time and patience.

'Did you know that, Commissario?'

'No.'

'Well, it is. Declared by the High Commission of the European Community.' When Brunetti proved resistant to this wonder, Patta asked, 'Aren't you curious to know what our part in this will be?'

'Who's "our"?'

After a pause to sort out the grammar, Patta answered, 'Why, Italy, of course.'

'There are lots of cities in Italy.'

'Yes. But few are as famous as Venice.'

'And few are as free of crime.'

Patta paused after this but then continued, as though Brunetti had been nodding and smiling in agreement to everything he said. 'As our part, we will be hosts, during the next few months, to the chiefs of police of our sister cities.'

'Which cities?'

'London, Paris, and Bern.'

'Hosts?'

'Yes. Since the chiefs of police will be coming here, we thought that it would be a good idea if they could work along with us, get an idea of what police work is like here.'

'And let me guess, sir. We're starting with Bern, and I get him, and then after his visit I'll be able to go and visit him in the mad whirl of Bern, that most exciting of capital cities, and you'll take over with Paris and London?'

Patta, if he was surprised to find it expressed this way, gave no sign. 'He's arriving tomorrow, and I've scheduled a lunchtime meeting for the three of us. Then I thought, in the afternoon, you might take him on a tour of the city. You could use a police launch.'

'Maybe out to Murano to look at the glass-blowing?'

Patta had nodded and begun to say that was a good idea before Brunetti's tone caught up with his words, and Patta stopped. 'It's part of the responsibilities of our office, Brunetti, to maintain good public relations.' Typically, Patta said that last phrase in English, a language he didn't speak.

Brunetti got to his feet. 'All right,' he said. He looked down at the still-seated Patta. 'Will there be anything else, sir?'

'No, I don't think so. I'll see you tomorrow for lunch, then?'

Chapter Ten

Outside, Brunetti found Signorina Elettra in silent confabulation with her computer. She turned and smiled when he emerged, apparently a silent declaration that she was prepared to forgive his provocative remarks about secret Swiss back accounts. 'And?' she asked.

'And I get to take the chief of the Bern police on a tour of the city. I suppose I should be lucky he hasn't asked me to take him into my house as a guest.'

'What does he want you to do with him?'

'I have no idea. Show him the city. Keep him here and let him have a look around. Maybe I ought to let him have a look at the people on line in front of the Ufficio Stranieri, asking for residence permits.' Though he was uncomfortable about feeling it, Brunetti could not completely disburden himself of a growing uneasiness about the hordes of people who crowded each morning into that long line: most of them were young males, and most of them came from countries that had no common link with European culture. Even as he found himself thinking this, dressing his ideas up in sophisticated language, he realized that they were, at bottom, exactly the same sentiments that formed the basis for the most xenophobic ravings of the members of the various Lege which promised to lead Italy back to ethnic and cultural purity.

Signorina Elettra broke into these grim musings. 'It might not be so bad, Dottore. The Swiss have been very helpful to us in the past.'

He smiled. 'Perhaps you could worm some computer passwords out of him, Signorina.'

'Oh, I'm not sure we need those, sir. The police codes were very easy to get. But the really useful ones, the ones for the banks — why, even I wouldn't bother to waste my time trying to get those.'

Without realizing where the idea came from, Brunetti said, 'Signorina, I'd like you to do something for me.'

'Yes, sir,' she asked, picking up a pen, quite as if he had never made a joke about Swiss bank accounts.

'There's a priest over at San Polo, Father Luciano something. I don't know his last name. I'd like you to find out if there's ever been any trouble with him.'

'Trouble, sir?'

'If he's ever been arrested or charged with anything. Or if he's been transferred often. In fact, see if you can find out where his last parish was and why he was sent here.'

Almost under her breath, she said, 'The Swiss banks would be easier.'

'Excuse me?'

'It's very difficult, to get this sort of information.'

'But if he's been arrested?'

'Things like that have a way of disappearing, sir.'

'Things like what?' Brunetti asked, interested by her bland tone.

'Things like when priests are arrested. Or when they drop into the public eye. Just remember that sauna in Dublin. How quickly did that drop out of the papers?'

Brunetti remembered the story that had appeared last year, though only in *Manifesto* and *L'Unità*, about the Irish priest who had died of a heart attack in a gay sauna in Dublin, given the last rites by two other priests who happened to be there at the same time. The story, a source of howling delight to Paola, had disappeared after a single day, and this from the leftist press.

'But certainly police files are different,' he maintained.

She glanced up and gave him a smile similar in its compassion to those Paola often used to end an argument. 'I'll get his name and have a look, sir.' She flipped to a new page. 'Anything else?'

'No, I don't think so,' Brunetti said and left her office, returning slowly to his own.

During the few years Signorina Elettra had worked at the Questura, Brunetti had become familiar with her sense of irony, but she could still say things that managed to leave him absolutely puzzled yet too embarrassed to ask for clarification, as had just happened with her remark about priests. He had never discussed religion or the clergy with Signorina Elettra, but, upon examination, he found that he believed her opinion wouldn't be much wide of Paola's.

Back in his office, he put thoughts of Signora Elettra and Holy Mother Church from his mind and reached for the phone. He dialled Lele Bortoluzzi's number, and when the painter answered on the second ring, Brunetti said he was calling about Doctor Messini again.

'How did you know I was back, Guido?' Lele asked.

'Back from where?'

'England. I had a show in London and just got back yesterday afternoon. I was going to call you today.'

'Call me about what?' Brunetti asked, too interested in this to bother with polite questions about the success of Lele's exhibit.

'It seems that Fabio Messini likes the ladies,' Lele answered.

'As opposed to the rest of us who don't, Lele?'

Lele, whose reputation in the city had been well known in his youth, laughed at this. 'No, I mean, he likes the company of young women and is prepared to pay for it. And it seems he's got two of them.'

'Two?'

'Two. One here in the city, in an apartment for which he pays the rent, a four-room apartment near San Marco, and another one out on the Lido. Neither of them works, but both of them dress very well.'

'Is he the only one?'

'Only one who what?'

'Visits them,' Brunetti said euphemistically.

'Hummm, I didn't think to ask that,' Lele said, his voice showing that he regretted this oversight. 'They are both very beautiful, it is said.'

'Is it? And who says this?'

'Friends,' Lele answered cryptically.

'What else do they say?'

'That he visits each of them two or three times a week.'

'How old is he, did you say?'

'I didn't say, but he's my age.'

'My, my,' Brunetti said in a neutral voice and then, after a pause, asked, 'Did they happen, your friends, to say anything about the nursing home?'

'Homes,' Lele corrected him.

'How many are there?'

'There seem to be five of them now, the one over here and four of them out on the mainland.'

Brunetti didn't say anything for so long that Lele finally asked, 'Guido, are you still there?'

'Yes, yes, Lele, I am.' He thought a moment and then asked, 'Did your friends know anything else about the nursing homes?'

'No, only that the same religious order works in all of them.'

'The Sisters of the Sacred Cross?' he asked, naming the order that ran the nursing home where his mother was and of which Maria Testa was no longer a member.

'Yes. In all, five of them.'

'Then how does he own them?'

'I didn't say that. I don't know if he actually owns them or if he's just the director. But he's in charge of all of them.'

'I see,' Brunetti said, already planning his next move. 'Thank you, Lele. Did they say anything else?'

'No,' Lele answered in a dry voice. 'Is there any other way I can be of use, Commissario?'

'Lele,' Brunetti said, 'I didn't mean to be rude. I'm sorry. You know how I am.'

Lele, who had known Brunetti since he was born, certainly did. 'Forget it, Guido. Come and visit sometime, all right?'

Brunetti promised that he would, said a warm goodbye, hung up the phone, immediately forgot the promise, and picked up the phone again, asking the police operator to find the number and connect him with the San Leonardo Casa di Cura, somewhere over by the Ospedale Giustiniani.

A few minutes later, he was speaking to the secretary of Dottor Messini, the director of the nursing home, and setting up an appointment at four that afternoon in order to discuss the transfer of his mother, Regina Brunetti, to that facility.

Chapter Eleven

Even though the area of the city around the Giustiniani Hospital was not far from Brunetti's home geographically, it was an area of the city with which he was not very familiar, no doubt because it did not stand between his home and any of the parts of the city where he would ordinarily have cause to go. He found himself over there only when he had occasion to pass through it on his way out to the Giudecca or occasionally, on a Sunday, when he and Paola went out to the Zattere to sit in the sun at one of the waterside cafès and read the papers.

What he knew of the area was as much legend as fact, as was so much of the information he and his fellow Venetians tended to have about their city. Behind that wall was the garden of the former movie star, married now to the industrialist from Torino. Behind that one was the home of the last of the Contradini family, rumoured not to have left the house in twenty years. And that was the door to the house of the last of the Dona Salvas, who used to be seen only at the opening night of the opera, always in the royal box, and then always dressed in red. He knew these walls and doors as other children could recognize the heroes of cartoons and television, and like those figures, these houses and *palazzi* spoke to him of youth and a different vision of the world.

Just as children outgrew the antics of Topolino or Braccio di Ferro and came to realize the illusion behind them, Brunetti had, over the course of his years as a police officer, come to learn the often dark realities that lurked behind the walls of his youth. The actress drank, and the industrialist from Torino had twice been arrested for beating her. The last of the Contradinis had indeed been inside for twenty years, kept behind a broad wall into the top of which glass fragments had been embedded and cared for by three servants who did nothing to contradict his belief that Mussolini and Hitler were still in power and the world thus saved from the filthy Jews. And the Dona Salva; few people realized that she had gone to the opera in the belief that she received there vibrations from the spirit of her mother, who had died in the same box sixty-five years before.

The nursing home stood behind yet another high wall. A bronze plaque announced its name and stated that visiting hours were from nine until eleven in the morning, every day of the week. After he rang the bell, Brunetti stepped back a few paces, but he could see no glass embedded into the top of the wall. It wasn't likely that anyone in a nursing home would have the strength to climb that wall, glass or not, Brunetti admonished himself, and the old and infirm had nothing but their lives that could any longer be stolen from them.

The door was opened by a white-habited nun who came to no higher than his shoulder. Instinctively, he bent down to speak to her and explained,

'Good afternoon, Sister, I have an appointment with Dottor Messini.'

She looked up at him with puzzled eyes. 'But the doctor is here only on Mondays,' she said.

'I spoke to his secretary this morning, and I was told I could come at four to discuss transferring my mother here.' He glanced down at his watch in an attempt to disguise his displeasure. The secretary had been precise about the time of the appointment, and Brunetti was irritated to find no one here.

She smiled, showing Brunetti for the first time how very young she was. 'Oh, then you must have an appointment with Dottoressa Alberti, the Vice-Director.'

'Perhaps,' Brunetti agreed amiably.

She stepped back and allowed Brunetti to come through the door and into a large square courtyard that had a capped well in the centre. In the sheltered space, rose plants were already in heavy bud, and he could smell the sweet scent of a dark lilac that bloomed in one corner. 'It's very beautiful here,' he volunteered.

'Yes, it is, isn't it?' she said, turning and leading him toward a doorway on the other side of the courtyard.

As they crossed the sun-filled courtyard, Brunetti saw them in the shadows created by the overhanging balcony that covered two sides of the courtyard. Lined up in a single row like a drawn-out *momento mori*, they sat, six or seven of them, motionless in their wheelchairs, staring ahead with eyes as hollow as those of Greek icons. He walked in front of them, but none of the old people registered his passing or paid any attention to him.

Inside the building, Brunetti found the walls a cheerful light yellow, all with railings running along them at waist height. The floors were spotless, marred only by the occasional tell-tale black scuff marks made by the rubber treads of wheelchairs.

'Down here, please, sir,' the young nun said, turning off to a corridor on their left. He followed her, having time only to note that what appeared to have once been the main banqueting hall, frescoed and chandeliered, still served that purpose, but did so now by means of formica-topped tables and moulded plastic chairs.

The nun stopped outside a door, knocked once, and hearing something from inside, opened it and held it open for Brunetti to enter.

The office into which Brunetti stepped had a row of four tall windows that gave out onto the courtyard, and the light that swept in bounced up from small flecks of mica in the Venetian pavement, filling the room with a magic glow. Because the single desk was placed in front of the windows, it was difficult for Brunetti at first to distinguish the person sitting behind it, but when his eyes grew accustomed to the light streaming up at him, he made out the form of a heavy-set woman in what looked like a dark smock.

'Dottoressa Alberti?' he asked, moving a bit forward and to the right so as to stand in a patch of shadow cast by a piece of wall that separated the windows.

'Signor Brunetti?' she said, rising from her desk

and coming around the side of it toward him. His first impression had been correct: she was a large woman, almost his height and probably close to his weight, most of which had settled on her shoulders and hips. Her face was round and high-coloured, the face of a woman who enjoyed food and drink. She had a surprisingly small nose, turned up at the end. Her eyes were amber and wide-spaced and certainly her best feature. Her smock was merely a successful attempt to drape her body in dark wool.

He extended his hand and shook hers, surprised to find it one of those dead-hampster hands that so many women used in place of a handshake. 'I'm pleased to meet you, Dottoressa, and grateful that you could find time to talk to me.'

'It's part of our contribution to the community,' she said simply, and it took Brunetti a moment to realize that she was entirely serious.

When Brunetti was seated in the chair in front of her desk and had refused her offer of coffee, he explained that, as he had told her secretary on the phone, he and his brother were considering moving their mother to the San Leonardo but wanted to know something about it before they decided to take that step.

'San Leonardo was opened six years ago, Signor Brunetti, blessed by the Patriarch, and staffed by the excellent sisters of the Order of the Sacred Cross.'

Brunetti nodded here, as if to suggest that he recognized the habit of the nun who had shown him into this office.

'We are a mixed facility,' she said.

Before she could go on, Brunetti said, 'I'm afraid I don't know what that means, Dottoressa.'

'It means that we have patients who are here as clients of the national health service, which is responsible for their upkeep. But we also have private patients. Could you tell me which sort of patient your mother would be?'

Long days spent in the halls of bureaucracy, earning for his mother the right to the treatment that forty years of his father's work had earned her, had made Brunetti fully aware that she was a patient who was covered by the state health service, but he smiled at Dottoressa Alberti and said, 'She'd be a private patient, of course.'

At this news, Dottoressa Alberti seemed to expand and fill an even larger space behind her desk. 'You realize, of course, that it makes no difference whatsoever in the way our patients are treated. We merely like to know so as to facilitate matters of billing.'

Brunetti nodded and smiled as if he believed her.

'And your mother's health?'

'Fine. Fine.' She seemed less interested in this answer than in the previous one.

'When were you and your brother thinking of moving her?'

'We thought that we'd like to do it before the end of the spring.' Dottoressa Alberti did her smiling and nodding when she heard this. 'Of course,' Brunetti added, 'I wouldn't like to do this until I had some idea of the facilities you offer.'

'Of course,' Dottoressa Alberti said, reaching to the left of her desk, where there lay a thin folder. 'I have all the information here, Signor Brunetti. It contains a full list of the services available to our patients, a list of our medical staff, a short history of the facility and the Order of the Sacred Cross, and a list of our patrons.'

'Patrons?' Brunetti asked politely.

'Those members of the community who have seen fit to speak well of us and who have permitted us to use their names. As a kind of recommendation of the high quality of care which we provide our patients.'

'Of course. I understand,' Brunetti said, measuring out a nod. 'And is there a list of your prices in there?'

Dottoressa Alberti, if she found this in any way brusque or tasteless, kept her opinion to herself and gave Brunetti an answering nod.

'Would it be possible for me to have a look around, Dottoressa?' When he saw her surprise, he added, 'To try to get an idea if our mother would be happy here.' As he said this, Brunetti turned away from her, as if interested in the books that lined her walls. He didn't want Dottoressa Alberti to see any evidence on his face of the double lie: his mother would never come to this facility, just as she would never again be happy.

'I see no reason why one of the sisters can't take you through the facility, Signor Brunetti, at least through parts of it.'

'That would be very kind of you, Dottoressa,' Brunetti said, getting to his feet with a pleasant smile.

She pushed a button on her desk, and after a few

minutes, the same young nun came into the office without knocking. 'Yes. Dottoressa?' she said.

'Sister Clara, I'd like you to take Signor Brunetti and show him the day room and the kitchen, and perhaps one of the private rooms, as well.'

'There's one last thing, Dottoressa,' he said, adding it as though he had just remembered it.

'Yes?' she asked.

'My mother is a very religious woman, very devout. If it's at all possible, I would like to have a few words with the Mother Superior.' When he saw her begin to object, he hurried on. 'It's not that I have any uncertainties; I've heard nothing but praise about San Leonardo's. But I did promise my mother that I'd speak to her. And I can't lie to her if I don't.' He made his smile boyish, pleading with her to understand his situation.

'Well, it's not common,' she began. She turned to Sister Clara. 'Do you think it's possible, Sister?'

The nun nodded, then said, 'I just saw Mother Superior coming from the chapel.'

Turning back to Brunetti, Dottoressa Alberti said, 'In that case, you might be able to have a few words with her. Sister, will you take Signor Brunetti there after he's seen Signora Viotti's room?'

The nun nodded and went back to the door. Brunetti stepped toward the desk and reached his hand across it. 'You've been very helpful, Dottoressa. Thank you.'

She got to her feet to shake his hand. 'You're entirely welcome, Signore. If I can be of any help in answering any further questions you might have, please feel free to call.' Saying that, she picked up the folder and handed it to Brunetti.

'Ah, yes,' he said, taking it with a grateful smile before turning toward the door. When he reached it, he turned and said a final thank you before following Sister Clara through the door.

Back in the courtyard, she turned left, re-entered the building, and started down a wide corridor. At the end, they came into a large open room in which sat a handful of old people. Two or three were engaged in conversations that seemed to have grown desultory with long repetition. A half dozen sat in their chairs, looking off at memory, or perhaps regret.

'This is the day room,' Sister Clara said somewhat unnecessarily. Leaving Brunetti, she walked over and picked up a magazine that had fallen from the hand of an old woman. She returned it to her and stayed a moment talking. Before she returned to Brunetti, he heard her say something encouraging to the woman in Veneziano.

When she came back, he addressed her in dialect, 'The home where my mother is now is also run by your order.'

'Which one?' she asked, not with real curiosity but from the habit of expressed concern that Brunetti assumed must develop if a person did what she did.

'In Dolo, the Casa Marina.'

'Ah yes, our order has been there for years. Why do you want to bring your mother here?'

'It would be closer for me and my brother. And this way our wives would be more willing to visit.'

She nodded, no doubt understanding just how

unwilling people were to visit the old, especially when they were not parents. She led Brunetti back down the hall and out into the courtyard.

'There was a sister who was there for years but who was transferred here, I think. About a year ago,' Brunetti said with careful off-handedness.

'Yes?' she asked with the same civil, bland curiosity. 'And who was that?'

'Suor'Immacolata,' he said, watching for her response from his greater height.

He thought that she missed a step, or else she put her foot down too heavily on the uneven pavement. 'Did you know her?' Brunetti asked.

He saw her struggle against the lie. Finally she said, 'Yes', but offered no explanation.

Pretending to be unaware of her response, Brunetti added, 'She was very good to my mother. In fact, my mother became very attached to her. My brother and I are very happy that she's here because she seems, well, she seems to be able to exert a calming influence on our mother.' Brunetti looked down at Sister Clara and added, 'I'm sure you understand how it is with some old people. They sometimes . . .' he let this trail off.

Opening a door, Sister Clara said, 'And this is the kitchen.'

Brunetti looked around, feigning interest.

Their inspection of the kitchen complete, she led him off in the opposite direction and up a flight of stairs. 'The female patients are up here. Signora Viotti is out with her son for the day, so you can have a look at her room.' Brunetti stopped himself from saying that he thought Signora Viotti should have something to say about this and followed her down the corridor, this one painted a light cream but with the same ubiquitous hand rails.

She opened a door and Brunetti looked into the room, saying whatever one says when presented with comfortable sterility. That done, Sister Clara turned toward the steps again.

'Before I see the Mother Superior, I'd like to say hello to Suor'Immacolata,' Brunetti said, then hastened to add, 'If it's possible, that is. I wouldn't want to take her away from her duties.'

'Suor'Immacolata is no longer here,' Sister Clara said in a tight voice.

'Oh, I'm sorry to hear that. My mother will be so disappointed. So will my brother.' He tried to make his voice sound philosophical and resigned when he said, 'But the Lord's work must be done, no matter where we are sent.' When the nun said nothing to this, Brunetti asked, 'Has she been sent to work in another nursing home, Sister?'

'She is no longer with us,' Sister Clara said.

Brunetti stopped in his tracks, as if astonished. 'Dead? Good heavens, Sister, that's terrible.' Then, as though remembering piety and its dictates, he whispered, 'May God have mercy on her soul.'

'May God have mercy on her soul, indeed,' Sister Clara said, turning to him. 'She's left the order. She hasn't died. She was caught by one of the patients stealing money from his room.'

'Good heavens,' Brunetti exclaimed, 'that's shocking.'

'When he caught her, she pushed him to the

ground and broke his wrist, and then she left, just disappeared.'

'Were the police called?'

'No, I don't think so. No one wanted to cause scandal.'

'When did this happen?'

'A few weeks ago.'

'Well, I think the police should be informed. A person like that ought not to be left walking around free. Taking advantage of the trust and weakness of old people. It's disgusting.'

Sister Clara made no comment in response to this. She led him down a narrow hall, turned right, and stopped in front of a heavy wooden door. She knocked once, heard a voice from within, opened the door and went inside. A few moments later, she came outside and said, 'Mother Superior will see you.'

Brunetti thanked her. '*Permesso?*' he said as he stepped inside. He closed the door behind him, the better to legitimize his presence in the room, and turned to look around him.

It was virtually empty, its only decoration an immense carved crucifix on the far wall. Beside that stood, though she looked as though she had just risen from the prie-dieu in front of it, a tall woman in the habit of the order. She wore a companion cross on her broad bosom and looked at Brunetti with neither curiosity nor enthusiasm.

'Yes?' she said, speaking as though he'd interrupted her from a particularly interesting conversation with the gentleman in the loincloth.

'I asked if I might speak to the Mother Superior.'

'I am the Mother Superior of the order. What is it you'd like?'

'I'd like some information about the order.'

'For what purpose?' she asked.

'The better to understand your holy mission,' Brunetti said in an entirely neutral tone.

She moved away from the crucifix and toward a stiff-backed chair that stood to the left of an empty fireplace. She lowered herself into it and gestured toward a smaller chair that stood to her left. Brunetti took his seat in it, facing her.

The Mother Superior said nothing for a long time, a tactic with which Brunetti was familiar, for it generally provoked the other person into speech, often rash speech. He sat and studied her face, the dark eyes bright with intelligence, the thin nose that bespoke either the aristocrat or the ascetic.

'Who are you?' she asked.

'Commissario Guido Brunetti.'

'Of the police?'

He nodded.

'It is not often that the police come to visit a convent,' she finally said.

'It would depend upon what's going on in the convent, I should think.'

'And what does that mean?'

'Precisely what it sounds like, Mother Superior. My presence here is prompted by what might be going on among members of your order.'

'Such as?' she asked scoffingly.

'Such as criminal slander, defamation of character, and the failure to report a felony, but that is only to mention those crimes of which I am a witness and prepared to testify.'

'I have no idea what you're talking about,' she said. Brunetti believed her.

'A member of your order today told me that Maria Testa, formerly known as Suor'Immacolata, formerly a member of your order, was expelled for attempting to steal money from one of her patients. I was further told that, in the attempt to commit this crime, she pushed the victim to the floor, breaking his wrist.' He paused, waiting for her to make a comment, but when she did not, Brunetti continued. 'If these things did happen, then a crime has been committed, and another crime has been committed by the failure to report the original crime to the police. In the event that these things did not happen, then the person who told me is subject to a charge of criminal slander.'

'Did Sister Clara tell you this?' she asked.

'That is irrelevant. What is important is that the accusation must reflect popular belief among the members of your order.' Brunetti paused and then added, 'If not fact.'

'It is not fact,' she said.

'Then why is this rumour current?'

She smiled for the first time, not a particularly attractive sight. 'You know how women are; they gossip, especially against one another.' Brunetti, who had always believed this to be true, but of men and not women, listened but made no response. She continued, 'Suor'Immacolata is not, as you suggest, a former member of our order. Quite the contrary. She is still bound by her vows.' Then, as if Brunetti

171

might not be aware of what they were, she enumerated them, raising the fingers of her right hand as she spoke. 'Poverty. Chastity. Obedience.'

'If she has chosen to leave, by what law is she still a member of your order?'

'By the law of God,' she answered in a sharp voice, as if she was more familiar with that sort of thing than he.

'Does this particular law have any legal force?'

'If it does not, then there is something wrong with a society that permits it not to.'

'I will gladly concede that there is a great deal that is wrong with our society, Mother Superior, but I will not concede that one of them is a law that permits a woman of twenty-seven to change her mind about a decision she made as an adolescent.'

'And how is it that you come to be aware of her age?'

Ignoring her question, Brunetti asked, 'Is there some reason why you maintain that Maria is still a member of your order?'

'I do not "maintain" anything,' she said with heavy sarcasm. 'I merely speak the truth of God. It is He who will forgive her sin; I will merely welcome her back to our order.'

'If Maria did not do the things of which she is being accused, why did she choose to leave the order?'

'I have no knowledge of this Maria of whom you speak. I know only Suor'Immacolata.'

'As you will,' Brunetti conceded. 'Why did she choose to leave your order?'

'She has always been wilful and rebellious. She has always found it difficult to submit herself to the will of God and the greater wisdom of her superiors.'

'Those, I assume, are meant to be synonyms?' Brunetti asked.

'Make jokes if you wish, but you do so at your peril.'

'I am not here to make jokes, Mother Superior. I am here to find out why she left the place where she was working.'

The nun considered this demand for a long time. As Brunetti watched, one hand rose up to finger the crucifix on her bosom, an entirely unconscious and involuntary gesture. 'There was talk of . . .' she began but didn't finish the sentence. She lowered her eyes, saw what her hand was about, and took it away from the cross. She glanced back at Brunetti. 'She refused to obey an order given to her by her superior, and when I suggested spiritual penance for her sin, she left.'

'Did you speak to her confessor?'

'Yes. When she left.'

'And did he tell you anything that she might have said to him?'

She managed to look shocked by this question. 'If she spoke to him in confession, of course he couldn't tell me. The vow is sacred.'

'Only life is sacred,' Brunetti shot back, regretting his words immediately.

He saw her bite back a reply and got to his feet. 'Thank you,' Brunetti said. If she was surprised by the abruptness with which he seemed to be terminating their interview, she gave no sign of it. He went to the door and opened it. When he glanced back to say goodbye, she was still sitting stiff in her chair, her hand fingering the crucifix.

Chapter Twelve

He cut his way back toward the apartment, stopped and got some mineral water, and was home by seven-thirty. When he opened the door, he knew immediately that everyone else was at home: Chiara and Raffi were in the living room, laughing at something on television, and Paola was in her study, singing along with Rossini.

He took the bottles to the kitchen, said hello to the children, and went down the hall to Paola's study. A small CD player stood on the bookshelf; Paola sat with the small, square libretto in her hand, sat and sang.

'Cecilia Bartoli?' he asked as he went in.

She looked up, astonished that he had recognized the voice of the singer she was helping with the aria, not suspecting that he had seen the singer's name on the new CD of *Barbiere* she had bought a week ago.

'How'd you know that?' she asked, forgetting for a moment about singing along with '*Una voce poco fa*'.

'We keep an eye on everything,' he said, then corrected himself. 'An ear, that is.'

'Oh, don't be a fool, Guido,' she said but laughed in the saying. She closed the libretto and tossed it on the desk beside her, leaned over, and switched off the music.

'You think the kids would like to go out to dinner?' he asked.

'No, they're watching some stupid movie that won't be over until eight, and I've already got something cooking.'

'What?' he asked, realizing that he was very hungry.

'Gianni had some beautiful pork today.'

'Good. How are you cooking it?'

'With porcini.'

'And polenta?'

She smiled at him. 'Of course. No wonder you're getting that stomach.'

'What stomach?' Brunetti asked, pulling in the one he had. When she didn't answer, Brunetti said, 'It's the end of the winter.' To divert her, perhaps to divert himself from discussion of his stomach, he explained the events of the day, since he had received the phone call from Vittorio Sassi that morning.

'Have you called him back?' Paola asked.

'No, I've been too busy.'

'Why don't you do it now?' she asked. She left him there to do it from the phone in her study and went down to the kitchen to put on water for the polenta.

He came out about ten minutes later.

'Well?' she asked when he came in, handing him a glass of Dolcetto.

'Thanks,' he murmured and took a small sip. 'I told him how she was and where she was.'

'What kind of man does he sound like?'

'Decent enough to help her find a job and a place to live. And worried enough to call me when this happened.'

'What do you think it was?'

'It could have been an accident, or it could have been something worse,' Brunetti said, sipping at his wine.

'You mean somebody trying to kill her?'

He nodded.

'Why?'

'That would depend on whom she's been to see since she spoke to me. And what she told them.'

'Would she be that rash?' Paola asked. The only things she knew about Maria Testa had come from what Brunetti had said about Suor'Immacolata over the years, and they had always been in praise of her patience and charity as a nun, hardly the sort of information that would give her any idea of how the young woman might behave in a situation such as the one Brunetti had described.

'I don't think she'd even think it was rash. She's been a nun most of her life, Paola,' he said as though that would explain everything.

'What is that supposed to mean?'

'That she doesn't have a very clear idea of how people behave. She probably hasn't been exposed to human evil or to deceit.'

'You said she was Sicilian, didn't you?' Paola asked.

'That's not funny.'

'I didn't mean it as a joke, Guido,' Paola said, voice injured. 'I'm quite serious. If she grew up in that society . . .' She turned away from the stove. 'How old did you say she was when she joined?'

'Fifteen, I think.'

'Then, if she grew up in Sicily, she had sufficient exposure to human behaviour to accept the possibility of evil. Don't romanticize her. She's not a plaster saint who will collapse at the first sight of impropriety or misbehaviour.'

Brunetti couldn't keep the resentment out of his voice when he shot back, 'Killing five old people can hardly be considered misbehaviour.' Paola made no rejoinder, merely stared at him and then turned to add salt to the boiling water.

'All right, all right, I know there's not much proof,' he temporized, and then when Paola refused to turn around, he corrected even that. 'All right, no proof. But then why would there be a rumour that she had stolen the money and hurt one of the old people? And why would she have been hit and left by the road?'

Paola opened the package of dry corn meal that stood next to the pot and grabbed up a handful. As she spoke, she trickled a fine stream into the boiling water with one hand, stirring with the other. 'It could have been a hit and run,' she said. 'And women alone don't have much to do except gossip,' she added.

Brunetti sat with his mouth open. 'And this,' he finally said, 'this from a woman who considers herself a feminist? Heaven save me from hearing what women who are not feminists say about women who live alone.'

'I mean it, Guido. Women or men, it's all the

same.' Undisturbed by his opposition, she continued to dribble the corn meal into the boiling water, slowly stirring all the while. 'Leave people alone long enough, and all they can do is gossip about one another. It's worse if there are no diversions.'

'Like sex?' he asked, hoping to shock her or at least to make her laugh.

'Especially if there is no sex.'

She finished adding the corn meal, and Brunetti considered what they had both just said.

'Here, stir this while I set the table,' she said, standing aside and leaving the place in front of the stove free. She held the wooden spoon out to him.

'I'll set the table,' he said, getting up and opening the cabinet. Slowly, he laid out the plates, glasses, and silverware. 'We having salad?' he asked. When Paola nodded, he pulled down four salad plates and placed them on the counter. 'Dessert?' he asked.

'Fruit.'

He pulled down four more plates.

He sat back in his place and picked up his glass. He took a sip, swallowed, and said, 'All right. Maybe it was an accident, and maybe it's entirely accidental that they're speaking badly of her in the *casa di cura*.' He set the glass down and poured some more wine into it. 'Is that what you think?'

She gave the polenta another stir and placed the wooden spoon across the open top. 'No, I think someone tried to kill her. And I think someone planted the story about taking the money. Everything you've ever said about her tells me it's impossible that she would lie or steal. And I doubt that anyone who knew her well would believe it.

Not unless the story came from someone in a position of authority.' She picked up his glass and took a sip, then set the glass down.

'It's funny, Guido, I was just listening to the same thing.'

'What same thing?'

'There's a wonderful aria in *Barbiere* – and don't interrupt me and say that there are many wonderful arias in *Barbiere*. It's the one where, what's his name, Basilio, the music teacher, talks about "*una calunnia*", the way once a slander is started, it will grow until the accused person' – and here she astonished Brunetti by bursting into the final words of the bass aria, but in her own bright soprano – '*Avvilito, calpestrato, sotto il pubblico flagello per gran sorte va a crepar.*'

Before she was finished, both children were at the kitchen door, looking in, astonished, at their mother. When Paola finished, Chiara blurted out, 'But *Mamma*, I never knew you could sing.'

Paola looked at her husband, not her daughter, when she answered, 'There's always something to discover about the people you think you know well.'

Toward the end of the meal, the subject of school came up and, as day must lead to night, that led Paola to ask about Chiara's R.E. class.

'I'd like to stop going,' Chiara said, taking an apple from a bowl of fruit at the centre of the table.

'I don't see why you don't let her stop,' Raffi interrupted. 'It's just a waste of time, anyway.'

Paola didn't grace his contribution with a

response but, instead, asked, 'Why do you say that, Chiara?'

She shrugged.

'I believe you have been graced with the power of speech, Chiara,' Paola said.

'Oh, come on, *Mamma*. Once you start using that tone with me, I know you're not going to listen to anything I say.'

'And what tone is that, if I might ask?' enquired Paola.

'That one,' Chiara shot back.

Paola looked to the males in her family for support against this unwarranted attack from her last-born child, but they turned implacable eyes upon her. Chiara continued to peel her apple, bent on creating a single strip out of the peel, now certainly long enough to reach the end of the table.

'I'm sorry, Chiara,' Paola said.

Chiara shot her a glance, cut off the last of the peel, sliced a piece of apple, and placed it on her mother's plate.

Brunetti decided to reopen negotiations. 'Why do you want to stop going to the classes, Chiara?'

'Raffi's right. It's a waste of time. I memorized the catechism the first week, and all we do is recite it back to him when he asks us questions. It's boring, and I could be reading or doing my other home-work. But the worst thing is that he doesn't like it if we ask questions.'

'What sort of questions?' Brunetti asked, accepting the last piece of her apple and thus setting Chiara free to begin peeling another one.

'Well,' she said, attention on the knife, 'today he

was talking about how God is our father and when he was talking about God, he kept saying "He" and "Him". So I raised my hand and asked if God was a spirit. And he said yes, He was. So I asked if it was right that a spirit was different from a person because it didn't have a body, wasn't material. And when he agreed, I asked how, if God was a spirit, He could be a man, if He didn't have a body or anything.'

Brunetti glanced across Chiara's lowered head, but he was too late and there was no trace of a smile of triumph on Paola's face. 'So what did Padre Luciano say?'

'Oh, he got mad and yelled at me. Said I was showing off.' She looked up at Brunetti, the apple momentarily forgotten. 'But I wasn't, *Papà*. I wasn't showing off at all. I really wanted to know. It doesn't make any sense to me. I mean, God can't be both things, can—' Chiara caught herself before using the questionable pronoun and asked instead, 'Can it be like that?'

'I don't know, angel, it's been a long time since I studied that stuff. I guess God can be whatever God wants to be. Maybe God's so great that even our little rules about material reality and our tiny little universe don't mean anything to God. You ever think of that?'

'No, I never did,' she said, pushing her plate away. She considered it for a while, then said, 'I suppose it's possible.' Another speculative silence. 'Can I go and do my homework now?'

'Of course,' Brunetti said, leaning over to ruffle her hair. 'If you have any trouble with your maths problems, the really hard ones, just bring them right to me.'

'And what will you do, *Papà*, tell me how you can't help because maths is so different from when you went to school?' Chiara asked with a laugh.

'Isn't that what I always do with your maths homework, *cara*?'

'Yes. I suppose it's the only thing you can do, huh?'

'I'm afraid so,' Brunetti said, pushing back his chair.

Chapter Thirteen

Prompted by the theme of religion that he seemed unable to prevent from invading both his personal and his professional life, Brunetti that night devoted himself to the reading of the early Church Fathers, a form of entertainment to which he was not much given. He began with Tertulian but found that his immediate dislike for that man's rantings drove him to consult the writings of Saint Benedict. But then he came upon a passage declaring that, 'The husband who, transported by immoderate love, has intercourse with his wife so ardently in order to satisfy his passion that even had she not been his wife, he would have wished to have commerce with her, is committing a sin.'

'Commerce?' Brunetti asked himself aloud, looking up from the page and managing to startle Paola, who sat beside him, half asleep over the notes for the class she was to give the next day.

'Humm?' she asked in mild interrogation.

'We really let these people educate our children?' he asked and then read the passage out to her.

He felt, rather than saw, her shrug. 'What's that mean?' he asked.

'It means that, if you put people on a diet, they start thinking about food. Or if you make someone stop smoking, all they think about is cigarettes. It seems logical enough to me that if you tell a person he can't have sex, he's going to be obsessive about the subject. Then to give him the power to tell other people how to run their sex lives, well, that's just asking for trouble. In a way, it's like having a blind person teach Art History, isn't it?'

'Why haven't you ever said any of this to me?' he asked.

'We made a deal. I promised that I would never interfere with the religious education of the children.'

'But this is lunacy,' he said, pounding his hand down on the open pages of the book.

'Of course it's lunacy,' she replied in an entirely calm voice. 'But is it any more lunatic than most of what they see or read?'

'I don't know what you mean.'

'Madonna. Sex clubs, phone sex. You name it, it's just the other side of the coin to the maniac who wrote that,' she said, pointing dismissively to the book in his hands. 'In either case, sex becomes an obsession.' She turned her attention back to her notes.

After a few moments, Brunetti said, 'But,' and then stopped until she looked up at him. When he saw that he had her attention, he repeated, 'But do they really tell them things like this?'

'I told you, Guido, I leave all of that to you. It was you who insisted that they needed to learn about – if I recall your precise phrase – "Western Culture". Well, Saint Benedict – if it is he from whom that particularly infelicitous passage comes – Saint Benedict is part of Western Culture.'

'But they can't teach them this,' he insisted.

She shrugged. 'Ask Chiara,' she said and bent back over her notes.

Left alone to his fulminations, Brunetti resolved to do just that the following day. He closed the book, set it aside, and pulled another from the stack on the floor beside the sofa. He settled in with Josephus's *History of the Jewish War* and had just got to the description of the Emperor Vespasian's siege of Jerusalem when the phone rang.

He reached across to the small table beside him and picked up the receiver. 'Brunetti,' he said.

'Sir, this is Miotti.'

'Yes, Miotti, what is it?'

'I thought I should call you, sir.'

'What for, Miotti?'

'One of those people you and Vianello went to see has died, sir. I'm there now.'

'Who is it?'

'Signor da Prè.'

'What happened?'

'We aren't sure.'

'What do you mean, you aren't sure?'

'Maybe you'd better come and have a look, sir.'

'Where are you?'

'We're at his home, sir. It's at—'

Brunetti cut him off. 'I know where it is. What happened?'

'Water started to come through the ceiling into the apartment below him, so the neighbour went up to see what was wrong. He had a key, so he let himself in, and he found da Prè on the floor of the bathroom.'

'And?'

'It looks like he fell and broke his neck, sir.'

Brunetti waited for further explanation, but when none was forthcoming, he said, 'Call Dottor Rizzardi.'

'I've already done that, sir.'

'Good. I'll see you in about twenty minutes.' Brunetti hung up and turned to Paola, who was no longer reading but curious to learn the other half of the conversation she had just overheard. 'Da Prè. He fell and broke his neck.'

'The little hunchback?'

'Yes.'

'Poor man, what rotten luck,' was her immediate response.

Brunetti's took longer to come and, when it did, reflected the difference in both their dispositions and their professions. 'Perhaps.'

Paola ignored this and looked down at her watch. 'It's almost eleven.'

Brunetti dropped Josephus on top of St Benedict and got to his feet. 'I'll see you in the morning, then.'

Paola touched the back of his hand. 'Wear a scarf, Guido. It's cold tonight.'

He bent down and kissed the top of her head, got his coat, remembered to take his scarf, and left the house.

When he got to da Prè's address, he found a uniformed policeman standing across the street from the front door. Recognizing Brunetti, the officer saluted and, in response to his question, told him that Dr Rizzardi had already arrived.

Upstairs, another uniformed officer, Corsaro, stood just inside the open door of the apartment. He saluted Brunetti and stepped aside. 'Dottor Rizzardi is inside, sir.'

Brunetti entered and went toward the back of the apartment, from which both light and male voices emerged. He entered what must be the bedroom and saw a low bed, almost as small as a child's crib, against the wall. As he started across the room, he stepped into something soft and liquid. Immediately he stopped in his tracks and called out, 'Miotti!'

In an instant, the young officer appeared at a door on the far side of the room. 'What is it, sir?'

'Switch on the light.'

Miotti did that, and Brunetti looked down at his feet, vainly attempting to stifle an irrational fear that he was standing in blood. He breathed with relief when he saw that it was nothing more than a carpet soaked with the water that had flowed through the open door of the bathroom. Seeing this, he continued across the room and stopped at the lighted doorway, from which came the sounds of human motion.

Stepping inside, he saw Dr Rizzardi bent, as he had seen him too many times, over the supine body of a dead man.

Hearing the noise behind him, Dr Rizzardi got to his feet. He extended his hand, then paused to remove the thin rubber glove that covered it. Extending it anew, he said, '*Buona sera*, Guido.' He didn't smile, and even if he had, it would not have made much difference in the austere severity of his face. Too long an exposure to violent death in all its forms had honed away the flesh from nose and cheeks, as if his face were made of marble, and each death had chipped away yet another minuscule fragment.

Rizzardi stepped aside, allowing Brunetti to see the tiny body that lay below them. Grown even smaller in death, Da Prè seemed to lie beneath the feet of giants. He lay on his back, his head tilted wildly to one side but not touching the ground, as though he were some sort of clothed turtle that had been flipped over and abandoned on his shell by wanton boys.

'What happened?' Brunetti asked. As he spoke, he noticed that the legs of Rizzardi's trousers were soaked from the knee to the cuff and that his own shoes were growing damp from standing in the half centimetre of water that covered the floor all around them.

'It looks like he turned on the water for his bath and then slipped on the floor.' Brunetti looked. The tub was empty, the water no longer running. A round black rubber plug stood on the side of the tub.

Brunetti looked down again at the dead man. He was dressed in a suit and tie, but he wore no shoes or socks. 'Slipped on the tile in his bare feet?' he asked.

'Looks that way,' Rizzardi answered.

Brunetti backed out of the bathroom, and Rizzardi, his work finished, followed him. Brunetti looked around the bedroom, though he had no idea what he was looking for. He saw three windows, curtains drawn against the night, a few paintings on the walls, looking as though they'd been put there decades ago and never again noticed. The rug was a thick old Persian tribal, sodden now and colours dulled. A red silk dressing gown lay across the foot of the bed, and beneath it, just beyond the point where the water had reached, Brunetti saw da Prè's tiny shoes placed neatly side by side, his dark socks folded and laid on top of them.

Brunetti crossed the room, bent down, and picked up the shoes. Holding the socks in one hand, he turned the shoes over and looked at the soles. The black rubber of the heels and soles was shiny and bright, as is often the case with shoes that are worn only inside the house. The only sign of wear were two grey scuff marks on the outer edges of the heels. He set the shoes down and replaced the tiny socks back across them.

'I've never seen anyone die this way,' Rizzardi said.

'Wasn't there a movie or something, years ago, about someone with that disease that makes you look like an elephant? Didn't he die like that?'

Rizzardi shook his head. 'I never saw it. I've read about things like this, at least about the danger of a fall for people like this. But usually all they do is break their vertebrae.' Rizzardi stopped and glanced away, and Brunetti waited, assuming that he was casting his memory back through the medical literature. After a few moments, Rizzardi said, 'No, I'm wrong. It has happened. Not often, but it's happened.'

'Well, maybe you've got something here different enough to get your name into the medical text-books,' Brunetti said evenly.

'Perhaps,' Rizzardi answered, moving off toward his black doctor's bag that stood on a table by the door. He tossed the rubber gloves in and snapped it shut. 'I'll get to him first thing in the morning, Guido, but I'm not going to be able to tell you anything I don't know right now. His neck was broken when his head tilted back in the fall.'

'Would death be instant?'

'It would have to have been. The break is clean. He would have felt the shock of the fall on his back, but even before he could have felt any pain, he would have been dead.'

Brunetti nodded. 'Thanks, Ettore. I'll call you. Just in case you find anything else.'

'After eleven,' the doctor said and extended his hand again.

Brunetti shook it and the doctor left the room. Brunetti heard low voices as Rizzardi said something to Miotti, and then he heard the front door of the apartment close. Miotti came into the bedroom, and behind him came Foscolo and Pavese, the men from the lab.

Brunetti exchanged nods with them and said, 'I want all the prints you can get, especially in the bathroom, and especially around the tub. And photos from every angle.' He stepped aside so the men could see past him to what lay inside.

Pavese moved across the room and set his camera case down in a dry corner, pulled out the pieces of his tripod, and began to assemble it.

Brunetti knelt down, entirely careless now of the water. He braced his weight on both hands and leaned forward, tilting his head to one side to afford himself a traverse view of the floor just outside the bathroom door. 'If you can find a hair dryer,' he said to Foscolo, 'maybe you can dry up this water – don't wipe it – and then get some shots of the surface here.' He waved his hand in a broad circle that encompassed the entire area.

'What for, sir?' asked the photographer.

'I want to see if there are any scuff marks, any sign that he might have been dragged into the bathroom.'

'Like that, is it, sir?' Pavese asked as he turned the screws that held his camera to the head of the tripod.

Instead of answering, Brunetti pointed to some faint marks barely visible under the thin coating of water. 'Here. And here.'

'I'll get them, sir. Don't worry.'

'Thanks,' Brunetti said and pushed himself to his feet and turned to Miotti. 'Have you got a pair of gloves? I forgot to bring any.'

Miotti reached into his jacket pocket and brought out a package of plastic-wrapped gloves. He ripped it open and handed them to Brunetti. As he pulled them on, Miotti pulled out a second pair and did the same. 'If you'll tell me what we're looking for, sir . . .'

'I don't know. Anything that might look like someone did this to him or that they might have had reason to.' Brunetti liked the fact that Miotti did not remark that the explanation didn't go a great way to answering his question.

Brunetti went out into the living room and looked carefully at the room in which he had spoken to da Prè. The little boxes still covered every surface. He went to the sideboard and opened the top drawer between the two doors. It held more of the boxes, some of them wrapped in individual pieces of cotton wool, like square eggs in albino nests. The second held more of them, as did the third. The bottom drawer held papers. On top, there was one neat manila file containing papers arranged in almost military neatness, but beneath it lay more piles of papers, all tossed higgledy-piggledy, with none of them separated into files; some lay face down, some face up, some folded into quarters, some in half. Brunetti pulled the file and the loose papers out with both hands but then discovered that there was no clear surface on which to set them: the little boxes lay everywhere.

He finally settled on taking them into the kitchen and spreading them on the wooden table he found there. Not at all to Brunetti's surprise, the manila file contained copies of letters da Prè had sent to antique dealers and private owners, enquiring about the age, provenance, and price of snuff boxes. Below these were the bills of sale for what seemed like hundreds of the tiny boxes, sometimes purchased in lots of twenty or more.

He lay the file aside and went through the other papers, but if he hoped to find among them some hint of the reason for da Prè's death, Brunetti was disappointed. There were electric bills, a letter from da Prè's former landlord, a hand-out flyer from a furniture store in Vicenza, a newspaper article about

193

the effects of long-term use of aspirin, and package information that listed the side effects of different types of pain killers.

Over the sounds of the lab technicians in the other rooms and to the accompaniment of the intermittent flashes of light as they photographed the body, Brunetti turned his attention to the bedroom and kitchen, where he found nothing at all that might indicate anything more sinister than a careless accident. Miotti, who had found a box of discarded magazines and newspapers, had much the same success.

A bit after one, the orderlies from the hospital were allowed to remove the body, and by two the crime team had finished. Brunetti tried to replace all of the papers and objects that had been moved as he and Miotti had made their careful way through the apartment, but he had no idea where to put the countless little snuff boxes that had been dusted, moved aside, pushed to the rear, set down on the floor. He finally gave up and stripped off his gloves, telling Miotti to do the same.

When the crime crew saw that Brunetti was ready to leave, they gathered up their bags, cameras, cases, and brushes, glad to finish and get away from the dreadful little boxes that had caused them so many hours of work.

Brunetti paused long enough to tell Miotti not to bother to get to the Questura until ten, though he knew the young man would be there at eight, if not before.

Outside, the fog hit him in the face, this the deadest, dampest hour of the night. Wrapping his scarf around his neck, he walked back toward the Accademia stop, but when he got there, he saw that he had missed a boat by ten minutes and so there would be forty minutes before the next one. He chose to walk, winding his way back through Campo San Barnaba, past the sealed gates of the University, and up past the house of Goldoni, it too barred against the night. He saw no one until he got to Campo San Polo, where a green-clad guard was making his late rounds, a docile German Shepherd walking at his side. The two men nodded as they passed; the dog ignored Brunetti, pulling his master toward home and warmth. As he approached the underpass that led out of the *campo*, he heard a faint plopping sound. At the bridge, he looked down into the water and saw a long-tailed rat swimming slowly away from him. Brunetti made a sudden hissing sound, but the rat, like the dog, ignored him and made its slow way toward home and warmth.

Chapter Fourteen

Before he went to the Questura the next morning, Brunetti stopped at da Prè's building and spoke to Luigi Venturi, the neighbour who had found da Prè's body. From him, Brunetti learned nothing that could not have been learned in a phone call: da Prè had few friends; very seldom did he have visitors, and Venturi had no idea who they were; and the only relative da Prè had ever spoken of was the daughter of a cousin, who lived somewhere near Verona. The previous night, Venturi had heard or seen nothing at all out of the ordinary, not until water had begun to soak through the ceiling of his kitchen. No, da Prè had never spoken of any enemies who might want to do him an injury. Venturi gave Brunetti a strange look when he asked this question, and Brunetti hastened to assure him that the police were merely excluding this unlikely possibility. No, neither man was in the habit of opening the door without first finding out who was there. Further questioning revealed that Signor Venturi had been watching a soccer game on television for much of the evening, and the only time he had given any thought to da Prè or what might be happening in his apartment was when he went into his kitchen to make himself a cup of Orzoro before going to bed, saw the water seeping down his wall, and went up to see what was wrong.

No, the two men could not be said to be friends. Signor Venturi was a widower; da Prè had never married. But the fact that they lived in the same house had been enough for each to have entrusted the other with a set of keys, though neither of them had ever, until the previous night, had call to use them. Not only did Brunetti learn nothing more from Venturi; he was certain that there was nothing more to be learned.

Among the papers stuffed into the drawer in da Prè's house, there had been several letters from a lawyer with an office address in Dorsoduro, and Brunetti called him soon after he arrived at his own office. The lawyer had heard, in the way people in Venice always seemed to, of da Prè's death and had already tried to notify his cousin's daughter. She, however, was in Toronto for a week with her husband, a gynaecologist, who had gone there for an international conference. The lawyer said that he would continue to try to contact her, but he was by no means certain that this news would cause her to return to Italy.

Asked, the lawyer could give Brunetti almost no information about da Prè. He had been his lawyer for years, but they had never been more than attorney and client. He knew virtually nothing about da Prè's life, though when asked, he ventured that the value of the estate, beyond the apartment, would not be great at all: almost everything da Prè had was invested in the snuff boxes, and he had left those to the Museo Correr.

He called Rizzardi's office and, even before he could ask, the pathologist said, 'Yes, there was a small bruise on the left side of his chin as well as the one along his spine. Both are consistent with a fall. His neck snapped back when he fell, just as I told you last night. He died instantly.'

'But he could have been hit or pushed?'

'It's possible, Guido. But you're not going to get me to say that, at least not officially.'

Brunetti knew better than to argue, so he thanked the doctor and hung up.

The photographer, when Brunetti called, suggested he come down to the lab and have a look. When he did, Brunetti saw four large blow-ups, two in colour and two in black and white, pinned to the corkboard on the back wall of the lab.

Brunetti crossed the room until he stood in front of the photos. He stared at them, moving his head to bring himself nearer and nearer. When he was so close that his nose almost touched them, he saw two faint parallel lines in the bottom left quadrant of one of the photographs. He put his finger on the lines and turned to Pavese. 'These?'

'Yes,' said the photographer, coming up to stand beside him. Gently, he pushed Brunetti's finger aside with the erasered end of a pencil and traced the two faint lines.

'Scuff marks?' Brunetti asked.

'Could be. But they could be a lot of things.'

'You check the shoes?'

'Foscolo did. The backs of the heels are scuffed, but in lots of places.'

'Any hope of matching the marks on the shoes with these?' Brunetti asked.

Pavese shook his head. 'Not so that it would convince anyone.'

'But he could have been dragged into the bathroom?'

'Yes,' Pavese said, but just as quickly added, 'but so could a lot of things. A suitcase. A chair. A vacuum cleaner.'

'What do you think it is, Pavese?'

Before he answered, Pavese tapped the end of the pencil against the photo. 'All I know is what's in the photo, sir. Two parallel marks on the floor. Could be anything.'

Brunetti knew he was going to get nothing better than that from the photographer, so he thanked him and went back up to his office.

When he went in, he saw two notes in Signorina Elettra's handwriting. The first told him that someone called Stefania had asked him to call her. The second said that Signorina Elettra had some information about 'the matter of that priest'. Nothing more.

Brunetti dialled Stefania's number and, again, got the cheery greeting that suggested things were dead in the real estate market.

'It's Guido. You sell that place in Canareggio yet?'

Stefania's voice warmed. 'They're signing the papers tomorrow afternoon.'

'And are you lighting candles against *acqua alta*?'

'Guido, if I thought it would keep the waters

199

at bay until those papers are signed, I'd crawl to Lourdes.'

'Business that bad?'

'You don't want to know.'

'You selling it to the Germans?' he asked.

'*Ja*.'

'*Sehr gut*,' Brunetti answered. 'You find out anything about those apartments?'

'Yes, but nothing very interesting. All three have been on the market for months, but everything's complicated by the fact that the owner is in Kenya.'

'Kenya? I thought he was in Torino. That's the address in the will.'

'That might well be true, but he's been in Kenya for the last seven years, so he doesn't have residence in Venice any more. It's all become a tax nightmare, and no one wants to handle the apartments, especially in this market. You don't even want to know what a mess it is.'

No, Brunetti reflected, he didn't; it was enough to learn that the heir had been in Kenya for seven years.

Stefania asked, 'Is that enough for—' but her voice was cut off by the sound of a phone ringing in her office. 'It's the other line. I've got to go, Guido. Pray it's business.'

'I will. And thanks, Steffi. *Auf Wiedersehen*.'

She laughed and was gone.

He left his office and went down the stairs to Signorina Elettra's office. She looked up when he came in and gave him a small smile. Brunetti noticed that today she was wearing a severe, high-collared black suit. At the top, rather in the way a clerical collar peeps out from a priest's lapels, Brunetti saw a thin band of white cotton that had been bleached to blinding whiteness. 'Is that your idea of monastic simplicity?' Brunetti asked when he saw that the suit was made of raw silk.

'Ah, this,' she said, as if she were just waiting for the next charity drive to be able to get rid of it. 'Any resemblance to the clergy is entirely accidental, I assure you, Commissario.' She reached down to her desk, picked up a few sheets of paper, and offered them to him. 'After you read this, I'm sure you'll understand my desire that it be accidental.'

He took the papers and read the first two lines. 'Padre Luciano?' he asked.

'The very same. A much-travelled man, as you will see.' She turned back to her computer, leaving Brunetti to read through the papers.

The first page contained a brief history of Luciano Benevento, born in Pordenone forty-seven years ago. His schooling was listed, as was the fact that he entered the seminary when he was seventeen. There was a gap here, presumably while he received his priestly education, but the school report attached to the back of the papers did not suggest that he would have been an outstanding student.

While still a student in the seminary, Luciano Benevento came to the attention of the authorities for having been involved in some sort of disturbance on a train, a disturbance involving a child whose mother had left her with the seminary student while she went to another carriage to get them some sand-wiches. What had happened while she was away was never clear, and whatever confusion had ensued was attributed to the little girl's imagination.

After his ordination twenty-three years ago, Padre Luciano was posted to a small village in the Tirol, where he remained for three years, transferred when the father of a catechism student, a girl of twelve, began telling the villagers strange stories of Padre Luciano and the questions he asked his daughter in the confessional.

His next posting was in the south, where he remained for seven years, until he was sent to a home kept by the Church for priests who had problems. The nature of Padre Luciano's problem was not disclosed.

After a year there, Padre Luciano was assigned to a small parish in the Dolomites, where he served for five years without distinction under a pastor the severity of whose rule was said to be unequalled in Northern Italy. Upon the death of that pastor, Padre Luciano was named pastor in his place but was transferred from that village two years later, mention being made of a 'trouble-making, Communist mayor.'

From there, Padre Luciano had been sent to a small church on the outskirts of Treviso, where he had remained a year and three months before his transfer, a year ago, to the church of San Polo, from which pulpit he now preached and from which church he was sent to contribute his portion to the religious instruction of the youth of the city.

'How did you get this?' Brunetti asked when he had finished reading.

'The ways of the Lord are many and mysterious, Commissario,' was her calm response.

'This time I'm serious, Signorina. I'd like to know how you obtained this information,' he said, not responding to her smile.

She considered him for a moment. 'I have a friend who works in the Patriarch's office.'

'A clerical friend?'

She nodded.

'Who was willing to give you this?'

She nodded again.

'How did you manage that, Signorina? I would imagine this is information they would want kept out of the hands of the laity.'

'I would assume as much, Commissario.' Her phone rang but she made no move to answer it. After seven rings, it stopped. 'He's having an affair with a friend of mine.'

'I see,' he said. Then he asked neutrally, 'And you used that as blackmail?'

'No. Not at all. He's wanted to leave for months, just walk out and begin a decent life. But my friend has persuaded him to remain there.'

'At the Patriarch's office?'

She nodded.

'As a priest?'

She nodded again.

'Dealing with documents and reports as sensitive as this?'

'Yes.'

'For what purpose does your friend want him to remain there?'

'I would prefer not to tell you that, Commissario.'

203

Brunetti refused to repeat his question, but he also refused to move away from her desk.

'It's in no way criminal, what he does.' She considered what she had just said and added, 'Just the contrary.'

'I think I need to know that's true, Signorina.'

For the first time in the years they had worked together, Signorina Elettra looked upon Brunetti with open disapproval. 'If I gave you my word?' she asked.

Before he answered, Brunetti looked down at the papers in his hands, badly made photocopies of the original documents. Badly blurred, but still visible at the top, was the seal of the Patriarch of Venice.

Brunetti glanced up. 'I don't think that will be necessary, Signorina. I'd as soon doubt myself.'

She didn't smile, but the tension left her body and voice. 'Thank you, Commissario.'

'Do you think your friend could obtain information about a priest who is a member of an order, rather than a parish priest?'

'If you gave me his name, he could certainly try.'

'Pio Cavaletti, he's a member of the Order of the Sacred Cross.'

She noted the name and looked up. 'Anything else, sir?'

'There is one more thing. I've heard gossip about Contessa Crivoni.' Because Signorina Elettra was Venetian, Brunetti did not have to specify the nature of the gossip. 'About a priest. I have no idea who he is, but I'd like your friend to see if he can find out anything.'

Signorina Elettra made another note, looked up, and said, 'I won't give him this until I see him, but I should see him at dinner tonight.'

'At your friend's place?' Brunetti asked.

'Yes. We never discuss any of this over the phone.'

'For fear of what would happen to him?' Brunetti asked, uncertain of how seriously he meant the remark.

'Partly,' she said.

'And what else?'

'Fear of what would happen to us.'

He looked at her to see if she was joking, but her face was set and grim. 'You believe that, Signorina?'

'It is an organization that has never been kind to its enemies.'

'And is that what you are, an enemy?'

'With all my heart.'

Brunetti was about to ask her why, but he stopped himself. It was not that he did not want to know – quite the opposite – just he did not want to begin a discussion of this topic now, and not in the office, standing in front of a door through which Vice-Questore Patta could walk at any moment. Instead, he said, 'I'll be very grateful to your friend for any information he can give me.'

The phone rang again, and this time she picked it up. She asked who was speaking and then asked them to hold the line for a moment while she called the files up on her computer.

Brunetti nodded in her direction and went back up toward his office, the papers still in his hand.

Chapter Fifteen

And this, Brunetti thought as he walked back up to his office, was the man to whom he had, all unwittingly, entrusted Chiara's religious education. He could not say that they had done it together, for Paola had made it clear from the very beginning that she wanted no part of it. He had known, even back when the children were just beginning elementary school, that she opposed the idea, but the social consequences of an outright rejection of religious instruction would be endured by the children themselves and not by the parents making the decision for them. Where would a child whose parents rejected religious instruction sit while his or her peers were learning the catechism and the lives of the saints? What would happen to a child who did not join in the rites of passage marked by First Communion and Confirmation?

Brunetti recalled a legal case much in the headlines last year that concerned a perfectly respectable couple, childless, he a doctor and she a lawyer. The high court of Torino had rejected their application to adopt a child because both of them were atheists, and it was determined that these people would not, therefore, be suitable parents.

He had laughed at the story of those Irish priests

in Dublin, as if Ireland were some Third World country in the death grasp of a primitive religion, yet here in his own country signs of the same grasp were surely to be seen, if only to the jaundiced eye.

He had no idea what to do about Padre Luciano, for he knew he had no legal foothold. The man had never been charged with a crime, and Brunetti guessed it would be impossible to find anyone in his old parishes to speak out openly against him. The infection had been passed on for other people to deal with, a natural enough response, and those who were free of him were sure to remain silent, if only because this would assure that they would remain free of him.

Brunetti knew that his society took a jocund view of sex offences, viewing them as little more than excesses of male ardour. It was not a view he shared. What sort of therapy, he wondered, was given to priests like Padre Luciano at this home where he had been sent? If Padre Luciano's record since his stay there was any indication, whatever treatment he had been given had not proven effective.

Back at his desk, he tossed the papers down in front of him. He sat for a while, then got up and went over to look out the window. Seeing nothing there to interest him, he returned to his desk and pulled together all of the reports and papers having to do with Maria Testa and the various events that could in any way be related to what she had told him that quiet day, now weeks ago. He read through them all, taking an occasional note. When he was finished, he stared at the wall for a few minutes, then picked up the phone and asked to be connected to the Ospedale Civile.

To his surprise, he had no difficulty in being connected to the nurse in charge of the emergency ward, who told him, when he introduced himself, that 'the police's' patient had been moved to a private room. No, there had been no change in her condition: she was still unconscious. Yes, if he waited a moment, she would go and get the police officer who was in front of her door.

It turned out to be Miotti. 'Yes, sir?' he asked when Brunetti identified himself.

'Anything?'

'Quiet and more quiet.'

'What are you doing?'

'Reading, sir. I hope you don't mind.'

'Better than looking at the nurses, I suppose. Anyone come to visit her?'

'Only that man from the Lido. Sassi. No one else.'

'Did you talk to your brother, Miotti?'

'Yes, sir. Last night, as a matter of fact.'

'And did you ask him about that priest?'

'I did, sir.'

'And?'

'Well, at first he didn't want to say anything. I don't know if it's because he didn't want to spread gossip. Marco's like that, sir,' Miotti explained, as if asking his superior's forbearance about such weakness of character. 'But then I told him I really needed to know, and he told me that there was talk – just talk, sir – that he was involved with Opus

Dei. He didn't know anything for sure, just that he had heard things. You understand, sir?'

'Yes, I understand. Anything else?'

'Not really, sir. I tried to think of what you would want to know, what else you'd ask when I told you this, and I thought you'd want to know if Marco believed the talk, and so I asked him if he did.'

'And?'

'And he believes it, sir.'

'Thank you, Miotti. Go back to your reading.'

'Thank you, sir.'

'What is it you're reading?'

'*Quattroute*,' he said, naming the most popular of the automobile magazines.

'I see. Thank you, Miotti.'

'Yes, sir.'

Oh, sweet merciful Jesus on the cross, save us all. At the thought of Opus Dei, Brunetti could not prevent himself from giving inner voice to one of his mother's favourite prayers. If any mystery was wrapped up in an enigma, it was Opus Dei. Brunetti knew no more than that it was some sort of religious organization, half clerical, half lay, which owed absolute allegiance to the Pope and which was dedicated to some sort of renewal of power or authority for the Church. And, as soon as Brunetti considered what he knew about Opus Dei and how he knew it, he was aware that he could not be sure of the truth of any of it. If a secret society is, by definition, a secret, then anything that is 'known' about it might well be mistaken.

The Masons, with their rings and trowels and tiny cocktail waitress aprons, had always charmed Brunetti. He had little real information about them, but he had always considered them more harmless than menacing, and he had to realize that not a little part of this was the result of his having seen them too frequently neutralized by the beautiful fun of *The Magic Flute*.

But Opus Dei was a different matter altogether. He knew less about them – had to admit that he knew almost nothing about them at all – but even the sound of the name was a cold breath on the back of his neck.

He tried to distance himself from stupid prejudice and tried to remember anything that he had ever read or heard directly about Opus Dei, anything tangible and verifiable, but he came up with nothing. He found himself thinking about the Gypsies, for he 'knew' about the Gypsies in much the same way that he 'knew' about Opus Dei: as a result of things repeated, things passed on, but never a name or a date or a fact. The cumulative effect was the atmosphere of mystery that any closed society must exude to those who are not members.

He tried to think of anyone from whom he could get accurate information, but he could think of no one except Signorina Elettra's anonymous friend in the Patriarch's office. Surely, if the Church was nursing an adder to its bosom, then it was in that bosom where information must be sought.

She looked up when he came in, surprised to see him again. 'Yes, Commissario?'

'I have another favour to ask your friend.'

'Yes?' she asked, reaching for her notebook.

'Opus Dei.'

Her surprise, no more than a minimal widening of her eyes, was evident to Brunetti. 'What would you like to know about them, sir?'

'How they might be involved in what's going on here.'

'You mean these wills and that woman in the hospital?'

'Yes.' Then, almost as an afterthought, Brunetti asked, 'And could you ask him to see if there's any connection with Father Cavaletti?'

She made a note of this. 'And the priest whose name you don't know? Contessa Crivoni's priest, if I may call him that?'

Brunetti nodded and then asked, 'Do you know anything about them, Signorina?'

She shook her head. 'No more than anyone else does. They're secret, they're serious, and they're dangerous.'

'Don't you think that's exaggerating the case?'

'No.'

'Do you know if they have a' – Brunetti struggled for the proper term – 'chapter in this city?'

'I have no idea, sir.'

'It's strange, isn't it?' Brunetti asked. 'None of us has any accurate information, but that doesn't stop us from being suspicious and frightened of them?' When she said nothing, he insisted, 'It's strange, isn't it?'

211

'I take the opposite view, sir,' Signorina Elettra said.

'What's that?'

'I assume that, if we did know about them, we'd be even more frightened.'

Chapter Sixteen

In the papers on his desk, he found the home number of Dottor Fabio Messini, dialled it, and asked to speak to the doctor. The person who answered, a woman, said that the doctor was too busy to come to the phone and asked who was calling. Brunetti said no more than 'Police', at which name she agreed, with audible reluctance, to ask the doctor if he could spare a moment.

Many moments passed before a man's voice said, 'Yes?'

'Dottor Messini?'

'Of course. Who is this?'

'Commissario Brunetti.' Brunetti paused to let the rank sink in and then said, 'There are some questions we'd like to ask you, Dottore.'

'About what, Commissario?'

'Your nursing homes.'

'What about them?' Messini asked, sounding more impatient than curious.

'About some of the people who work there.'

'I don't know anything about staffing,' Messini said casually, making Brunetti immediately curious about the Philippine nurses who worked at the nursing home where his mother was living.

'I'd prefer not to discuss this on the phone,'

Brunetti said, knowing that a sense of mystery was often enough both to up the stakes and incite the curiosity of the person he was talking to.

'Well, you hardly expect me to come to the Questura, do you?' Messini asked, voice rich with the sarcasm of the powerful.

'Not unless you want your patients to be disturbed by a raid from the Guardia di Frontiere when they come to question your Philippine nurses.' Brunetti waited a hairbreadth before adding, 'Dottore.'

'I don't know what you're talking about,' insisted Messini in a voice that said quite the opposite.

'As you choose, Dottore. I had hoped this was something we could discuss like gentlemen and perhaps settle before it became an embarrassment, but it seems that's impossible. I'm sorry to have troubled you,' Brunetti said in a voice he strained to make sound cordially terminal.

'Just a moment, Commissario. Perhaps I spoke too soon, and it might be better that we met.'

'If you're too busy for it, Dottore, I understand perfectly,' Brunetti said briskly.

'Well, I am busy, but certainly I could find some time, perhaps this afternoon. Let me check my schedule here a moment.' The sound grew muffled as Messini covered the phone and spoke to someone at the other end. After a short pause, his voice returned. 'I find that my lunch appointment has been cancelled. Could I invite you to lunch, Commissario?'

Brunetti said nothing, waiting for the name of the restaurant, for that would indicate the size of the bribe Messini thought he would have to pay.

'Da Fiori?' Messini suggested, and by naming the best restaurant in the city giving evidence of sufficient importance that he felt free to assume a table would always be found for him. More interesting, it told Brunetti that it would be wise to check into the passports and work permits of the foreign nurses who staffed his nursing homes.

'No,' said Brunetti in the voice of a civil servant not in the habit of being bought off by lunch.

'I'm sorry, Commissario. I thought it would be a pleasant atmosphere in which to become acquainted.'

'Perhaps we could become acquainted in my office at the Questura.' Brunetti waited a split second and then gave a man-of-the-world laugh at his own joke and added, 'If that's convenient for you, Dottore.'

'Of course. Would two-thirty be convenient for you?'

'Perfectly.'

'I look forward to seeing you then, Commissario,' Messini said and hung up.

By the time of Dottor Messini's appointment three hours later, a list of the foreign nurses working in his nursing homes had been compiled. Though most, as Brunetti had recalled, were Philippine, two others were from Pakistan, and one from Sri Lanka. All of them were on Messini's computerized payroll, a system so easy to enter that Signorina Elettra said that even Brunetti could have called Messini's number and broken in from his home phone. Because the mysteries of her computer remained so impenetrable to him, Brunetti never knew when she was joking. Nor, as usual, did he bother to ask or even to speculate if her invasions were legitimate or not.

With their names, he went down to speak to Anita in the Ufficio Stranieri, and within the hour she brought the files up to his office. In all cases, the women had entered the country as tourists and had subsequently been granted extensions to their visas when they showed proof that they were studying at the University of Padova. Brunetti smiled when he saw the various departments in which they were enrolled, no doubt chosen to deflect just the sort of attention they were now receiving: history, law, political science, psychology, and agronomy. He laughed aloud at the inventiveness of the last choice, a course of· study not offered by the university. Perhaps Dottor Messini would prove to be a whimsical man.

The doctor was on time for his appointment; Riverre opened the door to Brunetti's office at two-thirty precisely and announced, 'Dottor Messini to see you, sir.'

Brunetti glanced up from the files on the nurses, nodded briefly to Messini, and then, almost as if it were an afterthought, got to his feet and waved a hand to the chair in front of his desk. 'Good afternoon, Dottore.'

'Good afternoon, Commissario,' Messini said, taking his place in the chair and glancing around Brunetti's office to get an idea of his surroundings and, presumably, of the man he had come to see.

Messini could have been a Renaissance nobleman, one of the rich, corrupt ones. A large man, he had reached the point in his life when muscle was swiftly turning to bulk, and that very soon to fat. His mouth was his best feature, lips firmly chiselled and full, turning up naturally at the corners in a smile that suggested good humour. His nose was shorter than it should have been for a head as large as his, and his eyes just that fraction too close together to leave handsomeness behind while stealing away beauty.

His clothing whispered wealth; his shoes gleamed the same word. His teeth, capped so well as to appear faded with age, showed themselves in a friendly smile as he finished examining the room and turned his attention to Brunetti.

'You said you had some questions about people who work for me, Commissario?' Messini's voice was casual and relaxed.

'Yes, Dottore, I do. I have questions about some of your nursing staff.'

'And what might those questions be?'

'How is it that they are working in Italy?'

'As I told you on the phone this morning, Commissario . . .' Messini began, taking a pack of cigarettes from the inside pocket of his jacket. Without asking, he lit a cigarette, looked around for an ashtray, and, finding none, placed the spent match on the edge of Brunetti's desk. 'I do not concern myself with questions of staffing. That is the business of my administrators. It's what I pay them to do.'

'And I'm sure you pay them generously,' Brunetti said with what he hoped was a suggestive smile.

'Very,' Messini said, noting both the remark and

the tone and taking heart from both. 'What seems to be the problem?'

'It seems that a number of your employees are without the proper permits that would allow them to work legally in this country.'

Messini raised his eyebrows in what could pass as shock. 'I find that difficult to believe. I'm sure that all of the proper permits have been granted and forms filled out.' He looked across at Brunetti, who was just barely smiling as he looked down at the papers in front of him. 'Of course, Commissario, if it is the case that some oversight has been made, that other forms are to be filled out, and that,' he paused, searching for the politest words – and found them, straight off – 'some application fees have still to be paid, I want to assure you that I will gladly do whatever is necessary to normalize my situation.'

Brunetti smiled, impressed by Messini's grasp of euphemism. 'That's very generous of you, Dottore.'

'That's very kind of you to say, but I think it is only correct. I want to do whatever I can to remain in favour with the authorities.'

'As I said, generous,' Brunetti repeated, giving a smile he tried to make look venal.

Apparently he succeeded, for Messini said, 'You have but to let me know about those application fees.'

'Actually,' Brunetti said, setting down the papers and looking across at Messini, whom he noted was having considerable difficulty with the ash on his cigarette, 'it's not about the nurses that I want to talk to you. It's about a member of the Order of the Sacred Cross.'

It was Brunetti's experience that dishonest people seldom managed to look innocent, but Messini looked both innocent and confused. 'The Sacred Cross? You mean the nuns?'

'There are also priests, I believe?'

It seemed that this came as news to him. 'Yes, I think there are,' Messini said after a pause. 'But only the nuns work in the nursing homes.' His cigarette was burnt down almost to the filter. Brunetti saw him look at the floor, discard the idea rather than the cigarette, and then very carefully balance it upright on the unburnt end next to the match on the desk.

'About a year ago, one of the sisters was transferred.'

'Yes?' Messini asked with mild interest, obviously confused by Brunetti's change of topic.

'She was moved from the nursing home in Dolo to one here in the city, the San Leonardo.'

'If you say so, Commissario. I know little about the staffing.'

'Other than the foreign nurses?'

Messini smiled. He was back on comfortable ground with talk of the nurses.

'I'd like to know if you know why she was transferred.' Before Messini could say anything, Brunetti added, 'You might consider your answer a sort of application fee, Dottor Messini.'

'I'm not sure I understand.'

'That makes no difference, Dottore. I'd like you to tell me what you know about the transfer of this sister. I doubt that she could be moved from one of

219

your nursing homes to another without your having heard something about it.'

Messini considered this for a moment, and Brunetti watched the play of emotion on the other man's face as he tried to understand what peril lay before him for whatever answer he might give. Finally he said, 'I have no idea what information you're looking for, Commissario, but whatever it is, I can't give it to you. All questions about staffing are handled by the chief of nursing. Believe me, if I could help you here, I would, but it's not something I am concerned with directly.'

Though it usually turned out that anyone who asked to be believed was lying, Brunetti thought that Messini was telling him the truth. He nodded and said, 'This same sister left the nursing home some weeks ago. Did you know that?'

'No.' Again, Brunetti believed him.

'Why is it that the Order of the Sacred Cross aids in the running of your nursing homes, Dottore?'

'That's a long and complicated story,' Messini said with a smile that someone else probably would have found entirely charming.

'I'm in no hurry, Dottore. Are you?' Brunetti's smile was utterly without charm.

Messini reached for his cigarette packet but put it back in his pocket without taking another one. 'When I took over directorship of the first nursing homes eight years ago, they were run entirely by the order, and I was hired only as medical director. But as time passed, it became more and more evident that, if they continued to run them as a charity, they would be forced to close.' Messini gave Brunetti a long stare. 'People are so ungenerous.'

'Indeed,' was all Brunetti permitted himself.

'In any case, I considered the financial plight of the institution – I was already committed to aiding the old and ill – and it was obvious to me that it could remain viable only if it became a private facility.' Seeing that Brunetti was following, he continued, 'And so there was a reorganization – what the world of business would probably call a privatization – and I became administrator as well as medical director.'

'And the Order of the Sacred Cross?' Brunetti asked.

'The chief mission of the order has always been the care of the old, and so it was decided that they would remain as an integral part of the staff of the nursing homes, but they would remain as paid employees.'

'And their salaries?'

'Paid to the order, of course.'

'Of course,' Brunetti echoed, but before Messini could object to his tone, he asked, 'And who receives those salaries?'

'I have no idea. The Mother Superior, probably.'

'To whom are the cheques made out?'

'To the order.'

Though Brunetti graced his answer with a polite smile, Messini was utterly disconcerted. None of this was any longer making sense to him. He lit another cigarette, placing the second match on the other side of the upright filter.

'How many members of the order work for you, Dottore?'

'That's a question you'll have to ask my bookkeeper. I would imagine about thirty.'

'And what are they paid?' Before Messini could summon up his bookkeeper again, Brunetti repeated the question, 'And what are they paid?'

'I think it's about five hundred thousand lire a month.'

'In other words, about a quarter of what a nurse would earn.'

'Most of them aren't nurses,' Messini maintained. 'They're aides.'

'And as they are members of a religious order, I imagine that you do not have to pay the government any taxes for their health or pension funds.'

'Commissario,' Messini said, anger welling up in his voice for the first time, 'it seems that you know all this already, and so I don't see the need to have me here to answer these questions. Further, if you are going to continue in this vein, I think it would be better if my lawyer were present.'

'I have only one more question, Dottore. And I assure you that there is no need for your lawyer's presence. I am not a member of the Guardia di Finanza, nor of the Guardia di Frontiere. Who you hire and how little you pay them is entirely your concern.'

'Ask it.'

'How many of your patients have left money to you or to the nursing home?'

Though Messini was surprised by the question, he answered it quickly. 'Three, I believe. I try to discourage it. The few times I learned that people were planning to do so, I spoke to their families and asked them to see that the person be persuaded to do otherwise.'

'That's very generous of you, Dottore. One might even say high-minded.'

Messini had tired of games, and so he told the truth and told it sharply. 'If one said that, one would be a fool.' He dropped his cigarette on the floor and stamped it out with his toe. 'Think what it would look like. At the first word of it, people would be lining up to take their relatives out and put them somewhere else.'

'I see,' Brunetti said. 'Could you give me the name of one of the people you dissuaded? Of their relatives, that is.'

'What are you going to do?'

'Call them.'

'When?'

'As soon as you leave here, Dottore. Before you have time to get to a telephone.'

Messini didn't even bother with the appearance of outrage. 'Caterina Lombardi. Her family lives in Mestre somewhere. Her son's name is Sebastiano.'

Brunetti wrote it down. Looking up, he said, 'I think that will be all, Dottore. I thank you for giving me your time.'

Messini stood but didn't extend his hand. Saying nothing, he went across the room and left the office. He did not slam the door.

Before Messini could have left the Questura or used his mobile phone, Brunetti had spoken to the wife of Sebastiano Lombardi, who confirmed Dottor

Messini's story about having suggested they persuade her husband's mother not to change her will in favour of the nursing home. Before she hung up, Signora Lombardi spoke with great praise of Dottor Messini and the humane and loving concern he had for all of his patients. Brunetti's agreement was as effusive as it was false. And on that note, their conversation ended.

Chapter Seventeen

Brunetti decided to spend the rest of his afternoon in the Marciana Library, though he left the Questura without bothering to tell anyone where he was headed. Before taking his degree in law at the University of Padova, Brunetti had spent three years studying in the department of history at Cá Foscari, where he had been turned into a reasonably competent researcher, as much at home among the many volumes in the Marciana as in the meandering aisles of the Archivio di Stato.

As Brunetti walked up the Riva degli Schiavoni, Sansovino's library came into sight in the distance, and as it always did, its architectural unruliness gladdened his heart. The great builders of the Serene Republic had had only manpower at their disposition: rafts, ropes, and pulleys, yet they had managed to create a miracle like that. He thought of some of the horrid buildings with which modern Venetians had defaced their city: the Bauer Grunwald Hotel, the Banca Cattolica, the train station, and he mourned, not for the first time, the cost of human greed.

He came down off the last bridge and then out into the Piazza, and all gloom fled, driven off by the power of a beauty that only man could create. The spring wind played with the enormous flags flying in front of the Basilica, and Brunetti smiled to see how much more imposing was the lion of San Marco, raging across his scarlet field, than were the three parallel bars of Italy.

He walked across the Piazza and under the Loggetta, then into the Library, a place which seldom saw a tourist, not the least of its many attractions. He passed between the two giant statues, showed his *tessera* at the reception window, and went into the reference hall. He searched the main catalogues for 'Opus Dei', and after a quarter of an hour had found references to four books and seven articles in various magazines.

When he handed his written requests to the librarian, she smiled and asked him to take a seat, saying it would take about twenty minutes to accumulate the materials. He made his way to a seat at one of the long tables, walking silently in this place where even the turning of a page was an intrusion. While he waited, he pulled down one of the Loeb Classical Library volumes completely at random and began to read the Latin text, curious to see how much of that language, if any, remained. He had chosen the letters of Pliny the Younger and paged through it slowly, looking for the letter describing the eruption of Vesuvio in which the writer's uncle had lost his life.

Brunetti was half-way through that account, marvelling at how little interest the writer appeared to take in what had come to be considered one of the great events of the ancient world and at how much of the language of that world he had managed to retain, when the librarian approached and set a pile of books and magazines down beside him.

He smiled his thanks, returned Pliny to his dusty seclusion, and turned his attention to the books. Two of them appeared to be tracts written by members of Opus Dei or, at least, by people favourably disposed both toward the organization and its mission. Brunetti glanced through them quickly, found that their enthusiastic rhetoric and incessant talk of 'holy mission' set his teeth on edge, and pushed them aside. The other two were more antagonistic in stance, and because of that, they were also more interesting.

Founded in Spain in 1928 by Don Josemaria Escriva, a priest with pretensions to noble blood, Opus Dei was dedicated to recapturing, or so it would seem, political dominion for the Catholic Church. One of its avowed purposes was the extension of Christian principles, and with them, Christian power, into the secular world. In order for this to be achieved, members of the order were dedicated to spreading the doctrines of both order and Church in their places of work, their homes, and the larger society in which they lived.

Early on it was judged the wiser path of wisdom for membership in the order to remain secret. Though its members hotly and consistently denied that this made Opus Dei a secret society, a certain impenetrability about its goals and activities was strictly maintained, and no accurate estimate could be given of its membership. Brunetti assumed that the usual justification for this would pertain: the existence of some sort of 'enemy' which sought the destruction of the society – to make no mention of the moral order of the universe. Because of the political power of many of its members and because of the protection and support offered it by the current Pope, Opus Dei neither paid taxes nor underwent legal scrutiny by the various agencies of government in any of the countries in which it currently pursued its sacred mission. Of the many mysteries surrounding the society, its finances proved the most impenetrable.

He flipped quickly through the remainder of the first book, with its discussion of 'numeraries', 'fidelities', and 'elect', then paged through the second. There was a great deal of speculation, an even greater amount of suspicion, but there was very little fact. In a way, these books seemed to be little more than the opposite side of the bright, shiny coin offered by the supporters of the order: much passion but little substance.

He turned to the magazines but was immediately disconcerted by the discovery that all of the articles had been carefully razored out of the magazines. He carried them back across the main reading room. The librarian still sat at her desk, and two dusty scholars dozed on the banks of the pools of light shed by table lamps. 'Some things have been cut out of these magazines,' he said as he put them down in front of her.

'The anti-abortion people again?' she asked with no surprise but considerable distress.

'No, the Opus Dei people.'

'Much worse,' she said calmly and reached across to pull the magazines toward her. As she opened each, it fell open at the missing pages. She shook her head at the signs of destruction and at the care that had been taken to do it. 'I don't know if we have the money to keep buying replacement copies of all of them,' she said as she placed the magazines aside gently, as if reluctant to cause them further pain.

'Is this common?'

'Just in the last few years,' she said. 'I suppose it's become the latest form of protest. They destroy any article that contains information they disapprove of. I think there was a movie like this, years ago, something about people burning books.'

'*Fahrenheit 451*. At least we don't do that,' Brunetti said, trying with a smile to convey this minimum comfort.

'Not yet,' she said and turned her attention to one of the scholars who had approached her desk.

Out in the Piazza, Brunetti stood and looked out over the Bacino of San Marco, then turned and studied the ridiculous domes of the Basilica. He had read once about some place in California where the swallows return every year on the same date. St Joseph's Day? Here, it was much the same, for the tourists all seemed to reappear in the second week of March, led by some inner compass that brought them to this particular sea. Each year, there were more and more of them, and each year the city made itself more and more hospitable to them rather than to its citizens. Fruit dealers closed, shoemakers went out of business, and all seemed transformed into masks, machine-made lace, and plastic gondolas.

Brunetti recognized this as his most unpleasant

mood, no doubt exacerbated by his encounter with Opus Dei, and knew that, to counter it, he had to walk. He set off back along the Riva degli Schiavoni, water to his right, hotels to his left. By the time he got to the first bridge, moving quickly under the late afternoon sun, he felt better. Then, when he saw the tugboats pulled up to the riva, lined up and in order, each with its Latin name, he felt his heart lift up and sail over toward San Giorgio in the wake of a passing vaporetto.

The sign for Ospedale SS Giovanni e Paolo decided him, and twenty minutes later he found himself there. The nurse in charge of the floor to which Maria Testa had been moved told him that there was no change in her condition and said that she had been moved to a private room, Number 317, just up the corridor and around to the right.

Outside Room 317 Brunetti found an empty chair and, on it, lying face down, the current issue of *Topolino*. Without thinking, without knocking, Brunetti opened the door to the room and went inside, where instinct pulled him swiftly to the side of the still-closing door as his eyes flashed around the room.

A blanket-covered form lay on the bed, tubes running up and down to plastic bottles above and below. The same thick bandage that enwrapped her shoulder was still in place, as was the one that swathed her head. But the person Brunetti saw when he approached the bed seemed a different one: her nose had been honed down to a thin beak, her eyes had sunk deeper into her skull, and her body almost didn't show beneath the covers, so thin had she become in just this short time.

Brunetti, as he had the last time, studied her face, hoping it would reveal something. She breathed slowly, with such a long pause between breaths that Brunetti began to fear that the next one would never come.

He glanced around the room and saw no flowers, no books, no sign of human occupancy. Brunetti found that strange and then was struck by the sadness of it. She was a beautiful woman at the dawn of her life, trapped and unable to do little more than breathe, and yet there was no evidence that anyone in the world was aware of that fact, nor that there existed a single soul who suffered at the thought that the dawn would never come.

Alvise, newly engrossed in his reading, sat in the chair outside the room and didn't bother to look up when Brunetti emerged.

'Alvise,' Brunetti said.

He looked up absently from the comic and, recognizing Brunetti, pushed himself instantly to his feet and saluted, the comic still in his hand. 'Yes, sir?'

'Where were you?'

'I kept falling asleep, sir, so I went down to get a coffee. I didn't want to fall asleep and let an intruder into the room.'

'And while you were away, Alvise? Didn't it occur to you that someone might have gone in while you were away?'

Had he been stout Cortez, silent, on a peak in Darien, Alvise could have been no more astounded by this suggestion. 'But they would have had to know when I was away.'

Brunetti said nothing.

'Wouldn't they, sir?'

'Who assigned you here, Alvise?' Brunetti asked.

'There's a roster in the office, sir; we come over here by turns.'

'When will you be relieved?'

Alvise tossed the comic onto his chair and looked at his watch. 'At six, sir.'

'Who's replacing you?'

'I don't know, sir. I just look at my own assignments.'

'I don't want you to leave this place again before you're relieved.'

'Yes, sir. I mean no, sir.'

'Alvise,' Brunetti said, pushing his face so close to Alvise's that he could catch the sharp odour of coffee and grappa on the man's breath, 'if I come back here and I find you either sitting or reading, or not here in front of this door, you will be dismissed from the force so fast you won't even have time to explain it to your union steward.' Alvise opened his mouth to object, but Brunetti cut him off. 'One word, Alvise, one word and you're finished.' Brunetti turned and walked away.

He waited till after dinner to tell Paola that the name of Opus Dei had entered into this investigation. He did this not from uncertainty about her discretion but because he dreaded the inevitable pyrotechnics of her response to the name. They came long after dinner, when Raffi had gone to his room to finish his Greek homework and Chiara to read, but when they came, they were no less explosive for having been delayed.

'Opus Dei? Opus Dei?' Paola's opening salvo soared across the living room, from where she sat sewing a button onto one of his shirts, and struck at Brunetti, slumped down in the sofa with his feet crossed in front of him on the low table. 'Opus Dei?' she shouted again, just in case one of the children hadn't heard. 'Those nursing homes are mixed up with Opus Dei? No wonder old people are dying; they're probably being killed so their money can be used to convert some heathen savages to Holy Mother Church.' Decades with Paola had accustomed Brunetti to the extremity of most of her positions; they had also taught him that, on the subject of the Church, she was immediately incandescent and seldom lucid. And never wrong.

'I don't know that they're mixed up in it, Paola. All I know is what Miotti's brother said, that there is talk the chaplain is a member.'

'Well, isn't that enough?'

'Enough for what?'

'Enough to arrest him.'

'Arrest him for what, Paola? That he disagrees with you on matters of religion?'

'Don't be smart with me, Guido,' she threatened, aiming the needle in her hand at him to show how serious she was.

'I'm not being smart. I'm not even trying to be. I can't go out and arrest a priest just because there's a rumour he belongs to a religious organization.' He knew that, in Paola's vision of justice, little more evidence of crime was necessary, but he refrained from making this observation, judging the time inappropriate.

It was clear from her silence that Paola had to accept the truth of what he said, but the vigour with which she stabbed the needle through the cuff of his shirt gave evidence of how much she resented that fact. 'You know they're power-hungry thugs,' she said.

'That might well be true. I know that many people believe it, but I have no first-hand evidence of it.'

'Oh, come on, Guido, everyone knows about Opus Dei.'

He sat up straighter and crossed his legs. 'I'm not sure they do.'

'What?' she asked, shooting him an angry glance.

'I think everyone thinks they know about Opus Dei, but it is, after all, a secret society. I doubt that anyone outside of the organization knows very much about it, or about them. Or at least not anything that's true.'

Brunetti watched Paola as she considered this, the needle quiet in her hand as she continued to stare down at the shirt. Though she was violent on the subject of religion, she was also a scholar, and it was this part that caused her to look up and across at him. 'You may be right.' She grimaced at her own admission and then added, 'But isn't it strange that so little is known about them?'

'I just said they're a secret society.'

'The world is full of secret societies, but most of

them are a joke: the Masons, the Rosicrucians, all those Satanic cults the Americans are always inventing. But people are really afraid of Opus Dei. The way they were afraid of the SS, the Gestapo.'

'Paola, wouldn't you say that's an extreme position?'

'You know I can't be rational on this subject, so don't ask me to be, all right?' Neither spoke for a moment, and then she added, 'But it really is strange, the way they've managed to create such a reputation about themselves while still managing to remain almost entirely secret.' She set the shirt aside and stuck the needle into the pincushion that sat beside her. 'What is it they want?'

'You sound like Freud,' Brunetti said with a laugh. ' "What do women want?" '

She laughed at the joke: contempt for Freud and all his works and pomps was part of the intellectual glue that held them together. 'No, really. What do you think it is they really want?'

'Beats me,' Brunetti was forced to admit. Then, after he had considered it for a while, he answered, 'Power, I suppose.'

Paola blinked a few times and shook her head. 'That's always such a frightening idea for me, that anyone would want it.'

'That's because you're a woman. It's the one thing women believe they don't want. But we do.'

She looked up, half-smiling, thinking this was another joke, but Brunetti, straight-faced, continued, 'I mean it, Paola. I don't think women understand how important it is for us, for men, to have power.' He saw that she was going to object, but he cut her off. 'No, it's got nothing to do with womb envy. Well, at least I don't think it does – you know, feeling we're inadequate because we don't have babies and have to make it up in other ways.' Brunetti paused, never having articulated this, not even to Paola. 'Maybe it's no more than that we're bigger, so we can get away with pushing other people around.'

'That's terribly simplistic, Guido.'

'I know. Doesn't mean it's wrong.'

She shook her head again. 'I just can't understand it. In the end, no matter how much power we have, we get old, we get weak, and we lose it all.'

Brunetti was suddenly struck by how much she sounded like Vianello: his sergeant argued that material wealth was an illusion, and now his wife was telling him that power was no more real. And what did that make him, the gross materialist yoked between two anchorites?

Neither of them spoke for a long time. Finally Paola glanced at her watch, saw that it was after eleven, and said, 'I've got an early class tomorrow.' At her hint, Brunetti stood, but even before she could get to her feet, the phone rang.

She started to get up to answer, but Brunetti moved more quickly, certain that it would be Vianello or someone from the hospital. 'Pronto,' he said, mastering both fear and excitement and keeping his voice calm.

'Is this Signor Brunetti?' a strange woman's voice asked.

'Yes, it is.'

'Signor Brunetti, I need to speak to you,' she began in a rush. But then, as though her spirit had been deflated, she paused for a moment and then said, 'No, could I speak to Signora Brunetti, instead?'

The tension in her voice was so strong that Brunetti didn't dare ask who it was, for fear that she would hang up. 'One minute, please. I'll get her,' he said and set the phone down on the table. He turned to Paola, still seated on the sofa, looking up at him.

'Who is it?' she asked in a low voice.

'I don't know. She wants to talk to you.'

Paola came to the table and picked up the receiver. '*Pronto*,' she said.

Not knowing what to do, Brunetti turned to walk away, but then he felt Paola's hand snap out and grab his arm. She shot one quick glance toward him, but then the woman on the other end said something, and Paola's attention was pulled away from him and she released him.

'Yes, yes. Of course you can call.' Paola, as was her habit, started to play with the coiled wire of the phone, wrapping it around her fingers in a series of living rings. 'Yes, I remember you from the meeting with the teachers.' She pulled the wires from her left fingers and began to wrap them around the right ones. 'I'm very glad you called. Yes, I think it was the right thing to do.'

Her hands grew still. 'Please, Signora Stocco, try to stay calm. Nothing's going to happen. Is she all right? And your husband? When will he be back? The important thing is that Nicoletta's all right.'

Paola glanced up at Brunetti, who raised his eyebrows interrogatively. She nodded twice, though he had no idea what that was supposed to mean, and shifted her weight to lean against him. He put an arm around her and continued to listen to her voice and the sharp crackle from the other end of the line.

'Of course, I'll tell my husband. But I don't think he can do anything unless you . . .' The voice cut her off. It went on for a long time.

'I understand, I understand completely. If Nicoletta's all right. No, I don't think you should talk to her about it, Signora Stocco. Yes, I'll speak to him tonight and call you tomorrow. Could you give me your number, please?' Leaning away from him, she jotted down a number and then asked, 'Is there anything I could do for you tonight?' She paused and then said, 'No, of course it's no trouble. I'm very glad you called.'

Another pause, and then she said, 'Yes, I'd heard rumours, but nothing definite, nothing like this. Yes, yes, I agree. I'll talk to my husband about it and I'll call you tomorrow morning. Please, Signora Stocco, I'm glad to be of help in any way I can.' More sounds from the other end.

'Try to get some sleep, Signora Stocco. The important thing is that Nicoletta is all right. That's all that matters.' After another pause, Paola said, 'Of course you can call again if you want to. No, it doesn't matter what time it is. We'll be here. Of course, of course. You're welcome, Signora. Good night.' She replaced the receiver and turned to him.

'That was Signora Stocco. Her daughter Nicoletta is in Chiara's class. R.E. class.'

'Padre Luciano?' Brunetti asked, wondering what new lightning bolt was to be hurled at him by the forces of religion.

Paola nodded.

'What happened?'

'She didn't say. Or she didn't know. She was helping Nicoletta with her homework tonight – her husband's in Rome for business all this week – and she said Nicoletta started to cry when she saw the religion book. When she asked her what was the matter, she wouldn't say. But after a while, the girl said that Padre Luciano had said things to her in the confessional and then that he had touched her.'

'Touched her where?' Brunetti asked, a question he asked as much as a father as a policeman.

'She wouldn't say. Signora Stocco decided not to make too much of it, but I think she's shaken. She was crying when she talked to me. She asked me to speak to you.'

Brunetti was already far ahead, thinking of what would have to happen before he could separate parent from policeman and act. 'The girl would have to tell us,' he said.

'I know. From what the mother said, I think that's unlikely.'

Brunetti nodded. 'Unless she does, there's nothing I can do.'

'I know,' Paola said. She was silent for a while and then added, 'But I can.'

'What do you mean?' Brunetti asked, surprised by the strength and suddenness of his fear.

'Don't worry, Guido. I won't touch him. I promise you that. But I will see that he's punished.'

'You don't even know what he did,' Brunetti said. 'How can you talk of punishment?'

She backed away a few paces and looked at him. She started to speak and then stopped. After a pause during which he saw her start to speak twice and stop, she stepped toward him and put her hand on his arm. 'Don't worry, Guido. I won't do anything that is illegal. But I will punish him and, if necessary, I will destroy him.' She watched his shock turn into acceptance that she meant what she'd said. 'I'm sorry,' she apologized, 'I always forget how you hate melodrama.' She looked at her watch and then up at him. 'As I said before, it's late and I have an early class.'

Leaving him there, Paola went down the corridor toward their bedroom and their bed.

Chapter Eighteen

Usually a sound sleeper, that night Brunetti was kept awake by dreams, animal dreams. He saw lions, turtles, and a peculiarly grotesque beast with a long beard and a bald head. The bells of San Polo counted out the intermittent hours for him, keeping him company as he endured the long night. At five, the realization came to him that Maria Testa must recover and begin to speak, and as soon as he saw that, he slipped into a sleep so peaceful and dreamless that even Paola's noisy departure failed to wake him.

He woke a little before nine and spent twenty minutes lying in bed, planning it, attempting vainly to hide from himself the fact that it was she who would run all of the risks attendant upon her resurrection. The desire to put it into action grew so strong that he was finally driven up and into the shower, then out of the apartment and toward the Questura. From there, he called the chief of neurology at the Ospedale Civile and from him received his first setback, for the doctor insisted that Maria Testa could not, under any circumstances, be moved. Her condition was still too uncertain and precarious to allow her to be disturbed. A long history of battles with the health system suggested to Brunetti that a more realistic explanation lay in the fact that the staff simply didn't want to be bothered by something they considered as inconsequential as this, but he knew it was useless to argue.

He asked Vianello to come up to his office and began by explaining his plan. 'All we do,' he concluded, 'is have a story put in the *Gazzettino* tomorrow morning, saying that she's come out of the coma. You know how they love that sort of thing – *Back from the Edge of the Grave*. Then, whoever was in that car, once they believe she's recovered and able to talk, they'll have to try again.'

Vianello studied Brunetti's face, as if seeing new things in it, but said nothing.

'Well?' Brunetti prompted.

'Is there time for the story to get in by tomorrow?' the sergeant asked.

Brunetti looked at his watch. 'Of course there is.' When Vianello looked no more content, Brunetti asked, 'What's wrong?'

'I don't like the idea of putting her at even greater risk,' the sergeant finally answered. 'Using her as bait.'

'Someone will be in the room, I told you.'

'Commissario,' Vianello began, and Brunetti was immediately on his guard, as he was whenever Vianello addressed him by his title and in that patient tone. 'Someone in the hospital will have to know what's going on.'

'Of course.'

'Well?'

'Well what?' Brunetti snapped. He had thought of all of this and knew the dangers, so the force of his reaction to Vianello's question was no more than a reflection of his own unease.

'That's a risk. People talk. All anyone has to do is go into the bar on the ground floor and start asking about her. Someone – an orderly, a nurse, a doctor even – is bound to say something about there being a guard in the room with her.'

'Then we don't tell them it's a guard. We say the guard's been removed. We can say they're relatives.'

'Or members of the order?' Vianello suggested, voice so level that Brunetti couldn't tell if he was being helpful or sarcastic.

'No one in the hospital knows she's a nun,' Brunetti said, though he seriously doubted this.

'I'd like to believe that.'

'What does that mean, Sergeant?'

'Hospitals are small places. It's not easy to keep a secret for long. So I think we should take it as given that they know who she is.'

After having heard Vianello use the word 'bait', Brunetti was unwilling to admit that was exactly what he wanted her to be. Tired of hearing Vianello give voice to all of the uncertainties and objections he had spent the morning attempting to deny or minimize, Brunetti asked, 'Are you in charge of the duty roster this week?'

'Yes, sir.'

'Good. Then continue with the shifts at the hospital, but I want them moved inside her room.' Remembering Alvise and the comic book, he said, 'Tell them they aren't to leave the room, for any reason, unless they get a nurse to stay in there with her while they're gone. And put me down for one of the shifts, starting tonight, from midnight until eight.'

'Yes, sir,' Vianello said and got to his feet. Brunetti looked down at the papers on his desk, but the sergeant made no attempt to leave. 'One of the strange things about this exercise programme,' he began, waiting for Brunetti to look up at him. When he did, Vianello continued, 'is that I need a lot less sleep. So I can split that shift with you, if you'd like. Then, we just have to use two officers for the other two, and it will be a lot easier to juggle the hours.'

Brunetti smiled his thanks. 'You want to begin the shift?' he asked.

'All right,' Vianello agreed. 'I just hope this doesn't keep on long.'

'I thought you said you needed less sleep.'

'I do. But Nadia isn't going to like it.'

Nor, Brunetti realized, was Paola.

Vianello got to his feet and made a waving motion with his right hand, whether a lazy salute or the sign one accomplice gives another was impossible to determine.

After the sergeant went downstairs to make up the duty roster and tell Signorina Elettra to call the *Gazzettino*, Brunetti decided to stir the waters even more. He called the San Leonardo nursing home and left a message for the Mother Superior, saying that Maria Testa – he was insistent in using her name – was recovering well in the Civil Hospital and hoped to be able to receive a visit from the Mother Superior sometime in the future, perhaps as early as next week. Before he hung up, he asked the nun he spoke to if she'd also pass the message on to Dottor

Messini. He found the number of the chapter house and, when he called, was surprised to have the call taken by an answering machine. He left much the same message for Padre Pio.

He thought of calling both Contessa Crivoni and Signorina Lerini, but he decided to let them learn the news of Suor'Immacolata's recovery from the newspaper.

When Brunetti went into Signorina Elettra's office, she looked up at him but didn't give her usual smile. 'What's wrong, Signorina?'

Instead of answering, she pointed to a manila folder on her desk. 'Padre Pio Cavaletti is what's wrong, Dottore.'

'As bad as that?' Brunetti asked, though he had no idea what he meant by 'that'.

'Read it, and you'll see.'

Brunetti picked up the slim folder and opened it with interest. It held photocopies of three documents. The first was a one-sentence letter from the Lugano Office of the Union Bank of Switzerland to 'Signor Pio Cavaletti'; the second was a letter addressed to 'Padre Pio', written in a hand that trembled across the page with sickness or age, perhaps both; the third carried the by-now-familiar crest of the Patriarchate of Venice.

He glanced again at Signorina Elettra, who sat quietly, hands neatly folded on the desk in front of her, waiting for him to finish reading. He turned back to the papers and read through them slowly.

'Signor Cavaletti. We acknowledge your 29 January deposit of 27,000 Swiss francs to your account with this bank.' The computer-generated bank form had no signature.

'Sainted Father, you have turned my sinful eyes to God. His grace is not of this world. You were right – my family is not of God. They do not know Him or recognize His power. Only you, Father, you and the other holy saints. It is you and the saints we must thank with more than words. I go to God knowing I have done this.' The signature was illegible.

'Permission is herewith granted to the pious union Opus Dei to establish and maintain in this city a mission of study and holy works under the direction of Padre Pio Cavaletti.' This one bore the signature and seal of the director of the office of religious foundations.

Having finished the three pages, Brunetti looked up. 'What do you make of these, Signorina?'

'I make of them exactly what they are, Dottore.'

'And that is?'

'Spiritual blackmail. Not much different from what they've been doing for centuries, just a little shabbier and on a smaller scale.'

'Where did they come from?'

'The second and third are from files kept in the office of the Patriarch. Not from the same file.'

'And the first?'

'From a reliable source,' was the only explanation she gave and, Brunetti saw, the only one she was going to give.

'I'll take your word for that, Signorina.'

'Thank you,' she said with simple grace.

'I've been reading about them, Opus Dei,' he

volunteered. 'Does your friend's friend, the one at the Patriarchate, know if they're very' – Brunetti wanted to use the word 'powerful', but something akin to superstition prevented him – 'if they're very much of a presence in the city?'

'He says it's very difficult to be certain about them or about what they do. But he's convinced that their power is very real.'

'That's just what people used to say about witches, Signorina.'

'Witches didn't own entire neighbourhoods in London, Dottore. Nor did they have a Pope who praised them for their "sacred mission". Nor did witches,' she began, pointing to the folder he still held, 'have ecclesiastical sanction to set up centres for study and holy works.'

'I never knew you had such strong feelings about religion,' he said.

'This has nothing to do with religion,' she snapped out.

'No?' His surprise was real.

'It has to do with power.'

Brunetti considered this for a moment. 'Yes, I suppose it does.'

In a more relaxed voice, Signorina Elettra said, 'Vice-Questore Patta asked me to tell you that the visit from the Swiss police chief has been postponed.'

Brunetti hardly heard her. 'It's what my wife says.' When he saw that she wasn't following him, Brunetti added by way of explanation, 'About power.' And as soon as she understood, he asked, 'Excuse me, what did you say about the Vice-Questore?'

247

'The visit from the Swiss police chief has been postponed.'

'Ah, I'd forgotten all about it. Thank you, Signorina.' Saying nothing else, he placed the folder on her desk and went back to his office to get his coat.

This time his ring was answered by a middle-aged man wearing something that was meant, Brunetti supposed, to look like a friar's habit but which succeeded only in making him look like a man in a badly hemmed skirt. When Brunetti explained that he had come to speak to Padre Pio, the doorkeeper folded his hands together and bowed his head but said nothing. He led Brunetti across the courtyard, where there was no sign of the gardener, though the scent of lilac was even stronger. Inside, the sharp odours of disinfectant and wax lurked under the sweet pall of lilac. On the way they passed a younger man walking in their direction. The two demi-clerics nodded silently to one another, and Brunetti saw it as so much pious posturing.

The man Brunetti had come to think of as the artful mute stopped outside the door to Padre Pio's office and nodded to Brunetti that he might enter. When he did, without bothering to knock, he found the windows closed, but this time he noticed the crucifix that hung on the far wall. Since it was a religious image that Brunetti disliked, he gave it no more than a cursory glance, taking no interest in whatever aesthetic value it might have.

A few minutes later, the door opened and Padre Pio came into the room. As Brunetti recalled, he wore the religious habit with ease, managing to look comfortable in it. Brunetti's attention was again pulled to the full lips, but this time he realized how the centre of the man lay in his eyes, greyish green and bright with intelligence.

'Welcome back, Commissario,' the priest said. 'Thank you for your message. Suor'Immacolata's recovery is in response to our prayers, I'm sure.'

Though tempted, Brunetti did not begin by asking that he be spared the rhetoric of religious hypocrisy and, instead, said, 'I'd like you to answer a few more questions.'

'Gladly. So long as – as I explained the last time – they do not require me to divulge information which is sealed.' Though the priest continued to smile, Brunetti sensed that he had registered the difference in Brunetti's mood.

'No, I doubt that any of this information is in any way privileged.'

'Good. But before you begin, there's no reason to stand. Let's at least be comfortable.' He led Brunetti to the same two chairs and, flicking back his habit with practised grace, lowered himself into the chair. He reached under his scapular with his right hand and began to finger his rosary. 'What is it you'd like to know, Commissario?'

'I'd like you to tell me about your work at the nursing home.'

Cavaletti gave a small laugh and said, 'I'm not sure that's what I'd call it, Dottore. I serve as chaplain to the patients and some of the staff. To bring people closer to their Maker is a joy; it is not work.' He looked away toward the other side of the room, but not before he had seen Brunetti's lack of response to these sentiments.

'You hear their confessions?'

'I'm not sure whether that's a question or a statement, Commissario,' Cavaletti replied with a smile, as if he wished to remove even the hint of sarcasm from his remark.

'It's a question.'

'Then I'll answer it.' His smile was indulgent. 'Yes, I hear the confessions of the patients, as well as of some of the staff. It's a great responsibility, especially the confessions of the old people.'

'And why is that, Father?'

'Because they are nearer to their time, to their earthly ending.'

'I see,' Brunetti said and then, as if it were the logical consequence of the previous answer, he asked, 'Do you maintain an account at the Lugano branch of the Union Bank of Switzerland?'

The lips remained curved in their peaceful smile, but Brunetti was watching his eyes, which tightened almost imperceptibly and just for an instant. 'What a strange question,' Cavaletti said, pulling his brows together in evident confusion. 'How does it relate to the confessions of these old people?'

'That's exactly what I'm trying to find out, Father,' Brunetti said.

'It's still a strange question,' Cavaletti said.

'Do you maintain an account at the Lugano branch of the Union Bank of Switzerland?'

The priest moved his fingers to a new bead and said, 'Yes, I do. Part of my family lives in the Ticino and I go to visit them two or three times a year. I find that it is more convenient to have the money there than to carry it back and forth with me.'

'And how much do you keep in this account, Father?'

Cavaletti looked off into the distance, doing sums, and finally answered, 'I'd guess about a thousand francs.' Then, helpfully, he added, 'That's about a million lire.'

'I know how to convert from lira to Swiss francs, Father. It's one of the first things a policeman in this country has to learn.' Then Brunetti smiled, showing the priest that this was a joke, but Cavaletti did not smile in return.

Brunetti asked his next question. 'Are you a member of Opus Dei?'

Cavaletti dropped his rosary and raised his hands in front of him at this, palms toward Brunetti in an exaggerated gesture of appeal. 'Oh, Commissario, what strange questions you ask. I wonder at the relationship that keeps them together in your head.'

'I'm not sure if that's a yes or a no, Father.'

After a long silence, Cavaletti said, 'Yes.'

Brunetti got to his feet. 'That will be all, Father. I thank you for your time.'

The priest, for the first time, could not hide his surprise and lost a few seconds staring up at Brunetti. But he scrambled to his feet and went with him to the door and held it open while Brunetti passed out of the room. As he walked down the corridor, Brunetti was conscious of two things: the eyes of the priest on his back and, as he approached the open door at the end, the rich scent of the lilacs, swirling in from the courtyard. Neither sensation gave him any pleasure.

Chapter Nineteen

Though Brunetti didn't believe there would be any danger to Maria Testa until the article had appeared in the *Gazzettino* – and he couldn't be sure that there would be any danger even then – he still pushed himself away from Paola and out of bed a little after three and got dressed. It was not until he was buttoning his shirt that his head cleared enough for him to hear the rain driving against the windows of their bedroom. He muttered under his breath and went over to the window, opened the shutter, and then quickly shoved it closed against the wet gusts that pushed into the room. At the doorway, he put on his raincoat and picked up an umbrella, then remembered Vianello and picked up another.

In Maria Testa's room, he found Vianello, groggy-eyed and bad-tempered, even though Brunetti arrived almost a half hour before he was expected. By mutual consent, neither of the men approached the sleeping woman, as if her complete helplessness served as a kind of burning sword to keep them at a distance. They greeted one another in hushed voices and then moved out into the corridor to speak.

'Has anything happened?' Brunetti asked, pulling

his raincoat off and propping both umbrellas against the wall.

'A nurse comes in every two hours or so,' Vianello answered. 'Doesn't do anything, so far as I can tell. Just looks at her, takes her pulse, and writes something on the chart.'

'Does she ever say anything?'

'Who, the nurse?' Vianello asked.

'Yes.'

'Not a word. I might as well be invisible.' Vianello yawned. 'Hard to stay awake.'

'Why don't you do some push-ups?'

Vianello gave Brunetti a steady look but said nothing.

'Thanks for coming, Vianello,' Brunetti offered by way of apology. 'I brought you an umbrella. It's pouring.' When Vianello nodded his thanks, Brunetti asked, 'Who's coming in the morning?'

'Gravini. And then Pucetti. I'll relieve Pucetti when his shift's over.' Brunetti noted the delicacy with which Vianello avoided naming the time – midnight – when he would relieve the younger officer.

'Thanks, Vianello. Go get some sleep.'

Vianello nodded and bit back an enormous yawn. He picked up the rolled umbrella.

As Brunetti opened the door to go back into the room, he turned and asked Vianello, 'Was there any trouble about the staffing?'

'Not yet,' Vianello said, stopping in the hall and looking back.

'How long?' Brunetti asked, not knowing what to call the falsification of the staffing chart.

'There's never any telling, is there, but I'd guess it'll be three or four days before Lieutenant Scarpa notices anything. Maybe a week. But no longer than that.'

'Let's hope they bite before that.'

'If there's anyone to bite,' Vianello said, finally voicing his scepticism, and turned away. Brunetti watched his broad back turn right at the first staircase and disappear, and then he let himself back into the room. He draped his raincoat over the back of the chair where Vianello had been sitting and propped the umbrella in a corner.

A small light burned beside her bed, barely illuminating the space around her head and leaving the rest of the room in deep shadow. Brunetti doubted that the overhead light would disturb the woman in the bed – indeed, it would be a good sign if it did – but he still didn't want to turn it on, and so he sat in the shadows and did not read, though he had brought along his copy of Marcus Aurelius, an author who had in the past provided great comfort in difficult times.

As the night wore on, Brunetti found himself running through the events that had taken place since Maria Testa had come into his office. Any one of them could be a coincidence: the cluster of deaths among the old people, the accident that had struck Maria from her bicycle, da Prè's death. But their cumulative weight removed from Brunetti's mind any possibility of accident or happenstance. And that possibility gone, then the three things were related, though he could not yet see how.

Messini dissuaded people from leaving money to him or to the nursing home, Padre Pio was named in none of the wills, and the sisters of the order could not own property. The Contessa was wealthy in her own right and had hardly needed her husband's estate; da Prè wanted nothing more than little boxes to add to his collection; and Signorina Lerini appeared to have renounced worldly pomp. *Cui bono? Cui bono?* All that remained was to discover who stood to profit from the deaths, and the path would open before him, as if illuminated by torch-bearing seraphim, and lead him to the killer.

Brunetti knew he was a man of many weaknesses: pride, indolence, and wrath, to name those he thought most evident, but he also knew that greed was not among them, and so, when confronted with its many manifestations, Brunetti always felt himself in the presence of the alien. He knew it was a common, perhaps the most common, vice, and he could certainly apprehend it with his mind, but it always failed to move his heart, and it left his spirit cold.

He looked across the room at the woman in the bed, utterly motionless and silent. None of the doctors had any idea of the extent of the damage that had been done, apart from the damage done to her body. One said it was unlikely that she would emerge from the coma. Another said she would probably come out of it in a matter of days. Perhaps one of the sisters who worked here had responded with greatest wisdom when she told him, 'Hope and pray, and trust in God's mercy.'

As he looked at Maria and remembered the depths of charity that had radiated from the nun's eyes as she spoke, another of the sisters came into the room. She walked over to the bed carrying a tray, set the tray on the table beside Maria's bed, reached down and picked up her wrist. Glancing at her watch, she held Maria's wrist for a few moments, then set it back on the covers and went to enter her findings on the chart that hung at the foot of the bed.

She picked up the tray and went toward the door. When she saw Brunetti, she nodded, but she did not smile.

Nothing except that happened for the rest of the night. The same nurse came back at about six, and when she did, she found Brunetti standing against the wall in an attempt to keep himself awake.

At twenty to eight, Officer Gravini, wearing high rubber boots, a raincoat, and jeans came in. Even before saying good morning, he explained to Brunetti, 'Sergeant Vianello told us not to wear our uniforms, sir.'

'Yes, I know, Gravini. It's fine, fine.' The only window of the room faced a covered passageway, and so Brunetti had no idea of the weather. 'How bad is it?' he asked.

'Pouring, sir. Supposed to keep on until Friday.'

Brunetti picked up his raincoat and put it on, regretting that he hadn't worn his boots last night. He had hoped to be able to go back home and have a shower before going to the Questura, but it would be mad to walk to the other side of the city, not when he was so close to his office. Besides, a few coffees would be just as good.

That proved not to be the case, and by the time he got up to his office, he was cranky and ready for trouble. That came after only a few hours, when he received a call from the Vice-Questore, telling him to come down to his office.

Signorina Elettra was not at her desk, and so Brunetti went into Patta's office without the forewarning she usually provided. This morning, sleepless, grainy-eyed, and with too much coffee in his stomach, he didn't care in the least whether he had that warning or not.

'I've had an alarming conversation with my lieutenant,' Patta said without preamble. At any other time, Brunetti would have taken quiet, sardonic satisfaction in Patta's accidental admission of what the entire Questura knew – Lieutenant Scarpa was Patta's creature – but this morning he was dulled by sleeplessness and so barely noted the pronoun.

'Did you hear me, Brunetti?' Patta asked.

'Yes, sir. But I find it difficult to imagine what sort of thing might alarm the lieutenant.'

Patta pushed himself back in his chair. 'Your behaviour, for one thing,' Patta shot back.

'What particular part of my behaviour, sir?'

Brunetti noticed that the Vice-Questore was losing his tan. And his patience. 'For this crusade you seem to be launching against Holy Mother Church, for one thing,' Patta said and then stopped, as if capable himself of hearing the exaggeration in the claim.

'Specifically, sir?' Brunetti asked, rubbing his palm along the side of his jaw and discovering a spot he had missed when he shaved with the electric razor he kept in his desk.

'With your persecution of men who wear the cloth. With the violence of your behaviour toward the Mother Superior of the Order of the Sacred Cross.' Patta stopped here, as if waiting for the seriousness of these accusations to sink in.

'And with my asking questions about Opus Dei? Is that on Lieutenant Scarpa's list, as well?'

'Who told you about that?' Patta asked.

'I assume that, if the Lieutenant is making a general list of my excesses, that would certainly be on it. Especially if, as I believe, the orders for him to do so come from Opus Dei.'

Patta slammed his hand down on his desk. 'Lieutenant Scarpa takes his orders from me, Commissario.'

'Am I to take it, then, that you too are a member?'

Patta pulled his chair closer to the desk and leaned over it, toward Brunetti. 'Commissario, I'm not sure that this is a place where you are the one to ask questions.'

Brunetti shrugged.

'Do I have your attention, Commissario Brunetti?' Patta asked.

'Yes, sir,' Brunetti said in a voice which, to his surprise, he did not have to struggle to make level and calm. He didn't care about any of this, suddenly felt himself free of Patta and Scarpa.

'There have been complaints about you, com-

plaints of a wide variety. The Prior of the Order of
the Sacred Cross has called to object to your treatment of members of his order. Further, he says you
are harbouring a member of the order.'

'Harbouring?'

'That she's been taken to the hospital and is now
conscious and no doubt beginning to spread slander
about the order. Is this true?'

'Yes.'

'And you know where she is?'

'You just said where she is, in the hospital.'

'Where you visit her and permit no one else to
do so?'

'Where she is under police protection.'

'Police protection?' Patta repeated in a voice that
could be heard, Brunetti feared, on the lower floors.
'And who authorized this protection? Why has there
been no mention of it on the duty rosters?'

'Have you seen the rosters, sir?'

'Don't worry about who's seen the rosters, Brunetti. Just tell me why there is no mention of her
name on them.'

'It was entered as "surveillance".'

Again, Patta roared back an echo of Brunetti's
word.

'For days, policemen have been sitting in the
hospital, doing nothing, and you dare to put it down
as "surveillance"?'

Brunetti stopped himself from asking Patta if he
wanted him to change the wording and put it down
as 'guarding' and chose the wiser course of silence.

'And who's there now?' Patta demanded.

'Gravini.'

'Well, get him out of there. The police in this city have better things to do than sit outside the room of some runaway nun who's gone and got herself into the hospital.'

'I believe she's in danger, sir.'

Patta waved a hand wildly in the air. 'I don't want to know about danger. I don't care if she's in danger. If she's seen fit to leave the protection of Holy Mother Church, then she should be ready to take responsibility for herself in this world she's so eager to enter.' He saw Brunetti start to object and raised his voice. 'Gravini is to be out of the hospital in ten minutes and back here in the squad room.' Again, Brunetti started to explain, but Patta cut him off. 'No policeman is to be there, outside that room. If they are, if anyone goes there, they will be relieved of their duties immediately.' Patta leaned even farther over his desk and added ominously, 'As will be the person who sent them there. Do you understand that, Commissario?'

'Yes, sir.'

'And I want you to stay away from members of the Order of the Sacred Cross. The Prior does not expect an apology from you, though I think that's extraordinary, after what I've heard about your behaviour.'

Brunetti knew Patta in this vein, though he had never seen him this unhinged. As Patta continued to talk, spiralling ever higher in pursuit of his own anger, Brunetti began to calculate the reason for the extremity of Patta's response, and the only satisfactory explanation he came up with was fear. If Patta was a member of Opus Dei, his response would be nothing stronger than outrage; he had seen that in Patta enough times to know that what was now being manifested was something else entirely and something far stronger. Fear, then.

Patta's voice called him back. 'Do you understand that, Brunetti?'

'Yes, sir,' Brunetti said, getting to his feet. 'I'll call Gravini,' he said and started toward the door.

'If you send anyone there, Brunetti, you're finished. Do you understand?'

'Yes, sir, I do,' he said. Patta had said nothing about anyone's being their on his own time, not that it would have made any difference to Brunetti if he had.

He called the hospital from Signorina Elettra's desk and asked to speak to Gravini. There followed a series of messages to and from the policeman, who refused to leave the room, even when Brunetti told the person at the hospital to tell him that it was an order from the Commissario. Finally, after more than five minutes, Gravini came to the phone. The first thing he said was, 'There's a doctor in the room with her. He won't leave until I get back.' Only then he asked if he was speaking to Brunetti.

'Yes, it's me, Gravini. You can come back here now.'

'Is it over, sir?' Gravini asked.

'You can come back to the Questura, Gravini,' Brunetti repeated. 'But go home and put your uniform on first.'

'Yes, sir,' the young man said and hung up, persuaded by Brunetti's tone to ask no more questions.

Before going back to his office, Brunetti went

into the officers' room and picked up a copy of that morning's *Gazzettino* he saw lying on a desk. He turned to the Venezia section, but the article about Maria Testa appeared nowhere. He turned to the first section, but nothing was there either. He pulled out a chair and spread the paper open on the desk in front of him. Column by column, he went slowly through both sections of the paper. Nothing. No story had appeared, and yet someone with enough power to frighten Patta had learned of Brunetti's interest in Maria Testa. Or, even more interesting, they had somehow come to learn that she had regained consciousness. As he climbed the stairs to his office, a brief smile flit for a second across Brunetti's face.

Chapter Twenty

At lunch, he found the mood of the entire family as subdued as the mood he brought back with him from the Questura. He attributed Raffi's silence to some difficulty in the course of his romance with Sara Paganuzzi; Chiara was perhaps still smarting under the cloud that had marred the perfection of her academic record. As always, it was the cause of Paola's mood that was the most difficult to assess.

There was none of the usual joking with which they displayed their boundless affection for one another. Instead, at one point, Brunetti found them discussing the weather, and then, as though that weren't grim enough, politics. All of them were visibly glad to see the meal end. The children, like cave-dwelling animals which had been frightened by signs of lightning on the horizon, scurried back to the security of their rooms. Brunetti, having already read the paper, went into the living room and con-tented himself with watching sheets of rain batter themselves against the rooftops.

When Paola came in, she carried coffee, and Brunetti decided to view it as a peace offering, though he was uncertain about what sort of treaty was going to accompany it. He took the coffee and thanked her. He took a sip and asked, 'Well?'

'I've spoken to my father,' Paola said as she took a seat on the sofa. 'He was the only one I could think of.'

'And what did you tell him?' Brunetti asked.

'I told him what Signora Stocco told me, and what the children have said.'

'About Padre Luciano?'

'Yes.'

'And?'

'He said he'd look into it.'

'Did you tell him anything about Padre Pio?' Brunetti asked.

She glanced up, surprised at the question. 'No, of course not. Why do you ask?'

'Just asking,' he said.

'Guido,' she began, setting her empty cup on the table, 'you know I don't interfere, not in any way, with your work. If you want to ask my father about Padre Pio or about Opus Dei, then you have to do it yourself.'

Brunetti had no desire to have his father-in-law interfere in this, not in any way. But he didn't want to tell Paola that his reluctance was based on his doubts about where Count Orazio's allegiance would lie, whether to Brunetti's profession or to Opus Dei itself. Just as Brunetti had no idea of the extent of the Count's wealth and power, he was equally ignorant of their source and of the connections or loyalties which would make them possible. 'Did he believe you?' he asked her.

'Of course he believed me. Why do you even ask that?'

Brunetti tried to shrug this away, but a glance

from Paola denied him that chance. 'It's not as if you've got the most reliable of witnesses.'

'What do you mean?' she asked, voice sharp.

'Children speaking badly of a teacher who gave one of them a bad grade. The words of another child, filtered through a mother who was obviously hysterical when she spoke to you.'

'What are you doing, Guido, trying to play Devil's Advocate? You showed me that report from the Patriarchate. What do you think this bastard's been doing all these years, taking thousand-lire bills from the poor box?'

Brunetti shook his head. 'No, I have no doubts, none at all, about what he's been doing, but that's not the same as having proof.'

A wave from Paola dismissed this as so much nonsense. 'I'm going to stop him,' Paola said with naked aggression.

'Or just move him?' Brunetti asked. 'As they've been doing for years?'

'I said I'm going to stop him, and that's what I'm going to do,' Paola repeated, enunciating every syllable, as if for the deaf.

'Good,' Brunetti said. 'I hope you do. I hope you can.'

To his vast surprise, Paola answered with a quotation from the Bible: ' "But whoso shall offend one of these little ones which believe in me, it were better for him that a millstone were hanged about his neck, and that he were drowned in the depth of the sea." '

'Where'd that come from?' Brunetti asked.

'Matthew. Chapter eighteen, verse six . . .'

'No,' Brunetti said, shaking his head from side to side. 'It's strange to hear you, of all people, quoting the Bible.'

'Even the Devil is said to have that capacity,' she answered, but smiling for the first time and, with that smile, brightening the room.

'Good,' Brunetti affirmed. 'I hope your father has the power to do something.' Brunetti half-expected her to answer that there was nothing her father could not do and surprised himself by realizing that he, as well, at least half-believed this.

Instead, she asked, 'And you, with your priests?'

'There's only one left,' he said.

'What does that mean?'

'Signorina Elettra's friend in the Patriarch's office said that Contessa Crivoni and the priest, who seems to be wealthy in his own right, have been having an affair for years. Apparently her husband knew about it.'

'He knew?' Paola asked in open surprise.

'He preferred young boys.'

'You believe this?' Paola asked.

Brunetti nodded. 'The fact that she had a husband provided them with cover. Neither she nor the priest would wish him dead.'

'So there really is only one left,' Paola said.

'Yes.' Brunetti told her about Patta's anger and his command that police protection be removed from Maria Testa. He made no attempt to disguise his certainty that Padre Pio and the powers standing behind him were the original source of that order.

'What are you going to do?' Paola asked when he finished explaining.

'I've spoken to Vianello. He's got a friend who works in the hospital as an orderly, and he's agreed to look in on her during the day.'

'Not much, is it?' she asked. 'And the nights?'

'Vianello's offered – I didn't ask him, Paola, he offered – to be there until midnight.'

'And that means you'll be there from midnight until eight?'

Brunetti nodded.

'How long will this go on?'

Brunetti shrugged. 'Until they decide to make a move, I suppose.'

'And how long will that be?' she asked.

'That depends on how frightened they are. Or how much they think she knows.'

'Do you think it's Padre Pio?'

Brunetti had always tried to avoid naming the person he suspected of a crime, and he tried to do so this time, but she could read his answer in his silence.

She got to her feet. 'If you've got to be up all night, why don't you try to get some sleep now?'

' "A wife is her husband's richest treasure, a help-meet, a steadying column. A vineyard with no hedge will be overrun; a man with no wife becomes a helpless wanderer," ' he quoted, happy to have, for once, beaten her at her best game.

She couldn't disguise her surprise, nor her delight. 'It is true, then?' she asked.

'What?'

'That the Devil really can quote Scripture.'

★

That night, Brunetti again dragged himself from the warm cocoon of his bed and dressed himself to the sound of the rain that still pounded down on the city. Paola opened her eyes, made a kissing motion in his direction, and was immediately asleep again. This time, he remembered his boots but didn't bother to take an umbrella for Vianello.

At the hospital, they again went out into the hallway to talk, though they had little to say. Lieutenant Scarpa had spoken to Vianello that afternoon and had repeated to him Patta's orders about staffing. Like Patta, he had said nothing about what officers chose to do with their own time, which had encouraged Vianello to speak to Gravini, Pucetti and even a repentant Alvise, all of whom had volunteered to fill in the hours of the day, Pucetti offering to relieve Brunetti at six in the morning.

'Even Alvise?' Brunetti asked.

'Even Alvise,' Vianello answered. 'The fact that he's stupid doesn't stop him from being good-spirited.'

'No,' Brunetti answered immediately, 'that seems to happen only in Parliament.'

Vianello laughed, pulled on his raincoat, and wished Brunetti good night.

Back in the room, Brunetti walked to within a metre of the bed and looked at the sleeping woman. Her cheeks had sunken in even more, and the only sign of life was the pale liquid which dripped slowly from a bottle suspended above her and into a tube which fed into her arm, that and the remorselessly slow rise and fall of her chest.

'Maria?' he called, and then, 'Suor'Immacolata?'

Her breast continued to rise and fall, rise and fall, and the liquid continued to drip, but nothing else happened.

Brunetti switched on the overhead light, pulled his edition of *Marcus Aurelius* from his pocket, and began to read. At two, a nurse came in and took Maria's pulse and entered it on the chart. 'How is she?' Brunetti asked.

'Her pulse is quicker,' the nurse said. 'That sometimes happens when there's going to be a change.'

'You mean, that she's going to wake up?' he asked.

The nurse didn't smile. 'It can be that,' she said and left the room before Brunetti had time to ask her what else it could be.

At three, he switched off the light and closed his eyes, but when his head fell forward on his chest, he forced himself to his feet and stood against the wall behind his chair. He leaned his head back and closed his eyes.

Sometime later, the door opened again, and a different nurse came into the darkened room. Like the one the previous night, she carried a covered tray. Saying nothing, Brunetti watched her as she made her way across the room until she stood beside the bed, just inside the pool of light cast by the bedside lamp. She reached up and moved the covers, and Brunetti, thinking it immodest to watch whatever it was she had been sent to do for the sleeping woman, lowered his eyes.

And saw the marks her shoes had left on the floor, each wet footprint carefully stamped out behind her. Even before he was conscious of what he was doing,

Brunetti launched himself across the space between them, his right hand raised above his head. While still a few steps from her, he saw the towel that covered the tray fall to the floor and saw the long blade of the knife hidden under it. He screamed aloud, a wordless, meaningless noise, and saw the face of Signorina Lerini as she turned toward this form hurtling out of the darkness toward her.

The tray crashed to the floor and she turned toward Brunetti, knife slashing out in a purely instinctive arc. Brunetti tried to wheel away from it, but he was moving too fast and was carried within her reach. The blade slashed through the cloth of his left sleeve and across the muscles of his upper arm. His scream was deafening, and he repeated it again and again, hoping it would bring someone to the room.

One hand grasped to the cut, he turned toward her, afraid that she would come at him. But she had turned back to the woman who lay on the bed and, as he watched, she pulled the knife back level with her hip. Brunetti forced himself toward her again, pulling his hand away from the cut on his arm. Again, he screamed the same wordless sound, but she ignored him and took a step closer to Maria.

Brunetti made a fist with his right hand, raised it above his head, and slammed it down on her elbow, hoping to knock the knife to the ground. He felt, then heard, the shattering of bone but didn't know if it was the bone of her arm or of his hand.

She turned then, arm limp at her side, knife still in her hand, and started to scream. 'Antichrist. I must kill the Antichrist. God's enemies shall be ground down into the dust and they shall be no more. His vengeance is mine. The servants of God shall not be harmed by the words of the Antichrist.' Vainly she tried to raise her hand, but as he watched, her fingers loosened and the knife fell to the floor.

With one hand, he grabbed at the cloth of her sweater and pulled her savagely away from the bed. She offered him no resistance. He shoved her toward the door, which opened as he neared it, allowing a nurse and a doctor to push into the room.

'What's going on here?' the doctor demanded, pausing at the door to switch on the overhead light.

'Even the light of day shall not allow His enemies to hide from His just wrath,' Signorina Lerini said in a voice made quick by passion. 'His enemies shall be confounded and destroyed.' She raised her left hand and pointed a shaking finger at Brunetti. 'You think you can prevent God's will from being obeyed. Fool. He is greater than all of us. His will shall be done.'

In the light that now filled the room, the doctor saw the blood that dripped from the man's hand and the flecks of spittle that flew from the mouth of the woman. She spoke again, this time to the doctor and the nurse. 'You've tried to harbour God's enemy, given her succour and comfort, even though you knew she was the enemy of the Lord. But one greater than you has seen through all of your plans to defy the law of God, and he has sent me to administer God's justice to the sinner.'

The doctor began to ask, 'What's going on . . .?' but Brunetti silenced him with a wave of his hand.

He approached Signorina Lerini and placed his

good hand gently on her arm. His voice became an insinuating murmur. 'The ways of the Lord are many, my sister. Another shall be sent to take your place, and all His works shall be fulfilled.'

Signorina Lerini looked at him then, and he saw the dilated pupils and gasping mouth. 'Are you too sent by the Lord?' she asked.

'Thou sayest it,' Brunetti answered. 'Sister in Christ, your former works will not go unrewarded,' he prompted.

'Sinners. They were both sinners and worthy of God's punishment.'

'Many say your father was a godless man, who mocked the Lord. God is patient and all-loving, but He will not be mocked.'

'He died mocking God,' she said, eyes suddenly filled with terror. 'Even as I covered his face, he mocked God.'

Behind him, Brunetti heard the nurse and doctor whispering together. He turned his head toward them and commanded, 'Quiet.' Stunned by his voice and by the lunacy audible in the woman's, they obeyed. He returned his attention to Signorina Lerini.

'But it was necessary. It was God's will,' he prompted her.

Her face relaxed. 'You understand?'

Brunetti nodded. The pain in his arm grew from minute to minute, and looking down, he saw the pool of blood beneath his hand. 'And the money?' he asked. 'There is always great need of it in order to fight the enemies of the Lord.'

Her voice grew strong. 'Yes. The battle is begun

and must be waged until we have won back the kingdom of the Lord. The earnings of the godless must be given to do God's holy work.'

He had no idea how long he could keep the nurse and doctor prisoner there, and so he risked saying, 'The holy father has told me of your generosity.'

She greeted this revelation with a beatific smile. 'Yes, he told me there was instant need. To wait could have taken years. God's commands must be obeyed.'

He nodded, as if he found it perfectly understandable that a priest should have commanded her to murder her father. 'And da Prè?' Brunetti asked, casually, as though it were only a detail, like the colour of a scarf. 'That sinner,' he added, though it was hardly necessary.

'He saw me, saw me that day I delivered God's justice to my sinning father. But only later did he speak to me.' She leaned toward Brunetti, nodding. 'He was a sinful man, as well. Greed is a terrible sin.'

Behind him, he heard shuffling footsteps, and when he looked around, both the nurse and the doctor were gone. He heard running steps disappear down the corridor and, in the distance, raised voices.

He profited from the confusion of their noisy departure to turn his questions back to da Prè and asked, 'And those others? The people there with your father. What were their sins?'

Before he could think of a way to clothe his questions in the rags of her lunacy, she turned puzzled, questioning eyes on him. 'What?' she asked. 'What others?'

Brunetti realized that her confusion bespoke her innocence, so he ignored her questions and said, 'And the little man? Da Prè? What did he do, Signorina? Did he threaten you?'

'He asked for money. I told him that I had merely done God's will, but he said there was no God and no will. He blasphemed. He mocked the Lord.'

'Did you tell the holy father?'

'The holy father is a saint,' she insisted.

'He is truly a man of God,' Brunetti agreed. 'And did he tell you what to do?' he asked.

She nodded. 'He told me God's will and I hastened to perform it. Sin and sinners must be destroyed.'

'Did he . . .?' Brunetti began, but then three orderlies and the doctor came crashing into the room, filling it with noise and shouts, and she was lost to him.

In the aftermath, Signorina Lerini was taken to the psychiatric ward, where, after the bones in her elbow were set, she was heavily sedated and placed under twenty-four-hour guard. Brunetti was put in a wheelchair and taken to the emergency room, where he was given an injection against pain and had fourteen stitches in his arm. The head of the psychiatric unit, called to the hospital by the nurse who had witnessed the scene, forbade anyone to speak to Signorina Lerini, whose condition he diagnosed, without having seen or spoken to her, as 'grave'. When Brunetti questioned them, neither the doctor nor the nurse who had heard his conversation with Signorina Lerini had any clear sense of it beyond a vague impression that it was filled with religious ravings. He asked if they could remember his asking Signorina Lerini about her father and da Prè, but they insisted that none of it had made any sense at all.

At quarter to six, Pucetti showed up at Maria Testa's room and found no sign of Brunetti, though the Commissario's raincoat was draped over a chair. When the officer saw the pool of blood on the floor, his first thought was for the safety of the woman. He moved quickly to the bed, and when he looked down, he was relieved to see that her chest was still moving as she breathed. But then, moving his eyes to her face, he saw that her eyes were open and she was staring up at him.

Chapter Twenty-One

Brunetti learned nothing about the change in Maria Testa's condition until almost eleven that morning and not until he arrived at the Questura, his wounded arm in a sling. Within minutes, Vianello came into his office.

'She's awake,' he said with no introduction.

'Maria Testa?' Brunetti asked, though he knew.

'Yes.'

'What else?'

'I don't know. Pucetti phoned here at about seven and left the message, but I didn't get it until a half hour ago. When I called your place, you had already left.'

'How is she?'

'I don't know. All he said was that she was awake. When he told the doctors that she was, three of them went into her room and told him to leave. He thinks they were going to do tests. That's when he called.'

'Didn't he say anything else?'

'Nothing, sir.'

'What about the Lerini woman?'

'All we know is that she's under sedation and can't be seen.' This was no more than Brunetti had known when he left the hospital.

'Thanks, Vianello,' he said.

'Is there anything you want me to do, sir?' Vianello asked.

'No, not at the moment. I'll go back to the hospital later.' He shrugged off his raincoat and tossed it over a chair. Before Vianello left, Brunetti asked, 'The Vice-Questore?'

'I don't know, sir. He's been in his office since he got in. He didn't get in until ten, so I doubt that he learned about any of this before then.'

'Thanks,' Brunetti repeated, and Vianello left.

Alone, Brunetti went back to his raincoat and pulled out a bottle of painkillers and went down to the men's room at the end of the corridor to get himself a glass of water. He swallowed down two pills, then a third, and put the bottle back into the pocket of his raincoat. He had had no sleep the night before and felt it now, the way he always did, in his eyes, which burned with grainy irritation. He leaned back in his chair but winced as the back of his arm hit the chair, forcing him forward.

Signorina Lerini had said 'both' men were sinners. Had da Prè, on one of his rare visits to his sister, seen her come from her father's room on the day he died? And had Brunetti's visit and the questions he asked set him thinking about that? If so, then the little man had overlooked, in his attempt to blackmail her, the sense of divine mission which filled and animated her, and in so doing had condemned himself. He had menaced God's plan and so he had to die.

Brunetti played the conversation with Signorina Lerini back in his mind. He had not dared, not standing in front of her and confronted with the madness in her eyes, to name the priest, and so he had only her assertion that the 'holy father' had told her what to do. Even her confession of the murders of her father and da Prè had been garbled with the ravings of her religious mania, so much so that the two witnesses to what was nothing less than a confession had no idea what they had heard. How, then, convince a judge to issue an order for her arrest? And, as he remembered those wild eyes and the tones of outraged sanctity with which she had spoken, he wondered if any judge would be willing to commit her for trial. Although he had seen his fair share of it, Brunetti hardly considered himself an expert on the subject of madness, but what he had seen last night felt like the real thing. And with the woman's lost sanity fled any chance of making a case against her or against the man Brunetti was sure had sent her about her sacred mission.

He called the hospital, but he could not succeed in being put through to the ward where Maria Testa was. He tilted forward and allowed his weight to pull him to his feet. A glance out the window told him that, at least, it had stopped raining. With his right arm, he draped his raincoat over his shoulders and left his office.

When Brunetti saw the out-of-uniform Pucetti sitting outside the door to Maria Testa's room, he remembered that, now that someone had tried to murder her, police protection could be provided.

'Good morning, sir,' Pucetti said, jumping to his feet and snapping out a formal salute.

'Good morning, Pucetti,' Brunetti responded. 'What's going on?'

'Doctors and nurses have been going in and out all morning, sir. None of them will answer me when I ask them anything.'

'Is there anyone in there now?'

'Yes, sir. A nurse. I think she took some food in. At least it smelled like that.'

'Good,' Brunetti said. 'She needs to eat. How long has it been?' he asked, really, for an instant, incapable of remembering how long this had been going on.

'Four days, sir.'

'Yes, yes. Four days,' Brunetti said, not really remembering but willing to believe the young man. 'Pucetti?'

'Yes, sir?' he asked, not saluting, though it was difficult for him to stop himself.

'Go downstairs and call Vianello. Tell him to get someone over here to relieve you, and tell him to put it on the duty roster. Then get yourself home and have something to eat. When are you on duty again?'

'Not until the day after tomorrow, sir.'

'Was today your day off?'

Pucetti looked down at his tennis shoes. 'No, sir.'

'Well, what was it?'

'I had some vacation time coming. So I took a couple of days. I thought I'd, er, I thought I'd give Vianello a hand here. No place to go in this rain, anyway.' Pucetti studied a speck on the wall to the left of Brunetti's head.

'Well, when you call Vianello, see if you can get

him to change that and put you back on duty. Save your vacation for the summer.'

'Yes, sir. Will that be all, sir?'

'Yes, I think so.'

'Then goodbye, sir,' the young man said and turned away toward the steps.

'And thanks, Pucetti,' Brunetti called after him. The only acknowledgement Pucetti made was to raise one hand in the air, but he didn't look back, and he didn't otherwise acknowledge Brunetti's thanks.

Brunetti knocked on the door.

'*Avanti*,' a voice called from inside.

He pushed the door open and went in. A nun he didn't recognize, wearing the now-familiar habit of the Order of the Sacred Cross, stood by the side of the bed, wiping Maria Testa's face. She glanced across at Brunetti but didn't speak. On the table beside the bed lay a tray, a half-eaten bowl of something that looked like soup in its centre. The blood – his blood – was gone from the floor.

'Good morning,' Brunetti said.

The nun nodded but said nothing. She took a half-step forward until, perhaps accidentally, she stood between him and the bed.

Brunetti moved to the left until Maria could see him. When she did, her eyes opened wide, and her brows pulled together as she fought to recall him. 'Signor Brunetti?' she finally asked.

'Yes.'

'What are you doing here? Is something wrong with your mother?'

'No, no. Nothing's wrong. I've come to see you.'

'What's wrong with your arm?'

'Nothing, nothing.'

'But how did you know I was here?' Hearing the panic that came creeping into her own voice, she stopped and closed her eyes. When she opened them, she said, in a voice that trembled with her effort to force it to remain calm, 'I don't understand anything.'

Brunetti drew nearer the bed. The nun shot him a glance and shook her head, a warning, if that's what it was, that Brunetti didn't heed.

'What is it you don't understand?' he asked.

'I don't know how I got here. They said I was hit by a car while I was riding a bicycle, but I don't have a bicycle. There are no bicycles at the nursing home, and I don't think we're supposed to ride them, even if there are. And they said I was out at the Lido. I've never been to the Lido, Signor Brunetti, never in my life.' Her voice grew higher and higher.

'Where do you remember being?' he asked her.

The question seemed to startle her. She raised a hand to her forehead, just as he had seen her do in his office that day, and again she was surprised not to find the comforting protection of her wimple. With the tips of her first two fingers, she rubbed at the bandage that covered her temple, summoning thought.

'I remember being at the nursing home,' she finally said.

'The one where my mother is?' Brunetti asked.

'Of course. That's where I work.' The nun, perhaps responding to the increasing agitation in

Maria's voice, stepped forward. 'I think you better not ask any more questions, Signore.'

'No, no, let him stay,' Maria implored.

Seeing the nun's indecision, Brunetti said, 'Perhaps it will be easier if I do the talking.'

The nun looked from Brunetti to Maria Testa, who nodded and whispered, 'Please. I want to know what's happened.'

Looking down at her watch, the nun said, in that brisk voice that people adopt when given a chance to impose their limited power, 'All right, but only five minutes.' That said, Brunetti hoped she would leave, but she did not, merely moved to the end of the bed and listened openly to their conversation.

'You were riding a bicycle when you were hit by a car. And you were on the Lido, where you were working in a private clinic.'

'But that's impossible,' Maria said. 'I told you I've never been on the Lido. Never.' As soon as she had spoken, she stopped and said, 'I'm sorry, Signor Brunetti. Tell me what you know.'

'You'd been working there for a few weeks. You had left the nursing home weeks before. Some people helped you find the job and a place to live.'

'A job?' she asked.

'At the clinic. Working in the laundry.'

She closed her eyes for a moment and when she opened them, said, 'And I don't remember anything about the Lido.' Again, her hand moved to her temple. 'But why are you here?' she asked Brunetti, and he could tell by her tone that she had remembered his job.

'You came to my office a few weeks ago, and you asked me to look into something.'

'What?' she asked with a puzzled shake of her head.

'Something that you thought was going on in the San Leonardo nursing home.'

'San Leonardo? But I've never been there.'

Brunetti saw her hands clench into fists on top of the covers and decided there was little sense in continuing like this. 'I think we better leave this now. Perhaps you'll remember what's happened. You need to rest, and you need to eat and get stronger.' How many times had he heard this same woman say things just like this to his mother?

The nun stepped forward. 'That's enough, Signore.' Brunetti was forced to agree.

He reached out with his good hand and patted the back of Maria's. 'It'll be all right. The worst of all of this is over. Just try to rest and eat.' He smiled and turned away.

Before he reached the door, Maria turned to the nun and said, 'Sister, I'm sorry to trouble you, but could you get me a—' and stopped in embarrassment.

'A bedpan?' the nun asked, making no attempt to lower her voice.

Head still bowed, Maria nodded.

Breath exploded from the nun's lips, and her mouth tightened in exasperation she did nothing to hide. She turned and went to the door, opened it, and held it while she waited for Brunetti.

From behind, in a small, frightened voice, Maria said, 'Please, Sister, may he stay here with me until you come back?'

The nun glanced at her, at Brunetti, but she said nothing. She left the room and closed the door.

'It was a black car,' Maria said with no preamble. 'I don't know the difference between them, but it was very big, and it came right at me. It wasn't an accident.'

Stupid with surprise, Brunetti asked, 'You remember?'

He started to approach the bed, but she held a warning hand toward him. 'Stay over there. I don't want her to know we talked.'

'Why?'

This time it was Maria's lips that tightened in irritation. 'She's one of them. If they know I remember, they'll kill me.'

He looked across the room and almost staggered at the contagious energy that radiated out from her. 'What are you going to do?' he asked.

'Survive,' she spat, and then the door opened and the nun was back, the uncovered bedpan carried in front of her. She swept past Brunetti without speaking and went toward the bed.

He said nothing, didn't risk turning back to take a last look at Maria, but left them there, together in the room.

As Brunetti walked down the corridor toward the psychiatric ward, he suddenly felt the pavement grow uncertain under his feet. Part of him knew it was nothing more than exhaustion, but that didn't stop him from searching the faces of the people who passed him to see if he could catch panic or fear in their eyes and thus comfort himself with the knowledge that it really was an earthquake. Suddenly frightened by the realization that he was seeking comfort in that possibility, he went into the bar on the ground floor and ordered a *panino* but left it untouched when it arrived. Not liking the taste but knowing it was what he needed, he drank a glass of apricot nectar, then asked for a glass of water and took two more painkillers. Looking around at the other people in the bar, with their bandages, splints, and casts, he felt at home for the first time that day.

When he set off again toward the psychiatric ward, he felt better, though he did not feel good. He crossed the open courtyard, cut past the radiology department, and pushed open the double glass doors of the psychiatric ward. And as he did so, from the other end of the corridor he saw a white-skirted figure coming toward him and, again, Brunetti wondered if he had taken leave of his senses or if he was trapped in some sort of psychological earthquake. But no, it was nothing more, and nothing less, than Padre Pio advancing toward him, his tall form enveloped in a dark woollen cape that was fastened at the neck, Brunetti saw with almost hallucinatory clarity, by a clasp made of an eight-eenth-century Austrian Maria Teresa Thaler.

It was difficult to judge which of them was the more surprised, but it was the priest who recovered sooner and who said, 'Good morning, Commissario. Would it be rash of me to assume we're here to see the same person?'

It took Brunetti a moment to speak, and when he did he said no more than her name, 'Signorina Lerini?'

'Yes.'

'You can't see her,' Brunetti said, no longer bothering to keep the antagonism from his voice.

Padre Pio's face blossomed into the same sweet smile with which he had greeted Brunetti during their first meeting at the chapter house of the Order of the Sacred Cross. 'But surely, Commissario, you have no right to keep a sick person, someone in need of spiritual consolation, from seeing her confessor.'

Her confessor. Of course. Brunetti should have thought of that. But before he could say anything, the priest continued, 'In any case, it's too late for you to be giving orders, Commissario. I've already spoken to her and heard her confession.'

'And given her spiritual consolation?' Brunetti asked.

'Thou hast said it,' Padre Pio answered with a smile that had never known sweetness.

A sickening taste rose in Brunetti's throat, but it had nothing to do with the apricot nectar he had just drunk. Like a sudden spasm, rage and disgust erupted in him, he as helpless to control them as the pills were to stop the pain in his arm. Hurling aside the experience of a generation, Brunetti reached out and grabbed a handful of the priest's cloak, glad to feel the fine cloth wrinkle under the pressure of his fingers. He pulled, not gently, and the priest, suddenly caught off balance, fell forward until only a handsbreadth separated them. 'We know about you,' Brunetti spat.

The priest threw up an angry hand that easily broke Brunetti's grip. He backed away, turned, and started toward the door. But then just as suddenly he stopped and came back toward Brunetti, his head shifting from side to side, snakelike. 'And we know about you,' he whispered, and was gone.

Chapter Twenty-Two

Out in Campo SS. Giovanni e Paolo, Brunetti stood in front of the entrance to the hospital for a few minutes, incapable of deciding whether to force himself to go to the Questura or to return home and get some sleep. He looked at the scaffolding that covered the front of the basilica and saw that the shadows had crawled half-way up the façade. He looked at his watch and could barely believe that it was already the middle of the afternoon. He didn't know where he had lost those hours: maybe he had fallen asleep in the bar, head resting against the wall at the back of his chair. At any rate, they were gone, those hours, flown away in the same way that years of Maria Testa's life had been stolen from her.

Deciding that it would be easier to go to the Questura, if only because it was closer, he crossed the *campo* and set out in that direction. Burdened by thirst and returning pain, he stopped in a bar on the way and had a glass of mineral water and took another of the pills. When he got to the Questura, he found the lobby curiously silent, and it wasn't until he realized it was Wednesday, the day the Ufficio Stranieri was closed to the public, that he understood the reason for this unwonted peace.

Reluctant to attempt the four flights of stairs to

his office, he decided to have done with it by speaking to Patta immediately and started toward the staircase that led to his office. As he made his way up the first flight, he was struck by how easy the upward motion really was and wondered, but couldn't remember, why he had been reluctant to go to his own office. He found himself thinking how pleasant it would be if he could simply fly up the steps, how much time it would save him every day, but then he found himself in Signorina Elettra's office, and he forgot about flying.

She glanced up from her computer when he came in, and when she saw his arm and the condition he was in, she got to her feet and came around her desk toward him. 'Commissario, what's the matter? What's happened?' The sincerity of her alarm was as visible as it was audible, so much so that Brunetti found himself strangely moved by it. How lucky women were that they could permit themselves to display emotion openly, he thought, and how sweet were those signs of their affection or concern.

'Thank you, Signorina,' he said, resisting the desire to place his hand on her shoulder as he thanked her for what she had no idea she was displaying. 'Is the Vice-Questore in?'

'Yes, he is. Are you sure you want to see him?'

'Oh, yes. Now's the perfect time.'

'Can I get you a coffee, Dottore?' she asked, helping him with his raincoat.

Brunetti shook his head. 'No, that's all right, Signorina. Thank you for asking, but I'll just have a word with the Vice-Questore.'

Habit and habit alone caused Brunetti to knock

on Patta's door. When he went in, Patta greeted him with the same sort of surprise Signorina Elettra had shown at seeing him, but where Signorina Elettra's surprise had been rich with concern, Patta's spoke only of disapproval.

'What's wrong with you, Brunetti?'

'Someone tried to kill me,' he answered, tossing the line away.

'They didn't try very hard, if that's all they managed.'

'Do you mind if I sit down, sir?' Brunetti asked.

Seeing this as little more than a ploy on Brunetti's part to call attention to his injury, Patta nodded with bad grace and pointed to a chair. 'What's been going on?' Patta demanded.

'Last night in the hospital—' Brunetti began, but Patta cut him off.

'I know all about what happened in the hospital. That woman went to kill the nun because she had the crazy idea she had killed her father,' Patta said, paused for a long moment, and then added, 'It's a good thing you were there to stop her.' Had he tried, Patta could not possibly have managed to sound more grudging.

Brunetti listened, surprised only by the speed with which Patta had been convinced. He knew that some such story would have to be given to explain Signorina Lerini's behaviour, but he hadn't thought it would be as barefaced as this.

'Could there be another explanation, sir?'

'Such as?' Patta asked with his wonted suspicion.

'That she knew something Signorina Lerini wanted kept secret?'

'What sort of a secret could a woman like that possibly have?'

'A woman like what, if I might ask?'

'A zealot,' Patta answered immediately. 'One of those women who think about nothing except religion and the Church.' Patta's tone gave no indication of whether he approved of this sort of behaviour in women or not. 'Well?' he prompted when Brunetti said nothing.

'Her father had no history of heart trouble,' Brunetti said.

Patta waited for Brunetti to say something more, and when he didn't, Patta demanded, 'What is that supposed to mean?' Still Brunetti didn't answer. 'Does that mean you think this woman killed her father?' He pushed himself back from his desk in an attempt to give visible form to his disbelief. 'Are you out of your mind, Brunetti? Women who go to daily mass don't kill their fathers.'

'How do you know she goes to daily mass?' Brunetti asked, surprised at his own ability to keep calm and rise above this discussion, as though he had been carried up to the same place where the answers to all those secrets were being kept hidden.

'Because I've had calls from both her doctor and her spiritual advisor.'

'What have they told you?'

'The doctor told me that it seems to be a breakdown, brought on by delayed grief at her father's death.'

'And her "spiritual advisor", as you call him?'

'What would you call him, Brunetti, something

else? Or is he part of this sinister scenario you seem to be inventing?'

'What did he say?' Brunetti repeated.

'He said that he agreed with the doctor's analysis. And then he told me that he wouldn't be surprised to learn that it was this delusion about the nun that had led to the attack in the hospital.'

'And I suppose, when you asked why he said this, he said he wasn't at liberty to tell you how he came by that information?' Brunetti asked, feeling himself move even farther and farther away from the conversation and the two men who were having it.

'How do you know that?' Patta asked.

'Ah, Vice-Questore,' Brunetti said, getting to his feet and waving an admonishing finger at Patta. 'You wouldn't expect me to break the vow of the confessional, would you?' He didn't wait to hear if Patta had anything to say to that but drifted over to the door and let himself out of the office.

Signorina Elettra was moving very quickly away from the door when he opened it, and he waved the same admonishing finger at her. But then he smiled and asked, 'Would you help me with my coat, Signorina?'

'Of course, Dottore,' she said, picking up the coat from the chair where it lay and holding it out for him.

When it was draped over his shoulders, he thanked her and started for the steps. There in the doorway stood Vianello, who had appeared there with angelic suddenness.

'Bonsuan's got the launch, sir,' he said.

Later, Brunetti remembered starting down the

steps beside Vianello, who took his good arm. And he remembered asking Vianello if he, too, ever thought about how easy it would be if they could fly up and down the steps in order to get to their offices, but then his memory of the day fled and went to take its rest with all the lost hours of Suor'-Immacolata's life.

Chapter Twenty-Three

The infection in Brunetti's arm was later attributed to the threads of Harris tweed that had been carried into his wound and left there by careless medical procedure. Of course, it was not the Civil Hospital which said this, for the surgeon there insisted that the infection was caused by a common strain of staph and to be expected in the wake of a wound that serious. But his friend Giovanni Grimani later told him that heads had rolled all over the emergency room as a result, and a surgical orderly had been transferred to the kitchens. Grimani did not say, at least not openly, that the surgeon had been at fault because he had hurried through the operation, though his tone led Brunetti and Paola to that belief. But none of this was known until long after the infection had grown so serious and Brunetti's behaviour so strange that he was taken back to the hospital.

Because of his father-in-law's generosity to that institution, the delirious Brunetti was taken to the Giustiniani Hospital, where he was put in a private room and where the entire staff, once they learned to whom he was related, proved attentive and polite. During the first days, as he lapsed in and out of consciousness and the doctors sought to find the proper antibiotic to defeat his infection, Brunetti was told nothing about the cause of his infection, and when that drug was finally found and the infection under control, and then gone, he displayed no interest in knowing who was at fault. 'What difference does it make?' Brunetti asked Grimani, thus destroying a good deal of the satisfaction the doctor felt in having displayed greater loyalty to friendship than to his profession.

During his stay, at least during his periods of lucidity, Brunetti had insisted that it was absurd to keep him in the hospital, and on the day that the tube was removed from his arm and the wound was judged to be healing cleanly, he insisted on being released. Paola helped him dress, telling him that it was so warm outside that he wouldn't need a sweater, though she had brought a jacket to drape over his shoulders.

When a weakened Brunetti and a glowing Paola emerged into the corridor, they found Vianello waiting. 'Good morning, Signora,' he said to Paola.

'Good morning, Vianello. How nice of you to come,' she said with manufactured surprise. Brunetti smiled at her vain attempt to appear casual, certain as he was that she had arranged with Vianello that he be there, just as he was sure that Bonsuan would have the police launch at the side entrance, motor running.

'You're looking very well, sir,' Vianello said by way of greeting.

When he dressed, Brunetti had been surprised to notice how loose his trousers felt. Apparently the fever had burned away a good deal of the weight he had put on that winter, and his lack of appetite had seen to even more of it. 'Thanks, Vianello,' he said, leaving it at that. Paola started down the corridor, and Brunetti turned to the sergeant and asked, 'Where are they?' not needing to explain.

'Gone. Both of them.'

'Where?'

'Signorina Lerini was taken to a private clinic.'

'Where?'

'Rome. At least that's what we were told.'

'Did you check?' Brunetti asked.

'Signorina Elettra confirmed it.' And even before Brunetti could ask, he explained, 'It's run by the Order of the Sacred Cross.'

Brunetti didn't know which name to use. 'And Maria Testa?' he finally asked, voting with that name for the decision he hoped she had made.

'She's disappeared.'

'What do you mean, disappeared?'

'Guido,' Paola said, coming back to them, 'can't this wait?' She turned away from them and started down the corridor, toward the side exit of the hospital and the waiting police launch.

Brunetti followed her, Vianello falling into step beside him.

'Tell me,' Brunetti said.

'We kept the guard there for the first few days after you came in here.'

Brunetti interrupted him. 'Did anyone try to see her?'

'That priest, but I said there were orders that she wasn't allowed any visitors. He went to Patta.'

'And?'

'Patta stalled for a day, then he said that we should ask her if she wanted to see him.'

'And what did she say?'

'I never asked her. But I told Patta that she said she didn't want to see him.'

'Then what happened?' Brunetti asked. But then they arrived at the door of the hospital. Paola stood just outside, holding it open for him, and as he stepped outside, she said, 'Welcome to springtime, Guido.'

And so it was. During the ten days he had been inside, spring had advanced magically and conquered the city. The air smelled of softness and growth, the mating calls of small birds filled the air above their heads, and a spray of forsythia thrust its way out of a metal grating in the brick wall across the canal. As Brunetti had known he would, Bonsuan stood at the helm of the police launch that was drawn up to the steps leading down to the canal. He greeted them with a nod and with what Brunetti suspected was a smile.

Muttering, '*Buon giorno*,' the pilot helped Paola aboard, then assisted Brunetti, who almost stumbled, so blinded was he by the explosion of sunlight. Vianello flipped the mooring rope free and stepped aboard, and Bonsuan took them out into the Canal of the Giudecca.

'And then what?' Brunetti asked.

'And then one of the nurses told her that the priest wanted to see her but that we'd kept him out. I spoke to the nurse later, and she said that she – the Testa woman, that is – seemed troubled that he wanted to see her. And the nurse said she seemed glad that we hadn't let him in.' A speedboat cut quickly past them on the right side, splashing water up toward them. Vianello jumped aside, but the water splashed harmlessly against the side of the launch.

'And then?' Brunetti asked.

'Then the mother superior of her order called and said she wanted her to be sent to one of their clinics. And then she was gone. We'd taken the guard off, though some of the boys and I still sort of hung around during the nights, just to keep an eye on things.'

'When did this happen?'

'About three days ago. The nurse went in one afternoon, and she wasn't there. Her clothes were gone and there was no sign of her.'

'What did you do?'

'We asked around the hospital, but no one had seen her. She's just disappeared.'

'And the priest?'

'Someone from their motherhouse in Rome called the Vice-Questore the day after she disappeared – this was before anyone except us knew about it – and asked if it was true that her confessor was being kept from her. He still thought she was there, so he caved in, said that he'd see to it personally that she speak to her confessor. He called me in to tell me she had to see him, and that's when I told him she was gone.'

'What did he do? Or say?'

Vianello thought about this for a while before he answered. 'I think he was relieved, sir. The man from Rome must have frightened him with something, he was so insistent that she see the priest. But when I told him she was gone, he seemed almost happy to hear it. In fact, he called the man in Rome while I was still there. I had to speak to him myself and tell him she was gone.'

'Do you know who he was, the man in Rome?'

'No, but when they called, the operator said the call was coming from the Vatican.'

'Do you have any idea where she's gone?' Brunetti asked.

'None.' Vianello's answer was immediate.

'Did you call that man out on the Lido? Sassi?'

'Yes. It was the first thing I did. He told me not to worry about her, but he wouldn't say anything more than that.'

'Do you think he knows where she is?' Brunetti asked. He had no desire to hurry Vianello and looked up toward Paola, who stood at the wheel of the boat, talking easily with Bonsuan.

Finally Vianello answered him. 'I think he must, but he doesn't trust anyone enough to tell them, not even us.'

Brunetti nodded and turned away from the sergeant and then looked out over the waters, toward San Marco, just now coming into sight on their left. He remembered that last day in the hospital with Maria Testa, remembered the fierce determination in her voice, and at the memory, he felt a surge of relief that she had decided to run. Brunetti would try to find her, but he hoped it would be impossible – for him and for anyone else. God keep her safe and give her strength for her *Vita Nuova*.

Paola, seeing that he was finished talking to

Vianello, moved back toward them. Just then, a gust of wind came from behind her and blew her hair back across her face, wrapping the blonde waves around from both sides.

Laughing, she raised both hands to her face and swept the hair up and away, then shook her head from side to side, as if surfacing from a long dive. When she opened her eyes, she saw Brunetti watching her and laughed again, this time even louder. With his good arm, he reached around her shoulder and pulled her toward him.

Reduced by surging love to adolescence, he asked, 'Did you miss me?'

Catching his mood, she answered, 'I pined desperately. The children haven't been fed. My students languish for lack of intellectual stimulation.'

Vianello left them to it and went up to stand beside Bonsuan.

'What have you been doing?' Brunetti asked, as if she hadn't spent most of her time at the hospital with him for the last ten days.

He felt her change of mood register in her body and pulled her around to face him. 'What is it?' he asked.

'I don't want to disturb your homecoming,' she said.

'Nothing could do that, Paola,' he said and smiled at the simple truth of that. 'Tell me, please.'

She studied his face for a moment and then said, 'I told you that I was going to ask my father for help.'

'About Padre Luciano?'

'Yes.'

'And?'

'And he's spoken to some people, friends of his in Rome. I think he's found an answer.'

'Tell me.'

She did.

The housekeeper answered the door to the rectory at Brunetti's second ring. She was a plain woman in her late fifties, with the smooth, flawless skin that he had often observed on the faces of nuns and other women of long preserved virginity.

'Yes?' she asked. 'How may I help you?' She might have once been pretty, with dark brown eyes and a broad mouth, but time had made her forget about that sort of thing or she had lacked the will for beauty, and so her face had faded and gone dull and soft.

'I'd like to speak to Luciano Benevento,' Brunetti said.

'Are you a parishioner?' she asked, surprised at the use of the priest's name without his title.

'Yes,' Brunetti answered after only a moment's hesitation and giving an answer that was at least geographically true.

'If you'll come into the study, I'll call Father Luciano.' She turned away from Brunetti, who closed the front door and followed her down the marble-paved hall. She opened the door to a small room for him, then disappeared down the hall, off in pursuit of the priest.

Inside, there were two armchairs placed close beside one another, perhaps to facilitate the intimacy of confession. A small crucifix hung on one wall, a picture of the Madonna of Cracow opposite it. A low table held copies of *Famiglia Christiana* and a few postal contribution forms for those who might be encouraged to make a donation to *Primavera Missionaria*. Brunetti ignored the magazines, the images, and the chairs. He stood in the centre of the room, mind clear, and waited for the priest to arrive.

The door opened after a few minutes, and a tall, thin man came into the room. Dressed in the long skirts and high collar of his office, he seemed taller than he was, an impression that was intensified by his erect posture and long-legged stride.

'Yes, my son?' he said as he came in. He had dark grey eyes, and from them radiated lines caused by frequent smiles. His mouth was broad, his smile one that invited confidence and trust. He smiled at Brunetti and came forward, offering his hand in brotherhood.

'Luciano Benevento?' Brunetti asked, hands at his side.

With a soft smile, he corrected Brunetti. 'Padre Luciana Benevento.'

'I've come to speak to you about your new assignment,' Brunetti said, consciously refusing to address the man by his title.

'I'm afraid I don't understand. What new assignment?' Benevento shook his head and made no attempt to disguise his confusion.

Brunetti pulled a long white envelope from the inside pocket of his jacket and handed it silently to the other man.

Instinctively, the priest took it, glanced down, and saw his name written across the front. He was comforted to see that, this time, his title was used. He opened it, glanced up at the silent Brunetti, and pulled out a sheet of paper. Holding it away from him a bit, he read through the paper. When he finished it, he looked at Brunetti and then back down at the paper, and then read it through a second time.

'I don't understand this,' he said. His right hand, the one which held the paper, fell to his side.

'I think it should be very clear.'

'But I don't understand. How can I be transferred? They're supposed to ask me about that, get my consent, before they do anything like this.'

'I don't think anyone's interested in what you want, not any longer.'

Benevento could do nothing to hide his confusion. 'But I've been a priest for twenty-three years. Of course, they have to listen to me. They can't just do this to me, send me away and not even tell me where.' The priest waved the paper angrily in the air. 'They don't even tell me what parish I'm going to go to, not even what province. They don't give me an idea of where I'm going to be.' He pulled his arm up and stuck the paper out toward Brunetti. 'Look at this. All they say is that I'm being transferred. That could be Naples. For heaven's sake, it could be Sicily.'

Brunetti, who was familiar with far more than the contents of the letter, didn't bother to look at it.

'What sort of parish is it going to be?' Benevento continued. 'What sort of people will I have? They can't just assume I'll go along with this. I'll call the Patriarch. I'll complain about this and see that it's changed. They can't just send me off to any parish they want, not like that, not after all I've done for the Church.'

'It's not a parish,' Brunetti said calmly.

'What?' Benevento asked.

'It's not a parish,' Brunetti repeated.

'What do you mean, it's not a parish?'

'Just what I said. You're not being assigned to a parish.'

'That's absurd,' Benevento said with real indignation. 'Of course I have to be assigned to a parish. I'm a priest. It's my job to help people.'

Brunetti's face was motionless through all of this. His silence provoked Benevento into demanding, 'Who are you? What do you know about this?'

'I'm someone who lives in your parish,' Brunetti said. 'And my daughter is one of the children in your catechism class.'

'Who?'

'One of the children from the middle school,' Brunetti said, seeing no reason to name his child.

'What's that got to do with anything?' Benevento demanded, his mounting anger audible in his voice.

'It has a great deal to do with it,' Brunetti said, nodding toward the letter.

'I don't have any idea what you're talking about,' Benevento said, then repeated his question, 'Who are you? Why are you here?'

'I'm here to deliver the letter,' Brunetti said calmly, 'and to tell you where you're going.'

'Why would the Patriarch use someone like you?'

Benevento asked, coming down with heavy sarcasm on the last word.

'Because he's been threatened,' Brunetti explained blandly.

'Threatened?' Benevento repeated in a quiet voice, looking at Brunetti with a nervousness he tried, badly, to disguise. There was little left of the benevolent priest who had come into the room only minutes before. 'What can the Patriarch be threatened about?'

'Alida Bontempi, Serafina Reato, and Luana Serra,' Brunetti said simply, giving him the names of the three girls whose families had complained to the Bishop of Trento.

Benevento's head flew back as though Brunetti had slapped him three times across the face. 'I don't know . . .' he began to say, but then he saw Brunetti's face and stopped speaking for a moment.

He smiled a man-of-the-world smile at Brunetti. 'You believe the lies of hysterical girls like that? Against a priest?'

Brunetti didn't bother to answer him.

Benevento grew angrier. 'Do you honestly mean to stand there and tell me that you believe the horrible stories those girls invented against me? Do you think that a man who has dedicated his life to the service of God could possibly do the things they said?' When Brunetti still didn't answer, Benevento slapped the letter angrily against the side of his leg and turned away from Brunetti. He walked over to the door, opened it, but then slammed it closed and turned back toward Brunetti. 'Where is it they think they're going to send me?'

'Asinara,' said Brunetti.

'What?' Benevento cried.

'Asinara,' Brunetti repeated, sure that everyone, even a priest, would know the name of the maximum security prison in the middle of the Thyyhenean Sea.

'But that's a prison. They can't send me there. I'm not guilty of anything.' He took two long steps across the room, as if he hoped to push some sort of concession out of Brunetti, even if only by force of his own anger. Brunetti stopped him with a look. 'What do they expect me to do there? I'm not a criminal.'

Brunetti met his eyes at that but said nothing.

Benevento shouted into the silence that radiated out from the other man. 'I'm not a criminal. They can't send me there. They can't punish me; I've never even had a trial. They can't just send me to prison because of what some girls say, without a trial or a conviction.'

'You haven't been convicted of anything. You've been assigned as chaplain.'

'What? Chaplain?'

'Yes. To care for the souls of sinners.'

'But they're dangerous men,' Benevento said in a voice he fought to keep calm.

'Precisely.'

'What?'

'They're men. There are no young girls on Asinara.'

Benevento looked wildly around the room, seeking some sane ear to listen to what was being done to him. 'But they can't do this. I'll leave. I'll go to Rome.' By the last sentence, Benevento was shouting.

'You're to leave on the first of the month,' Brunetti said with iron calm. 'The Patriarchate will provide a launch and then a car that will take you to Civitavecchia and see that you get on the weekly boat to the prison. Before that time, you are not to leave this rectory. If you do, you will be arrested.'

'Arrested?' Benevento blustered. 'For what?'

Brunetti didn't answer this question. 'You have two days to get ready.'

'And what if I choose not to go?' Benevento asked with the tones usually delivered from positions of high moral strength. Brunetti failed to respond, and so he repeated his question, 'What if I don't go?'

'Then the parents of those three girls will receive anonymous letters, telling them where you are. And what you've been doing.'

Benevento's shock was evident, and then his fear, so immediate and palpable that he couldn't prevent himself from asking, 'What will they do?'

'If you're lucky, they'll contact the police.'

'What do you mean, if I'm lucky?'

'Exactly what I said. If you're lucky.' Brunetti allowed a long silence to expand between them and then said, 'Serafina Reato hanged herself last year. She'd tried for a year to get someone to believe what she said, but no one would. She said that she did it because no one would believe her. They do now.'

Benevento's eyes opened wide for a moment, and his mouth contracted into a tight little circle. Both the envelope and the letter fell to the floor, but Benevento didn't notice.

'Who are you?' he asked.

'You have two days,' was Brunetti's answer. He stepped over the two pieces of paper that lay forgotten on the floor and went over toward the door. His hands ached from being kept in tight fists at his sides. He didn't bother to look back at Benevento when he left. Nor did he slam the door.

Outside, Brunetti walked away from the rectory and turned into a narrow *calle*, the first one he saw that would take him all the way down to the Grand Canal. At the end, his progress blocked by the water, he stood and stared across at the buildings opposite. A bit to the right was the *palazzo* where Lord Byron had lived for a time, and next to it the one where Brunetti's first girlfriend had lived. Boats passed, taking the day and his thoughts with them.

He felt no triumph in this cheap victory: if anything, he felt only a thick sadness at the man and his miserable, crippled life. This priest had been stopped, at least for as long as he could be kept on the island by Count Orazio's power and connections. Brunetti thought of the warning he had been given by the other priest and of the power and connections that lay behind that threat.

Suddenly, with a splash that sent water up onto Brunetti's shoes, a pair of black-headed gulls landed just at his feet, fighting over a piece of bread. They squabbled, beak to beak, pulling at the bread, cawing and screaming all the while. Then one of them gobbled it down, and after that the two of them grew quiet and bobbed peacefully on the waters side by side.

He stayed there for a quarter of an hour, until the stiffness went out of his hands. He put them in the pockets of his jacket and, bidding farewell to the gulls, went back up the *calle* and towards home.

For more of Donna Leon's elegant mystery series, look for the

Coming from Penguin in October 2007

Fatal Remedies

For Commissario Brunetti, it began with an early morning phone call. In the chill of the Venetian dawn, a sudden act of vandalism shatters the quiet of the deserted city. But soon Brunetti is shocked to find that the culprit waiting to be apprehended at the scene is someone from his own family. Meanwhile, Brunetti is under pressure from his superiors to solve a daring robbery with a link to a suspicious accidental death. Does it all lead back to the Mafia? And how are his family's actions connected to these crimes?

ISBN 978-0-14-311242-6

Acqua Alta

As Venice braces for a winter tempest and the onslaught of *acqua alta*—the rising waters from torrential rain—Commissario Guido Brunetti finds out that an old friend has been savagely beaten at the palazzo home of reigning diva Flavia Petrelli.

ISBN 978-0-14-200496-8

Blood from a Stone

Shortly before Christmas a man is killed in Venice's Campo Santo Stefano. An illegal immigrant from Senegal, he is one of the *vu cumpra* who sell fake fashion accessories while trying to stay ahead of the law. At first the crime seems like a simple clash between rival vendors, but as Commissario Guido Brunetti probes more deeply, he begins to suspect that this murder was the work of a professional. And why does his boss want him off the case?

ISBN 978-0-14-303698-2

Death and Judgment

A truck crashes on one of the treacherous mountain roads in the Italian Dolomites, spilling a terrible cargo. Meanwhile, a prominent international lawyer is found dead in the carriage of an intercity train at Santa Lucia. Can the two tragedies possibly be connected? Commissario Guido Brunetti digs deep into the secret lives of Italy's elite classes to find the answer. *ISBN 978-0-14-303582-4*

Death in a Strange Country
Brunetti confronts a grisly sight when the body of a young American is fished out of a fetid Venetian canal. Though all the signs point to a violent mugging, something incriminating turns up in the victim's apartment that suggests the existence of a high level conspiracy.

ISBN 978-0-14-303482-7

Doctored Evidence
After a wealthy elderly woman is found brutally murdered in her apartment, the authorities suspect her maid. But when the maid meets an untimely end trying to escape from border police, and it appears that the money she carried may not have been stolen, Commissario Guido Brunetti decides—unofficially—to take on the case himself. *ISBN 978-0-14-303563-3*

Dressed for Death
Brunetti's hopes of a refreshing family holiday in the mountains are dashed when a gruesome discovery is made in Marghera—a body so badly beaten that the face is completely unrecognizable. But when the victim's identity is revealed the investigation takes a very unexpected turn. *ISBN 978-0-14-303584-8*

A Noble Radiance
The new owner of a farmhouse at the foot of the Italian Dolomites is summoned to the house when his workmen disturb a macabre grave. Once on the job, Brunetti uncovers a clue that reignites an infamous cold case of kidnapping and disappearance involving one of Venice's oldest, most aristocratic families.

ISBN 978-0-14-200319-0

Through a Glass, Darkly
When the body of a night watchman is found in front of a blazing furnace at Dè Cal's glass factory along with an annotated copy of Dante's *Inferno,* Brunetti must investigate. Does the book contain the clues Brunetti needs to solve the murder and uncover who is ruining the waters of Venice's lagoon? *ISBN 978-0-14-303806-1*

Uniform Justice
Brunetti faces an unsettling case when a young cadet has been found hanged, a presumed suicide, in Venice's elite military academy. As he pursues his inquiry, he is faced with a wall of silence and finds himself caught up in the strange and stormy politics of his country's powerful elite. *ISBN 978-0-14-200422-7*